Hello, My Nam Poop

WONDERBOUND

Written by **BEN KATZNER**
Illustrated by **IAN McGINTY**
Colors by **FRED C. STRESING**
Letters by **ANDWORLD DESIGN**
Edited by **REBECCA TAYLOR**
Design by **SONJA SYNAK**

Publisher, **Damian A. Wassel**
Editor-in-Chief, **Adrian F. Wassel**
Art Director, **Nathan C. Gooden**
Managing Editor, **Rebecca Taylor**
Director of Sales & Marketing, Direct Market, **David Dissanayake**
Director of Sales & Marketing, Book Market, **Syndee Barwick**
Production Manager, **Ian Baldessari**
Branding & Design, **Tim Daniel**
Principal, **Damian A. Wassel Sr.**

WONDERBOUND

Missoula, Montana. www.readwonderbound.com
@readwonderbound

First Edition, First Printing, October, 2021
ISBN: 9781638490128
LCN: 2021938883

1 2 3 4 5 6 7 8 9 10
Printed in Canada by Avenue 4.

For information about foreign or multimedia rights, contact: rights@vaultcomics.com

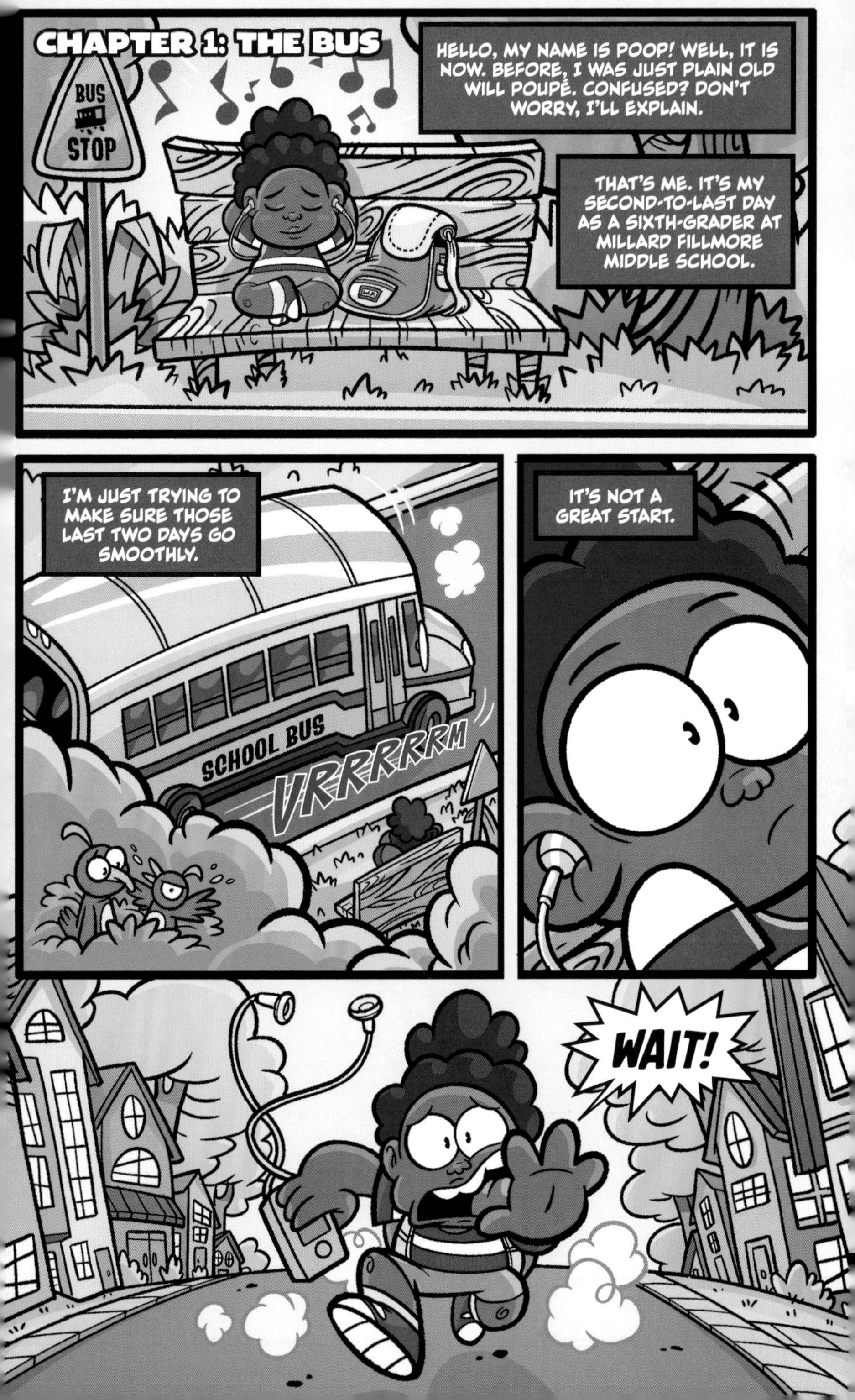
CHAPTER 1: THE BUS
HELLO, MY NAME IS POOP! WELL, IT IS NOW. BEFORE, I WAS JUST PLAIN OLD WILL POUPÉ. CONFUSED? DON'T WORRY, I'LL EXPLAIN.
BUS STOP
THAT'S ME. IT'S MY SECOND-TO-LAST DAY AS A SIXTH-GRADER AT MILLARD FILLMORE MIDDLE SCHOOL.
I'M JUST TRYING TO MAKE SURE THOSE LAST TWO DAYS GO SMOOTHLY.
SCHOOL BUS
VRRRRRRM
IT'S NOT A GREAT START.
WAIT!

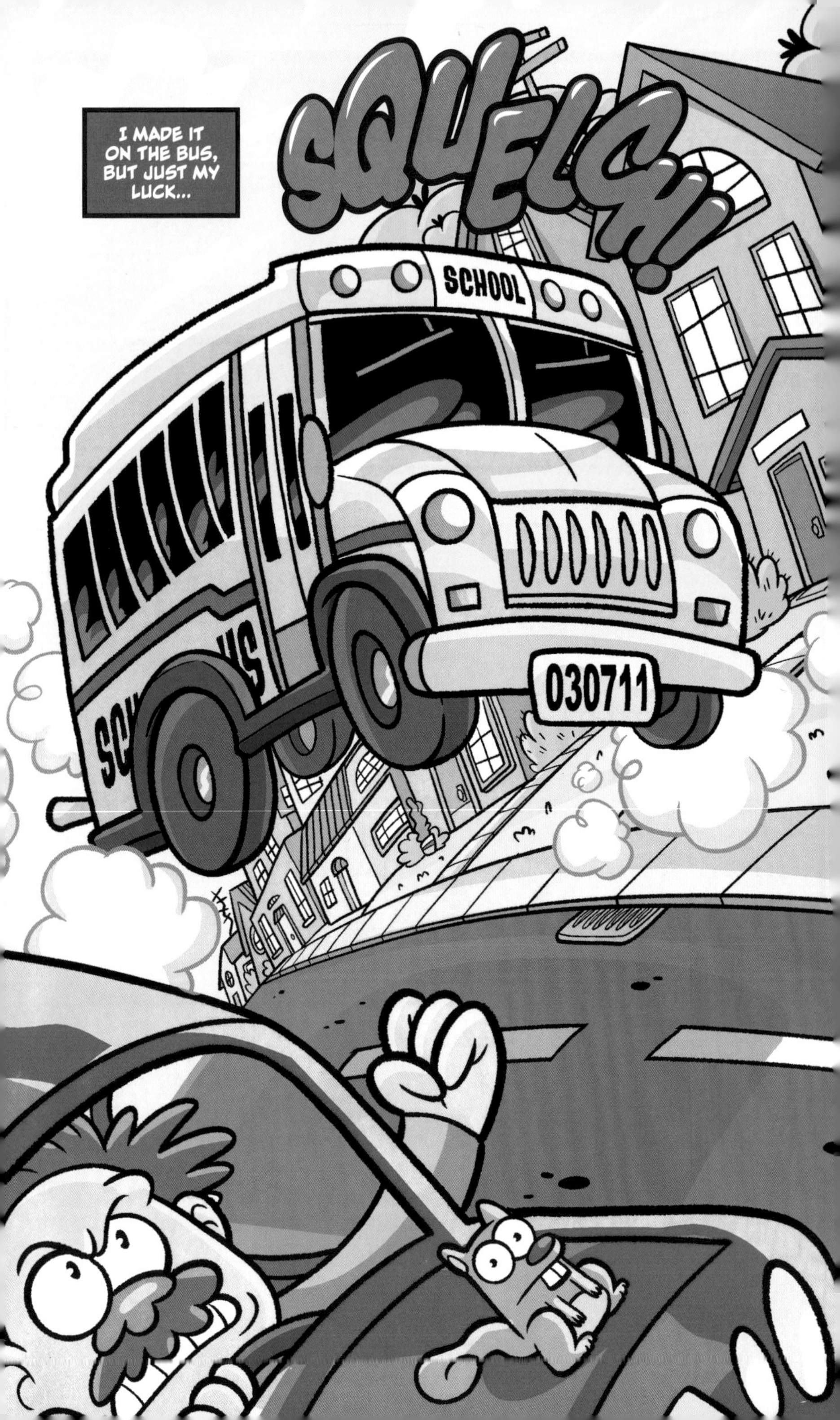
I MADE IT ON THE BUS, BUT JUST MY LUCK...
SQUELCH!
SCHOOL
030711

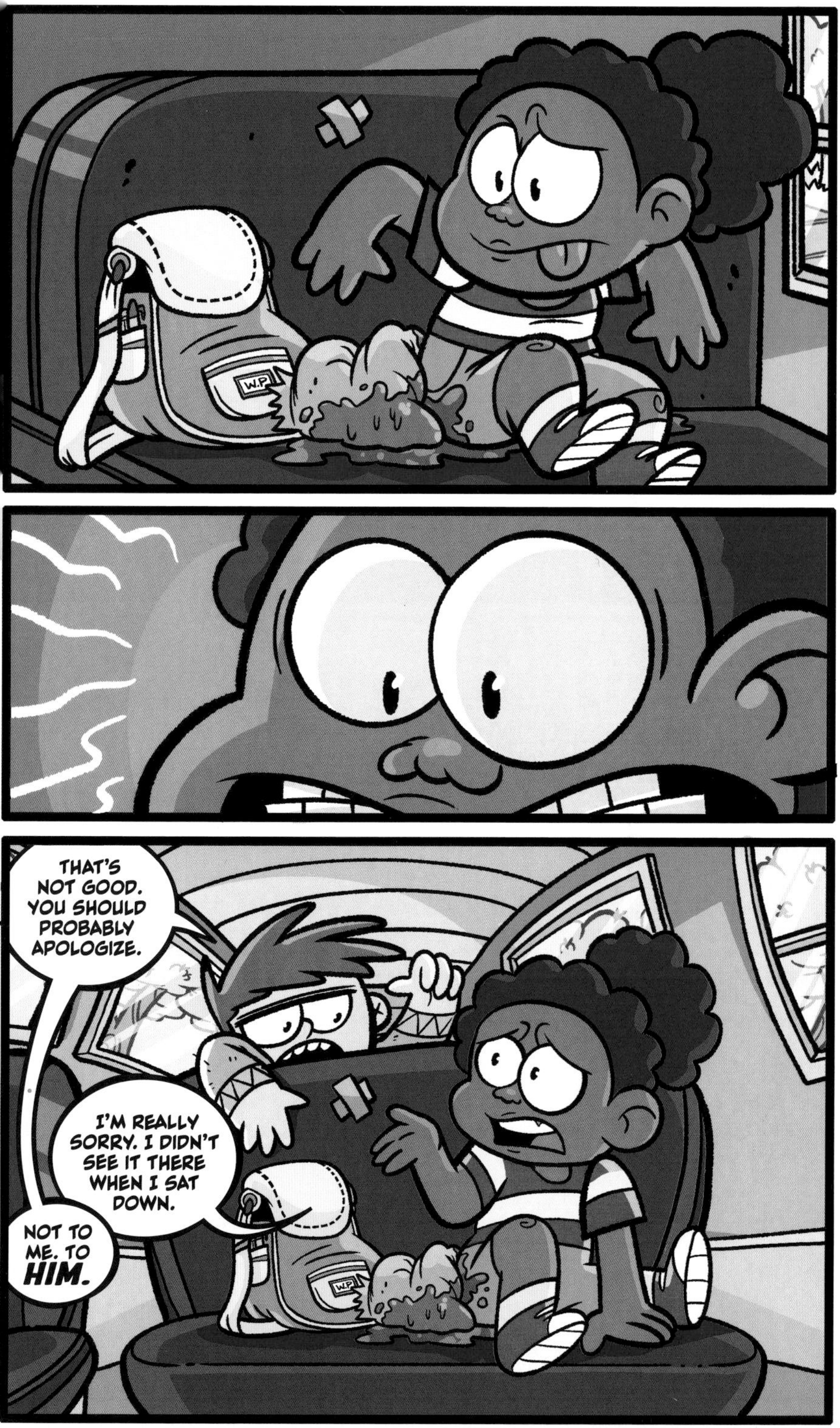
W.P.
THAT'S NOT GOOD. YOU SHOULD PROBABLY APOLOGIZE.
I'M REALLY SORRY. I DIDN'T SEE IT THERE WHEN I SAT DOWN.
NOT TO ME. TO **HIM.**
W.P.

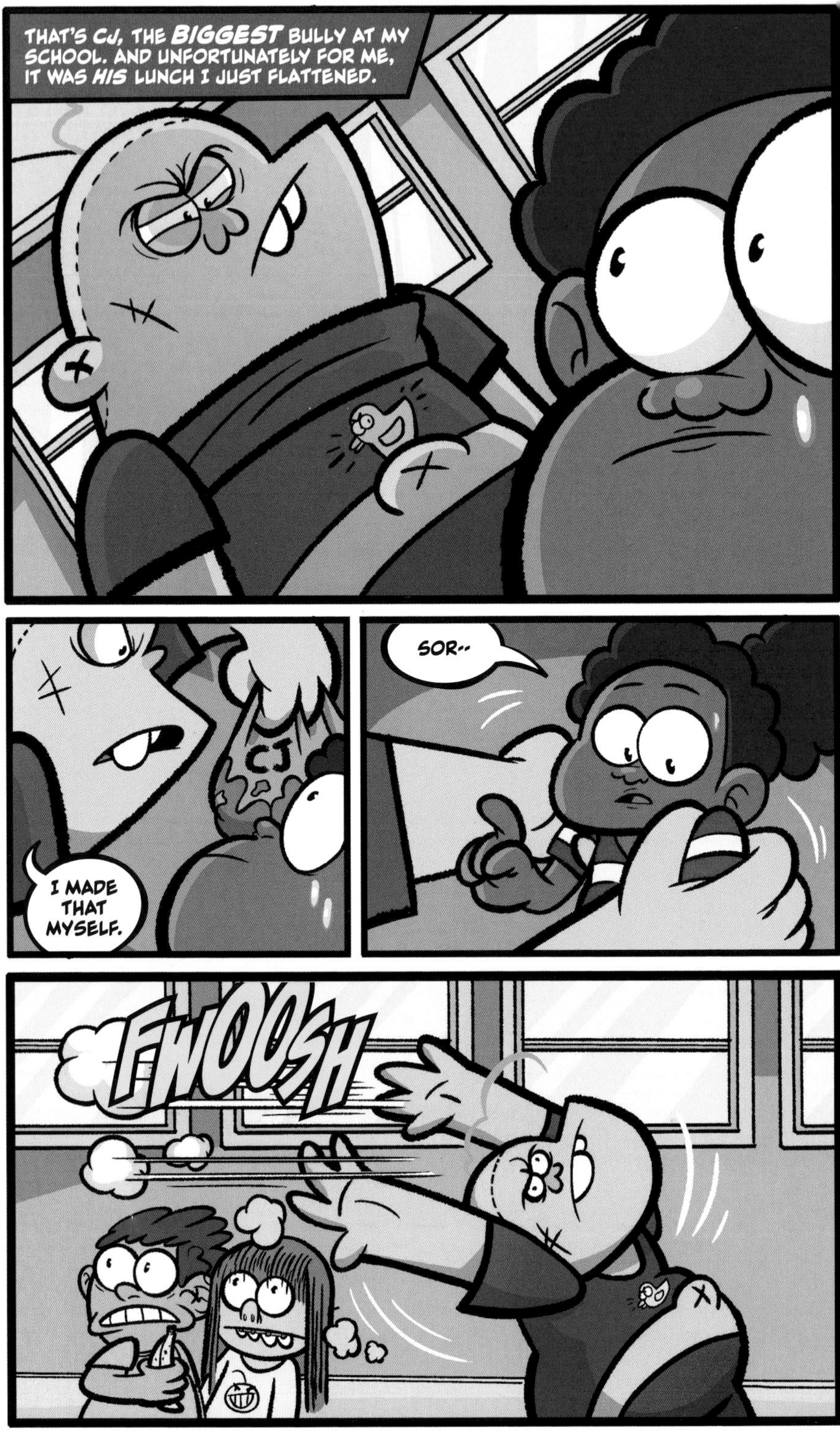
THAT'S CJ, THE BIGGEST BULLY AT MY SCHOOL. AND UNFORTUNATELY FOR ME, IT WAS HIS LUNCH I JUST FLATTENED.
CJ
I MADE THAT MYSELF.
SOR--
FWOOSH

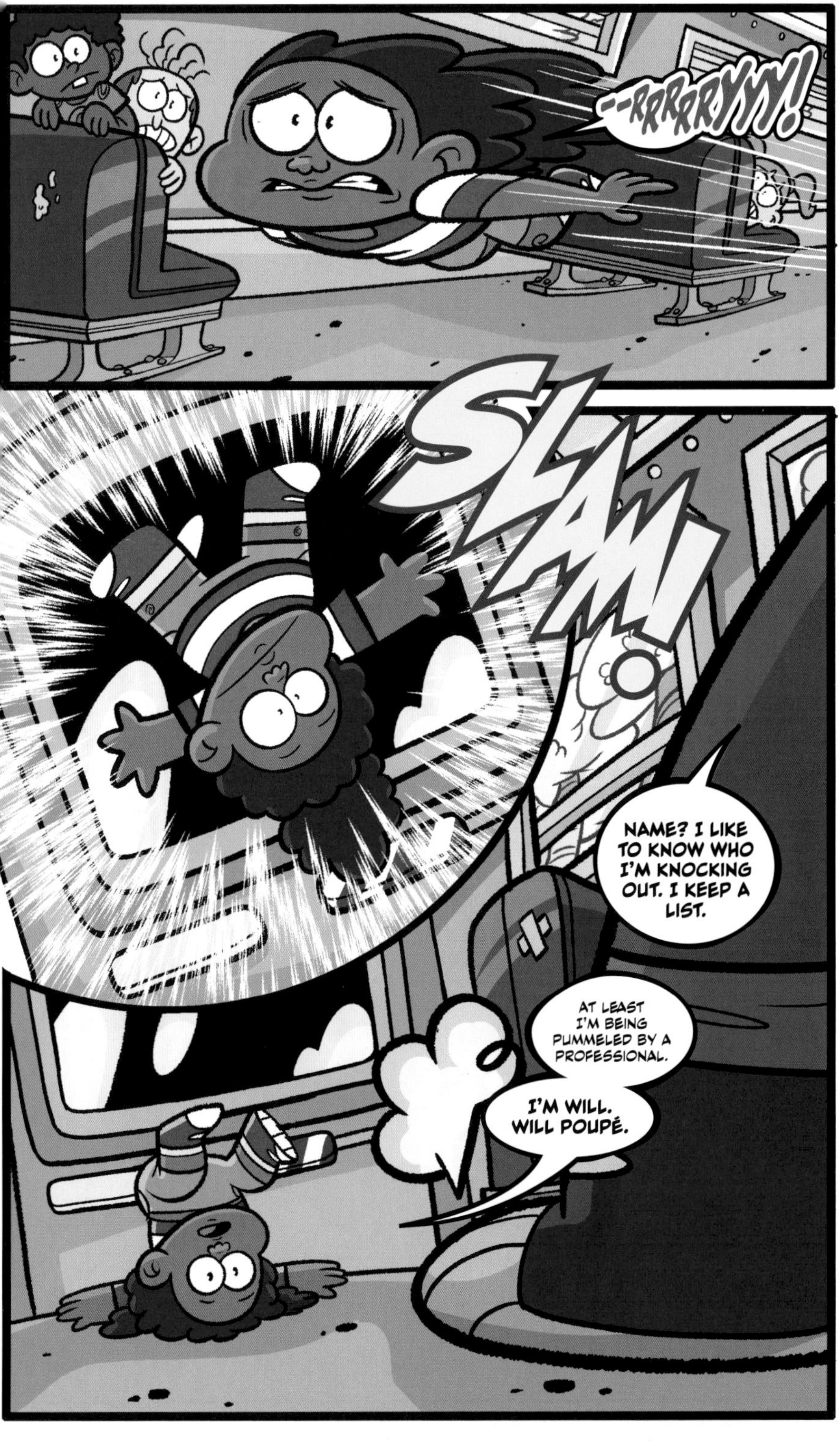
--RRRRRYYYY!
SLAM!
NAME? I LIKE TO KNOW WHO I'M KNOCKING OUT. I KEEP A LIST.
AT LEAST I'M BEING PUMMELED BY A PROFESSIONAL.
I'M WILL. WILL POUPÉ.

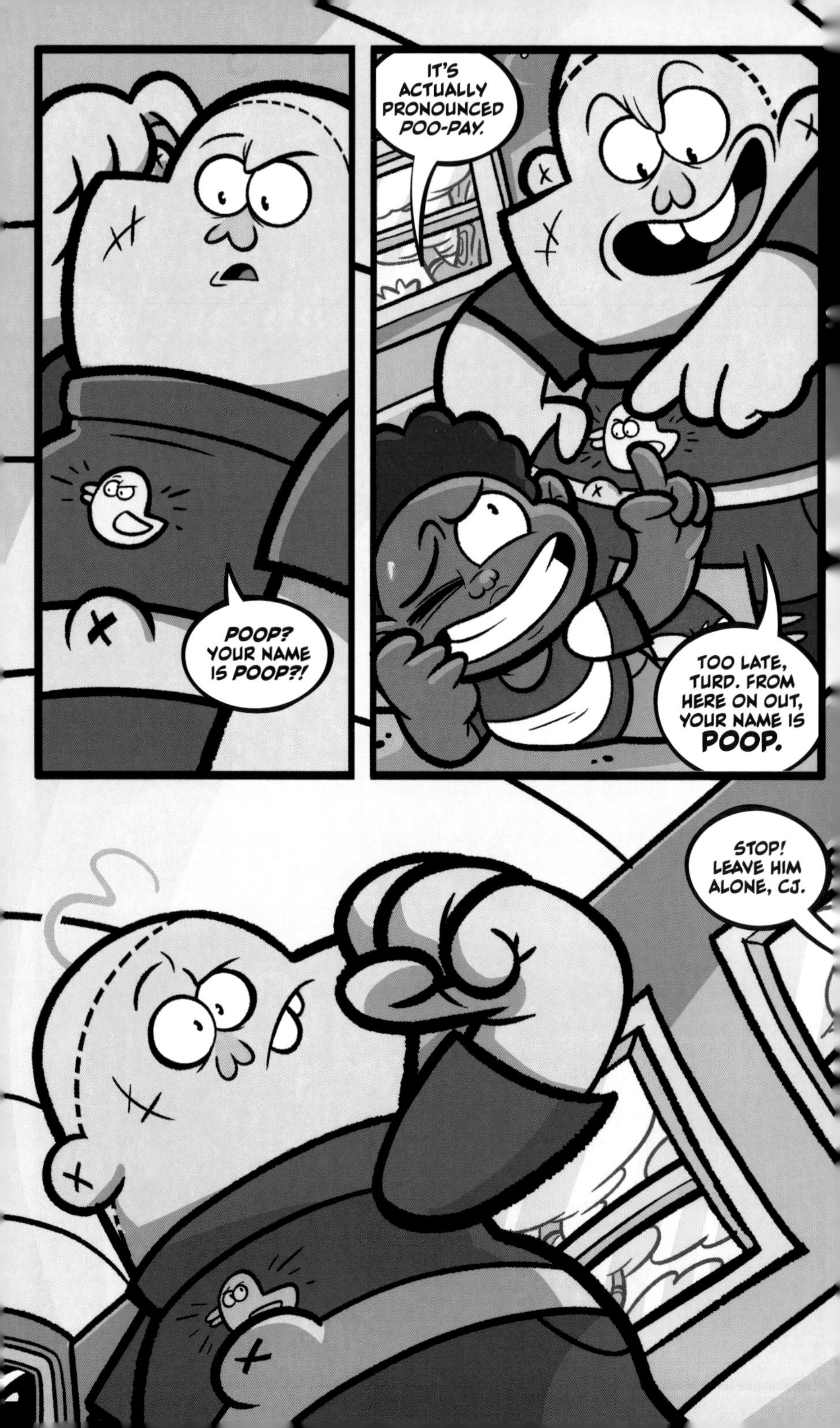
POOP? YOUR NAME IS POOP?!
IT'S ACTUALLY PRONOUNCED POO-PAY.
TOO LATE, TURD. FROM HERE ON OUT, YOUR NAME IS POOP.
STOP! LEAVE HIM ALONE, CJ.

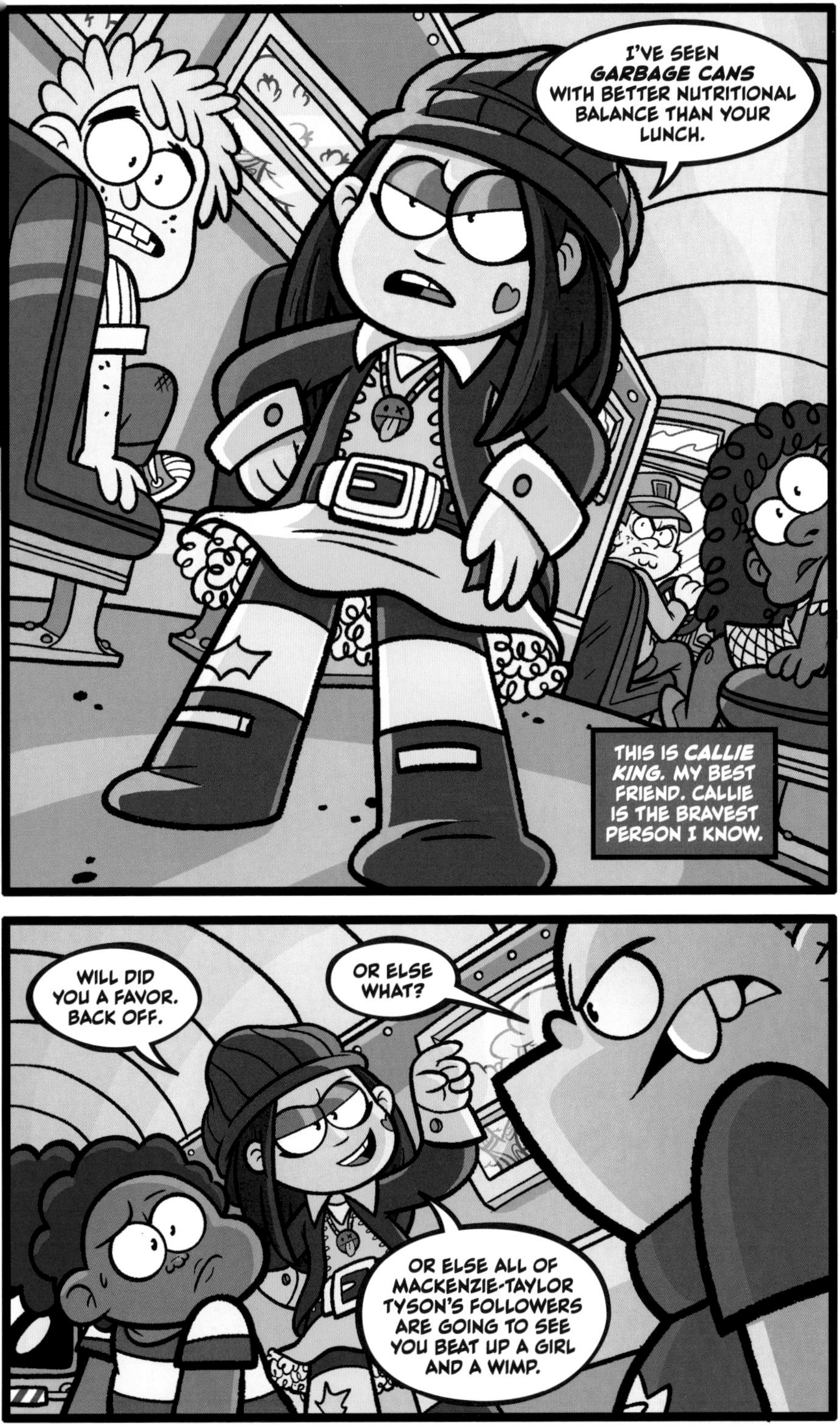
I'VE SEEN GARBAGE CANS WITH BETTER NUTRITIONAL BALANCE THAN YOUR LUNCH.
THIS IS CALLIE KING. MY BEST FRIEND. CALLIE IS THE BRAVEST PERSON I KNOW.
WILL DID YOU A FAVOR. BACK OFF.
OR ELSE WHAT?
OR ELSE ALL OF MACKENZIE-TAYLOR TYSON'S FOLLOWERS ARE GOING TO SEE YOU BEAT UP A GIRL AND A WIMP.

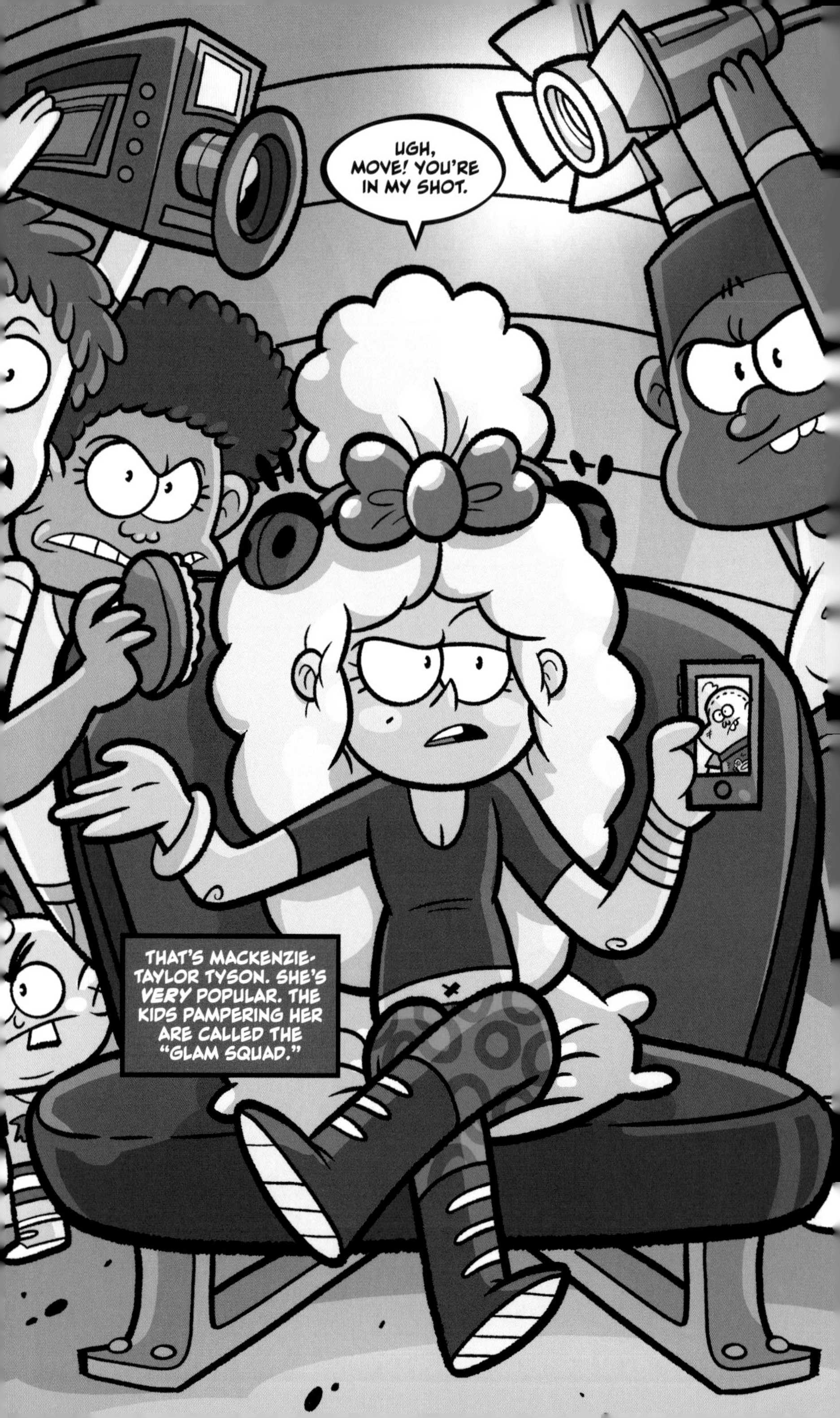
UGH, MOVE! YOU'RE IN MY SHOT.
THAT'S MACKENZIE-TAYLOR TYSON. SHE'S *VERY* POPULAR. THE KIDS PAMPERING HER ARE CALLED THE "GLAM SQUAD."

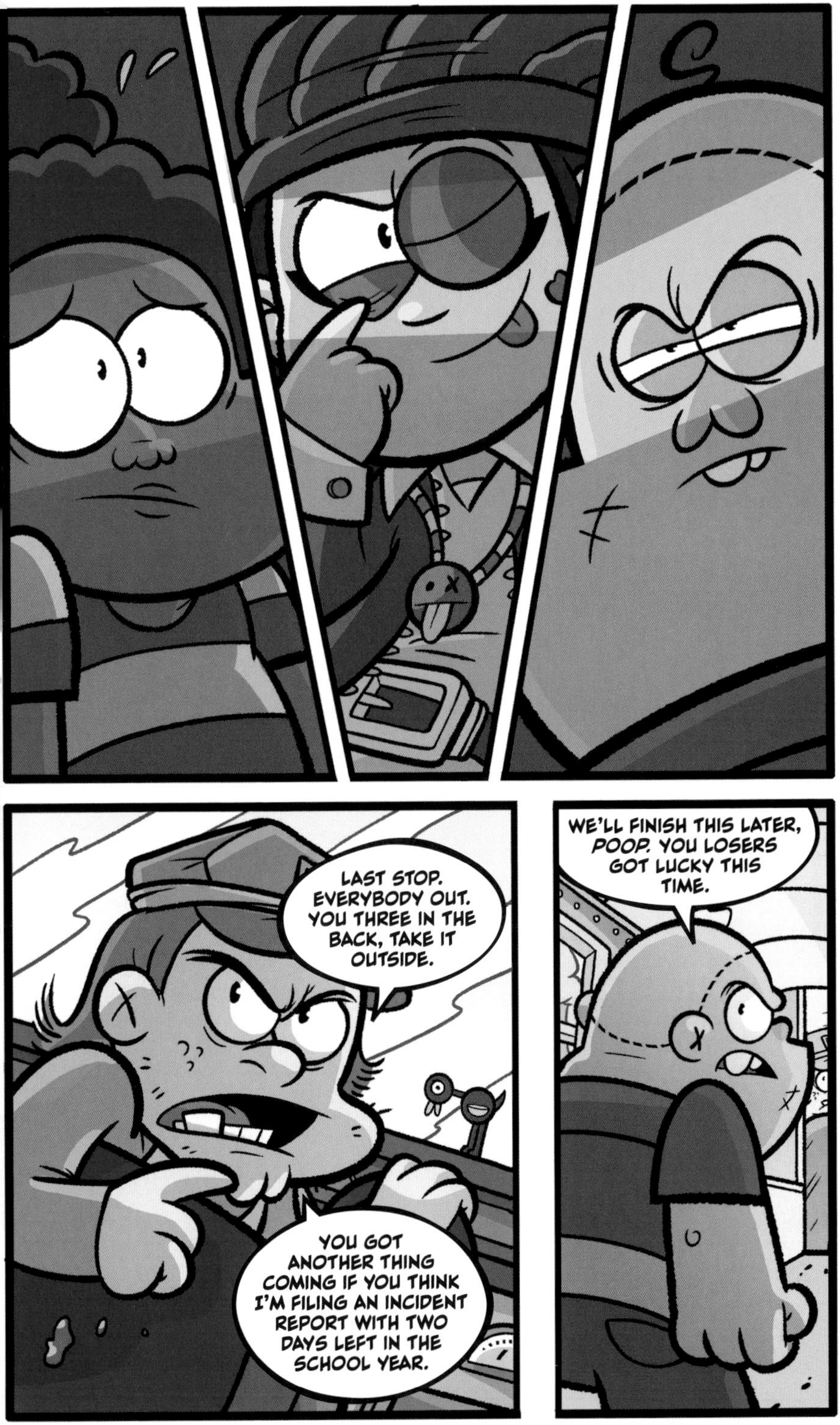
LAST STOP. EVERYBODY OUT. YOU THREE IN THE BACK, TAKE IT OUTSIDE.
YOU GOT ANOTHER THING COMING IF YOU THINK I'M FILING AN INCIDENT REPORT WITH TWO DAYS LEFT IN THE SCHOOL YEAR.
WE'LL FINISH THIS LATER, *POOP.* YOU LOSERS GOT LUCKY THIS TIME.

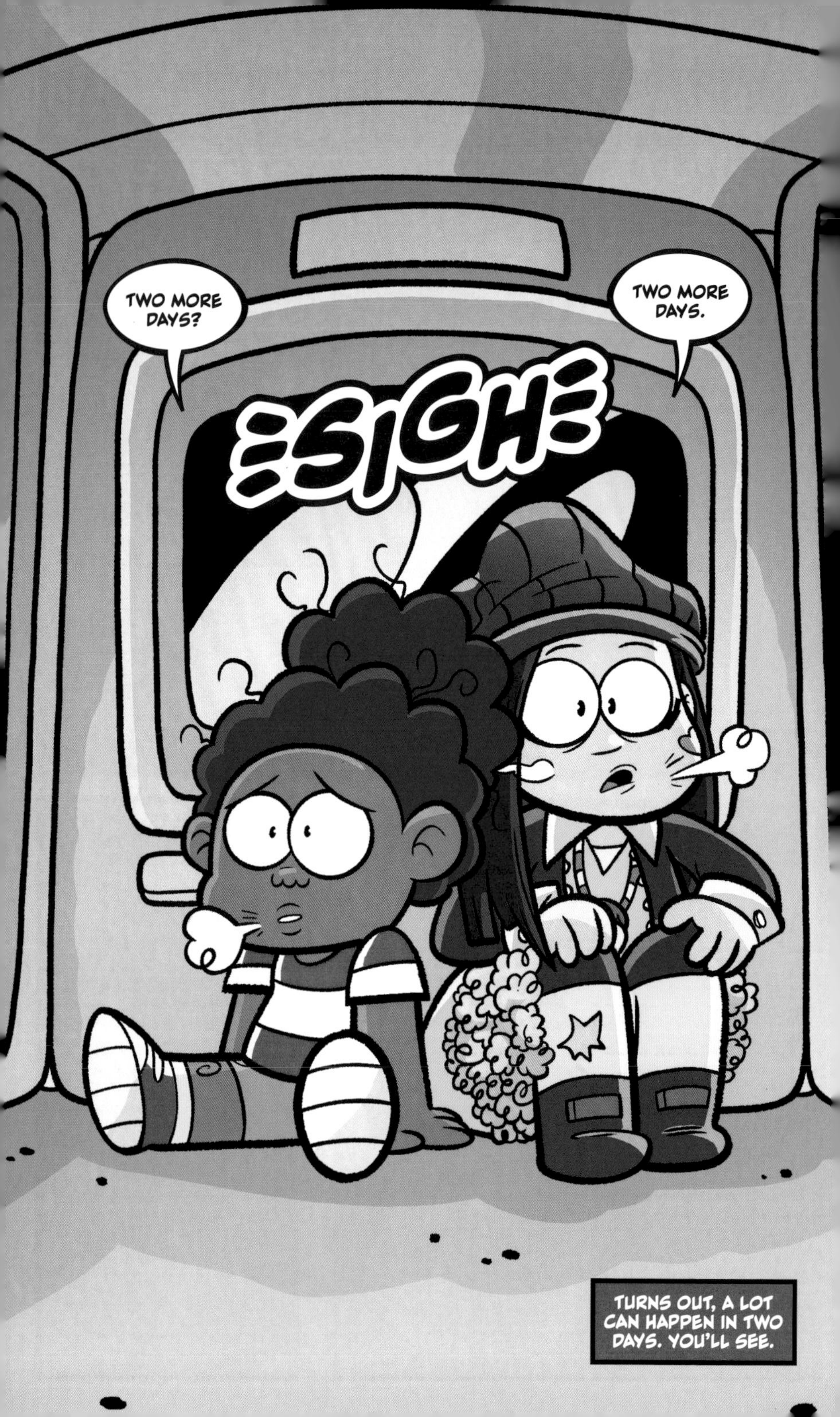
TWO MORE DAYS?
TWO MORE DAYS.
SIGH
TURNS OUT, A LOT CAN HAPPEN IN TWO DAYS. YOU'LL SEE.

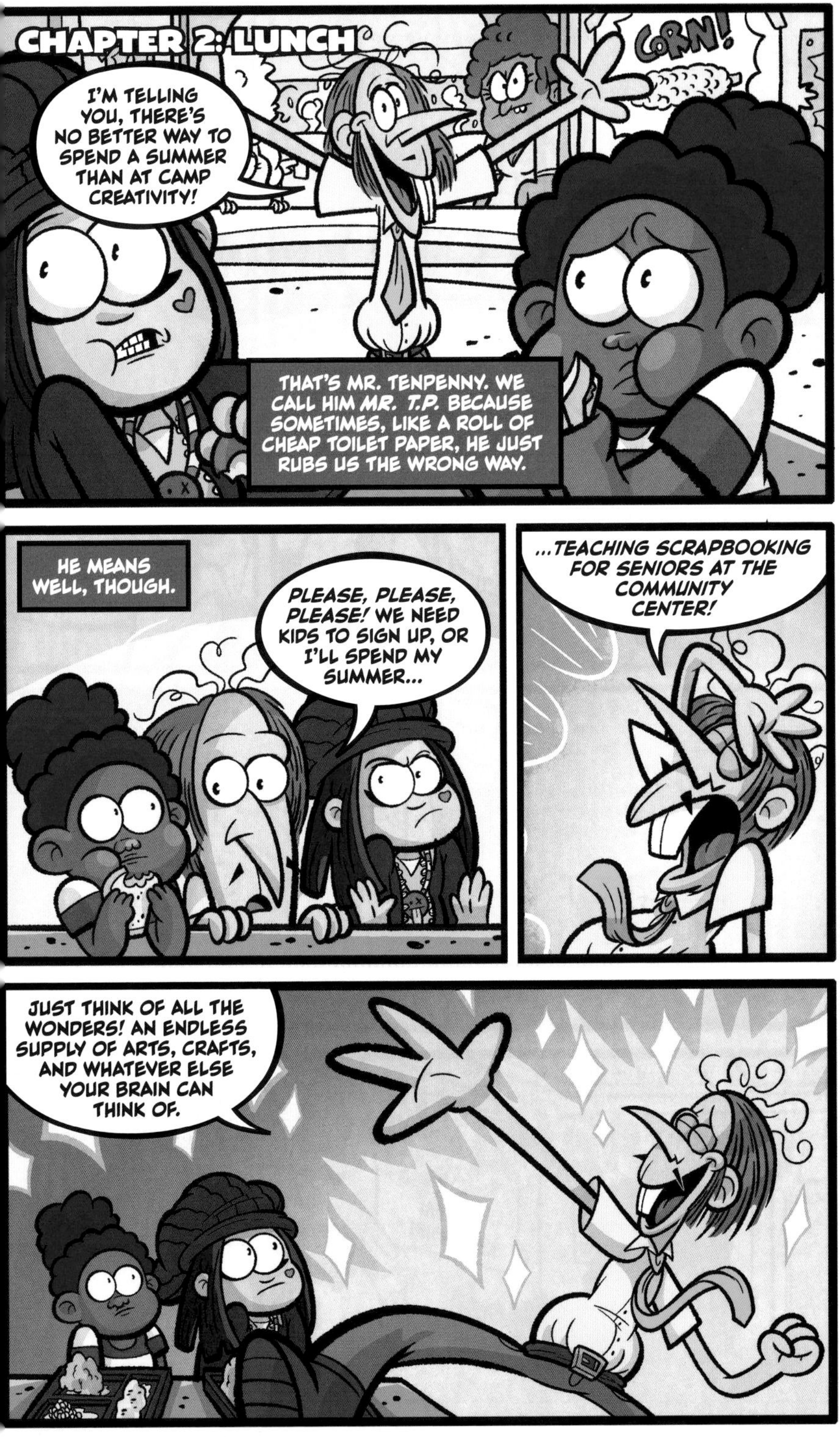
CHAPTER 2: LUNCH
CORN!
I'M TELLING YOU, THERE'S NO BETTER WAY TO SPEND A SUMMER THAN AT CAMP CREATIVITY!
THAT'S MR. TENPENNY. WE CALL HIM MR. T.P. BECAUSE SOMETIMES, LIKE A ROLL OF CHEAP TOILET PAPER, HE JUST RUBS US THE WRONG WAY.
HE MEANS WELL, THOUGH.
PLEASE, PLEASE, PLEASE! WE NEED KIDS TO SIGN UP, OR I'LL SPEND MY SUMMER...
...TEACHING SCRAPBOOKING FOR SENIORS AT THE COMMUNITY CENTER!
JUST THINK OF ALL THE WONDERS! AN ENDLESS SUPPLY OF ARTS, CRAFTS, AND WHATEVER ELSE YOUR BRAIN CAN THINK OF.

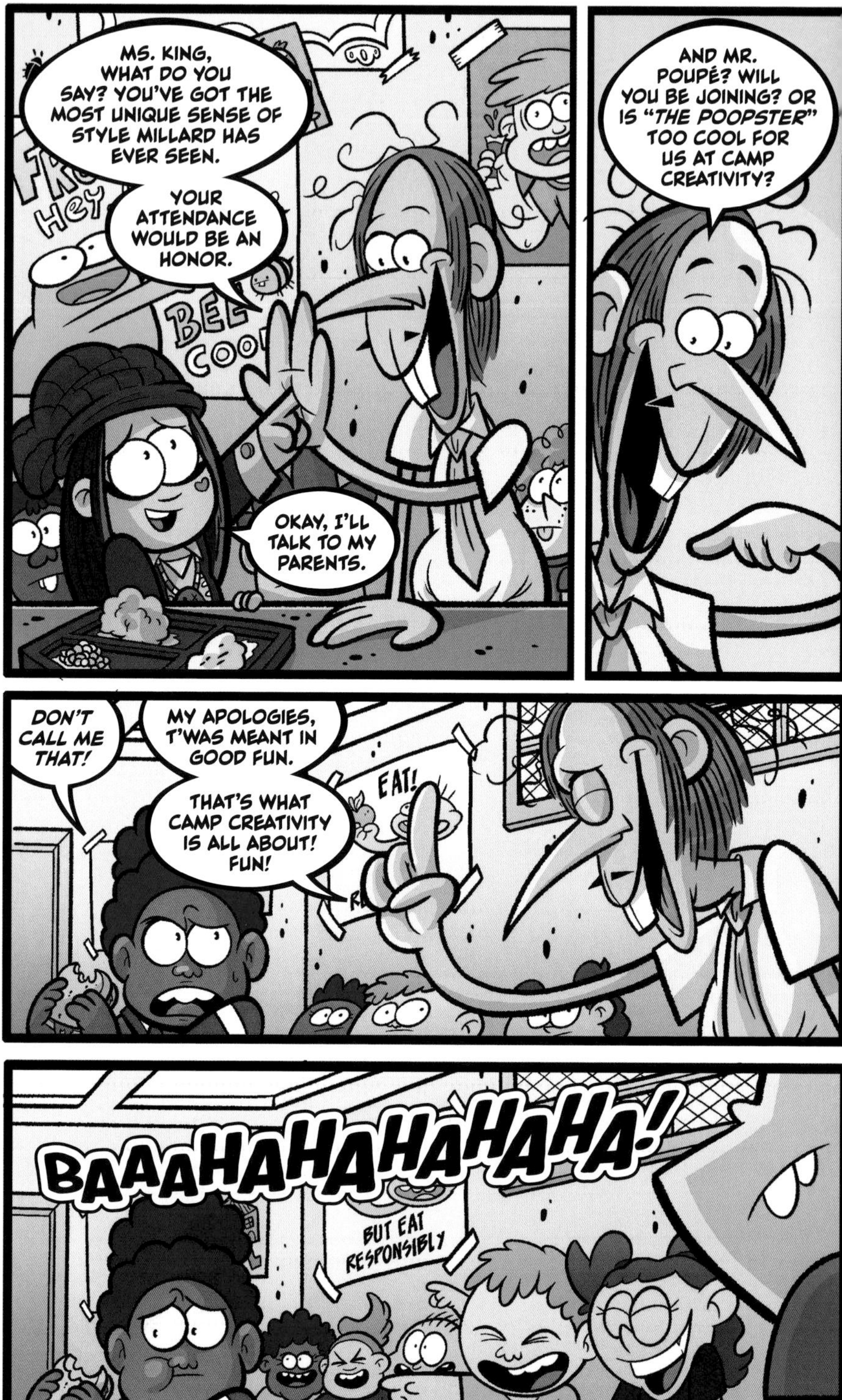
MS. KING, WHAT DO YOU SAY? YOU'VE GOT THE MOST UNIQUE SENSE OF STYLE MILLARD HAS EVER SEEN.
YOUR ATTENDANCE WOULD BE AN HONOR.
OKAY, I'LL TALK TO MY PARENTS.
AND MR. POUPÉ? WILL YOU BE JOINING? OR IS "*THE POOPSTER*" TOO COOL FOR US AT CAMP CREATIVITY?
DON'T CALL ME THAT!
MY APOLOGIES, T'WAS MEANT IN GOOD FUN.
THAT'S WHAT CAMP CREATIVITY IS ALL ABOUT! FUN!
EAT!
BAAAHAHAHAHAHAHA!
BUT EAT RESPONSIBLY

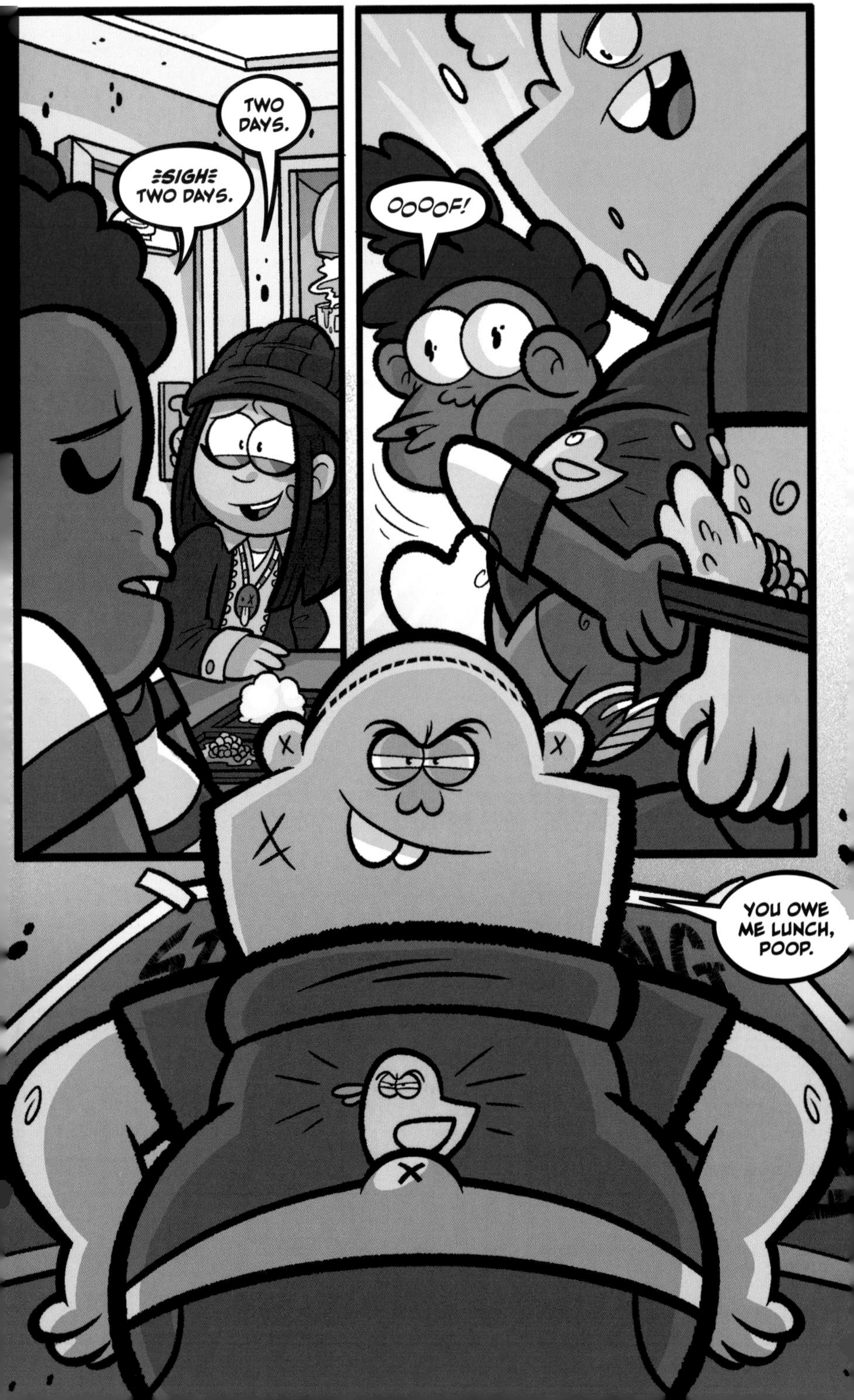

≡SIGH≡ TWO DAYS.
TWO DAYS.
OOOOF!
YOU OWE ME LUNCH, POOP.

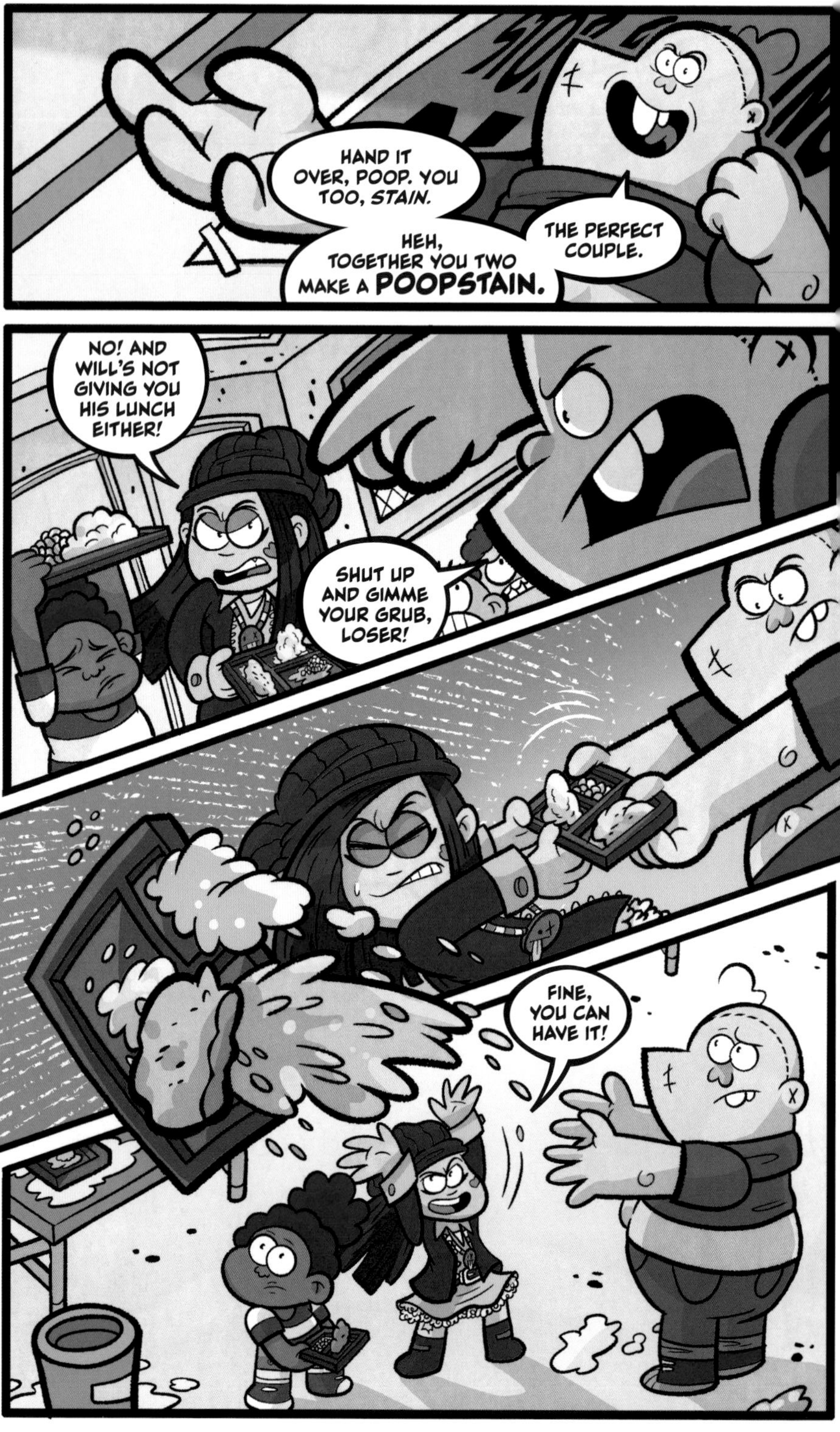
HAND IT OVER, POOP. YOU TOO, STAIN.
HEH, TOGETHER YOU TWO MAKE A POOPSTAIN.
THE PERFECT COUPLE.
NO! AND WILL'S NOT GIVING YOU HIS LUNCH EITHER!
SHUT UP AND GIMME YOUR GRUB, LOSER!
FINE, YOU CAN HAVE IT!

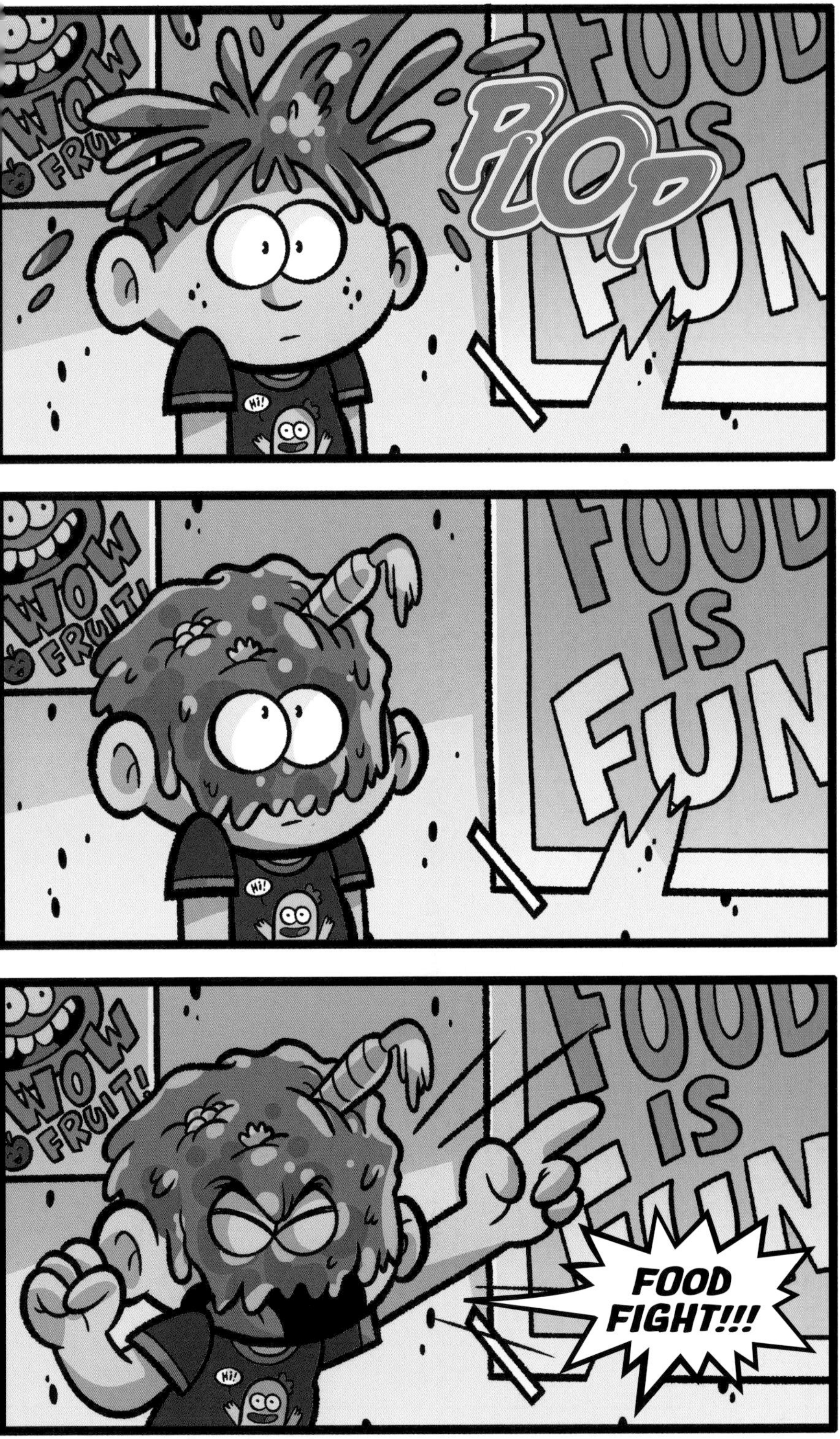
PLOP
WOW FRUIT!
FOOD IS FUN
HI!
FOOD FIGHT!!!

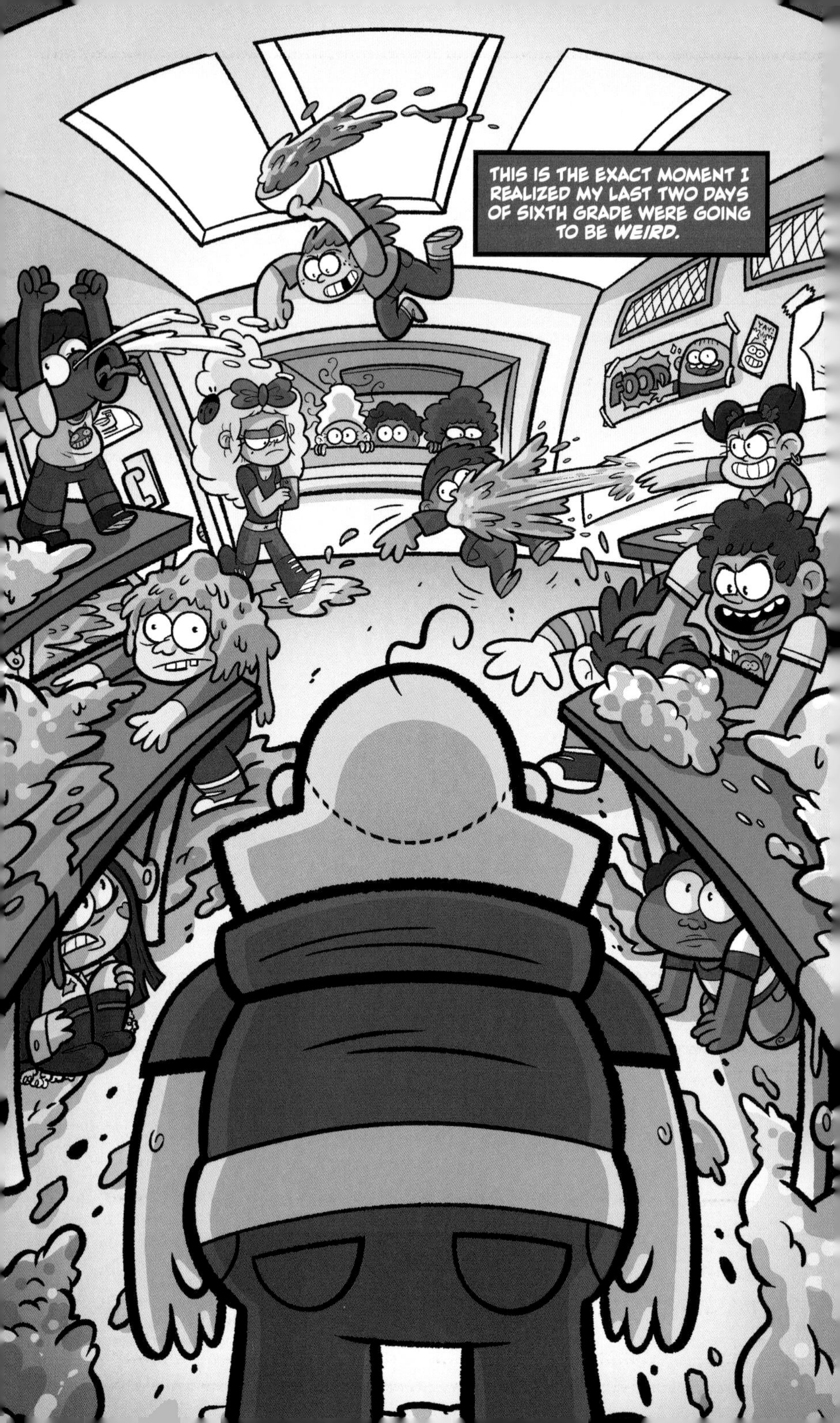
THIS IS THE EXACT MOMENT I REALIZED MY LAST TWO DAYS OF SIXTH GRADE WERE GOING TO BE *WEIRD.*
FOOD
YAY!

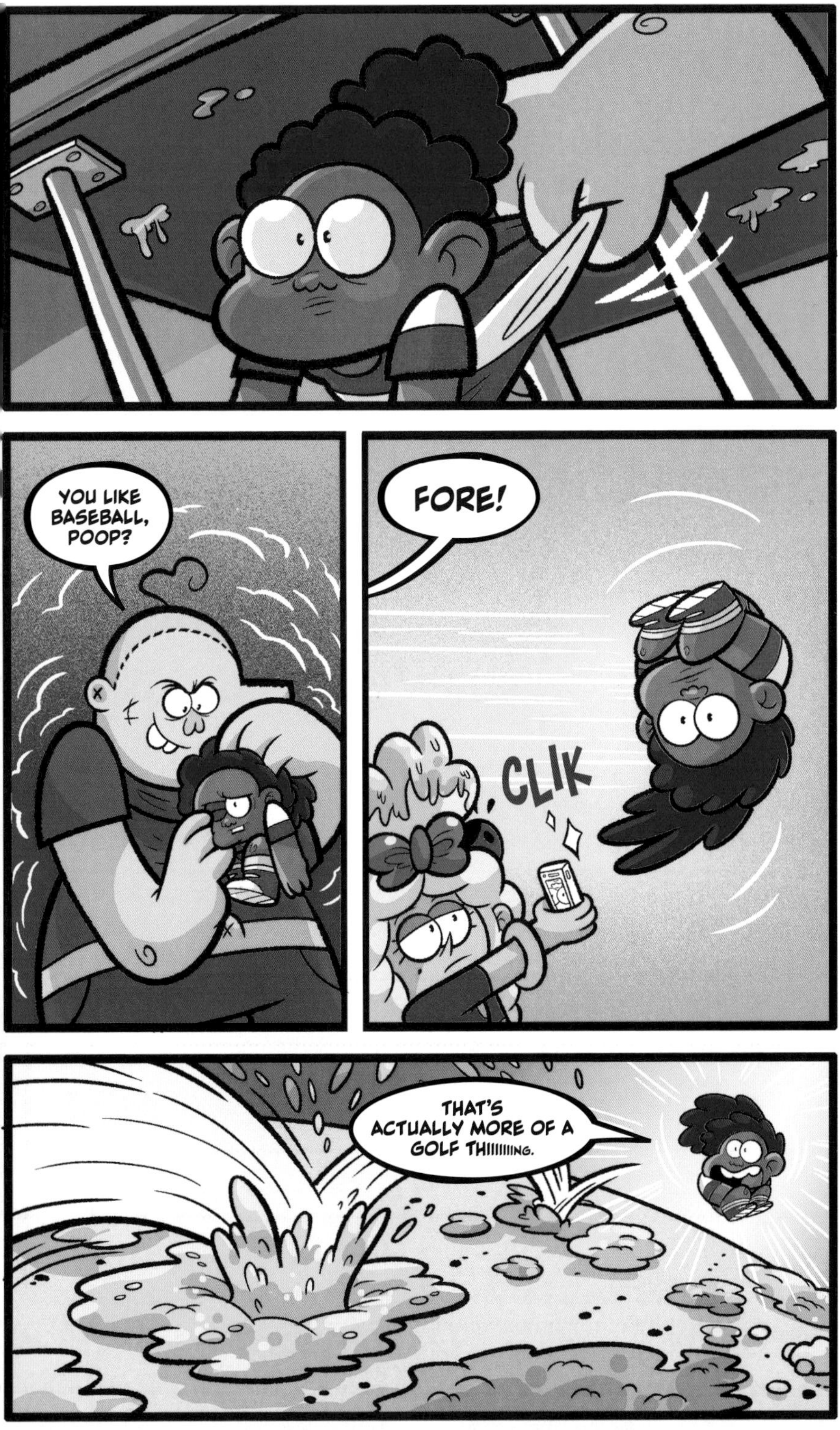
YOU LIKE BASEBALL, POOP?
FORE!
CLIK
THAT'S ACTUALLY MORE OF A GOLF THIIIIIIING.

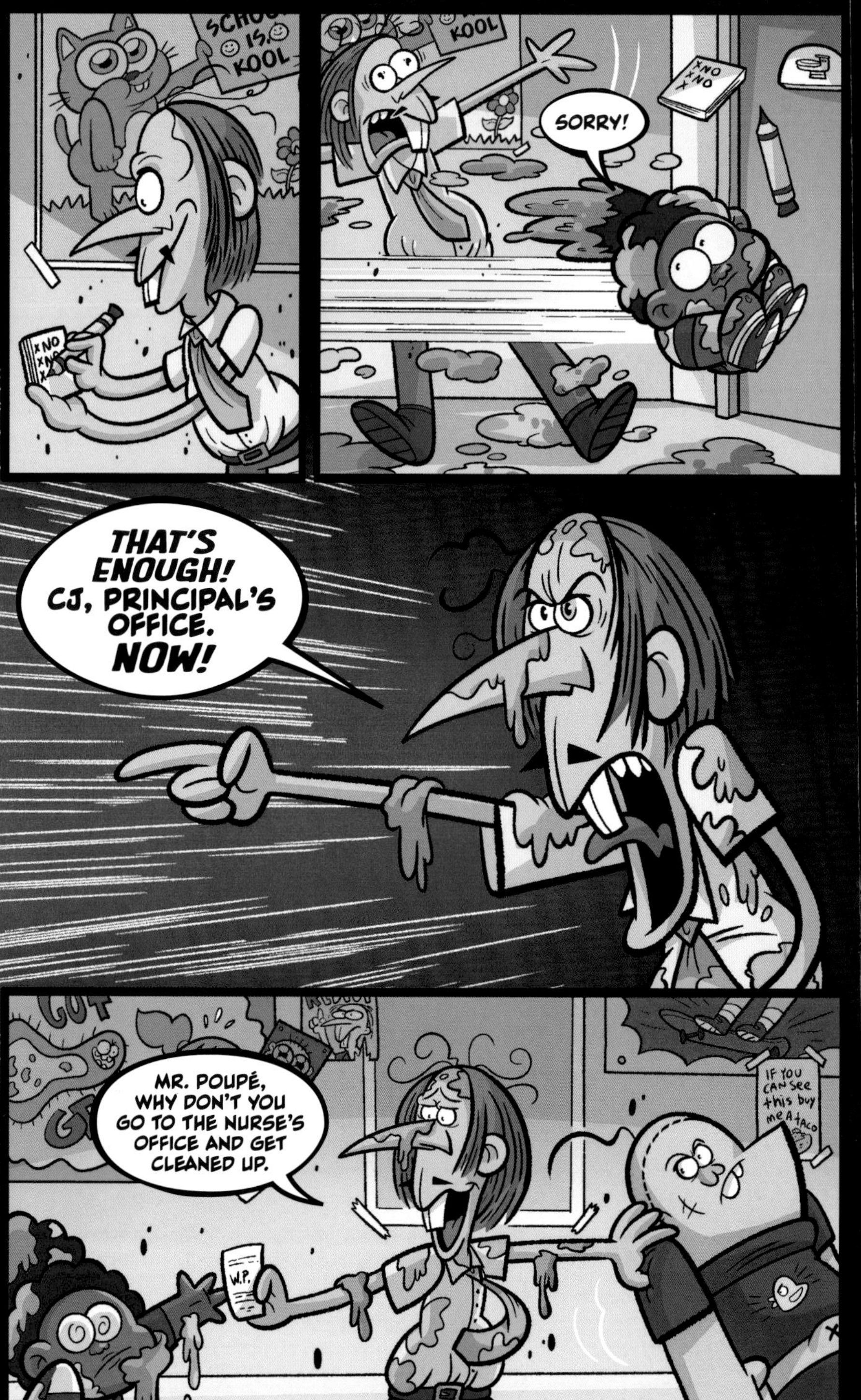
SORRY!
THAT'S ENOUGH! CJ, PRINCIPAL'S OFFICE. NOW!
MR. POUPÉ, WHY DON'T YOU GO TO THE NURSE'S OFFICE AND GET CLEANED UP.
IF YOU CAN see this buy me A taco

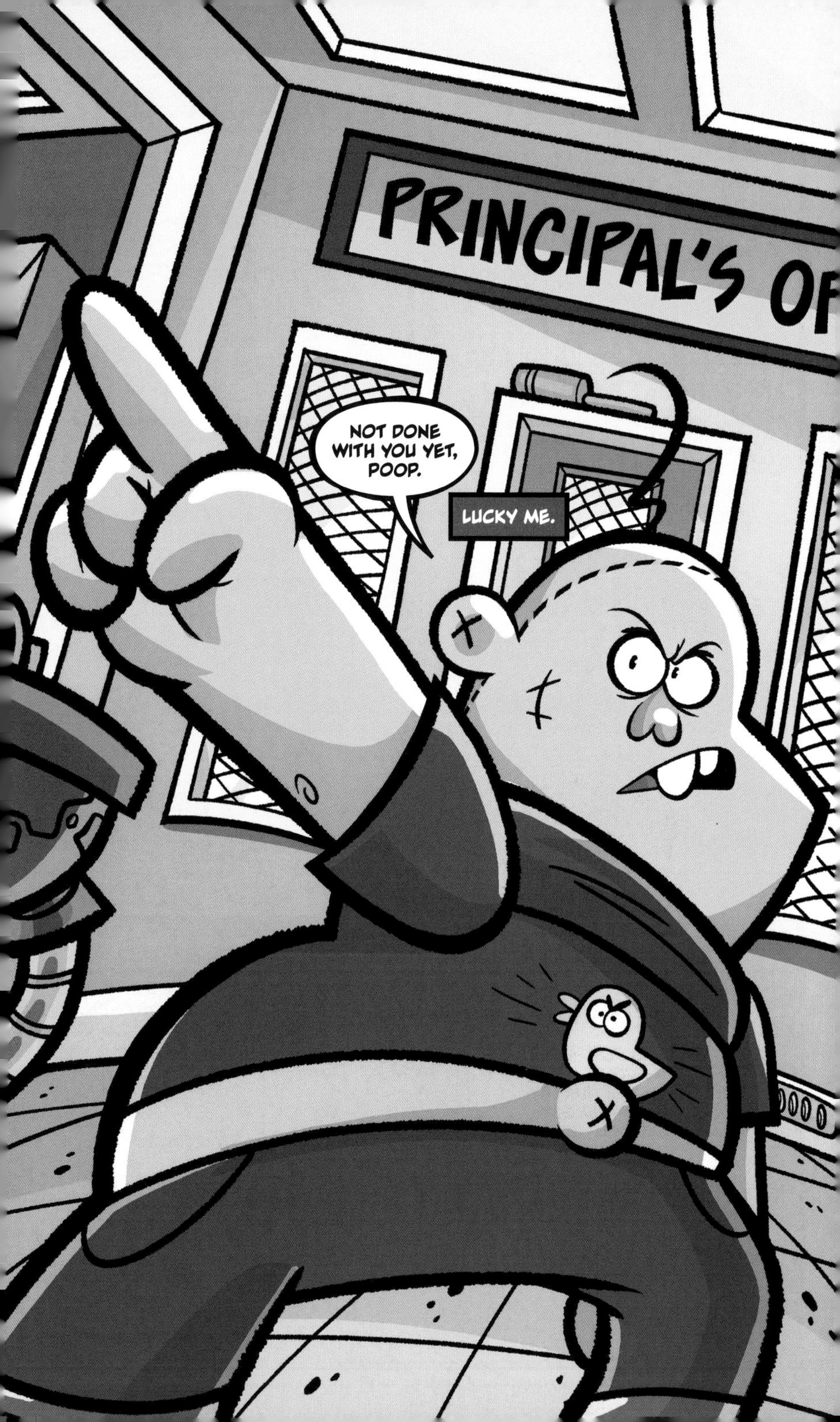
PRINCIPAL'S OF
NOT DONE WITH YOU YET, POOP.
LUCKY ME.

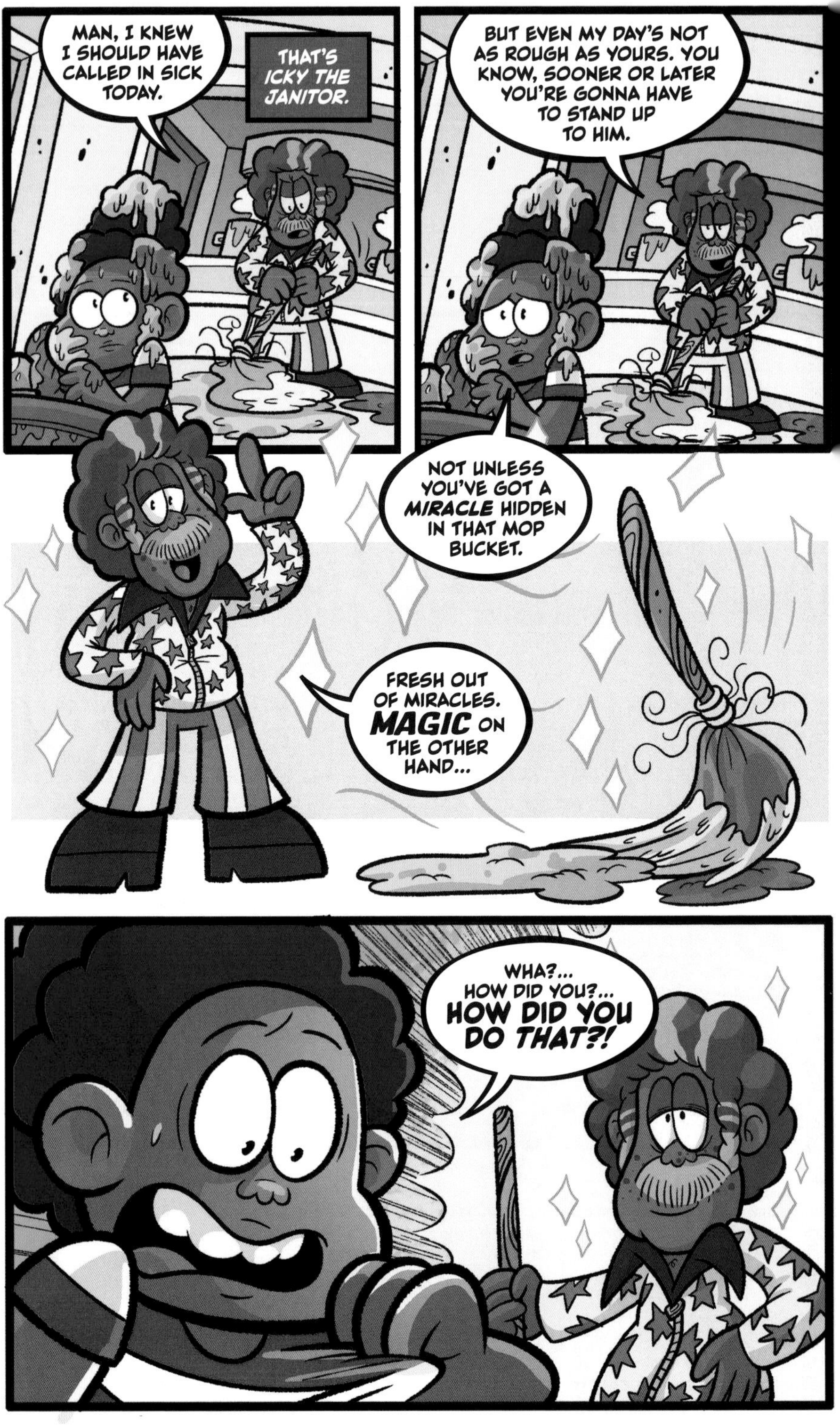
MAN, I KNEW I SHOULD HAVE CALLED IN SICK TODAY.
THAT'S *ICKY THE JANITOR.*
BUT EVEN MY DAY'S NOT AS ROUGH AS YOURS. YOU KNOW, SOONER OR LATER YOU'RE GONNA HAVE TO STAND UP TO HIM.
NOT UNLESS YOU'VE GOT A *MIRACLE* HIDDEN IN THAT MOP BUCKET.
FRESH OUT OF MIRACLES. **MAGIC** ON THE OTHER HAND...
WHA?... HOW DID YOU?... **HOW DID YOU DO *THAT*?!**

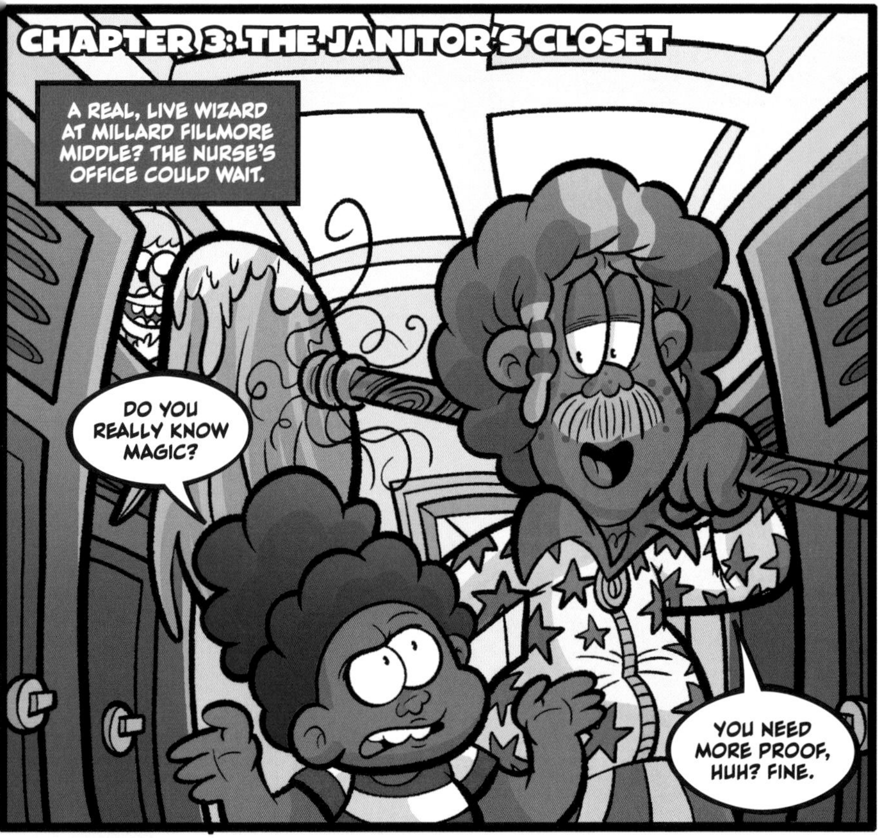
CHAPTER 3: THE JANITOR'S CLOSET
A REAL, LIVE WIZARD AT MILLARD FILLMORE MIDDLE? THE NURSE'S OFFICE COULD WAIT.
DO YOU REALLY KNOW MAGIC?
YOU NEED MORE PROOF, HUH? FINE.

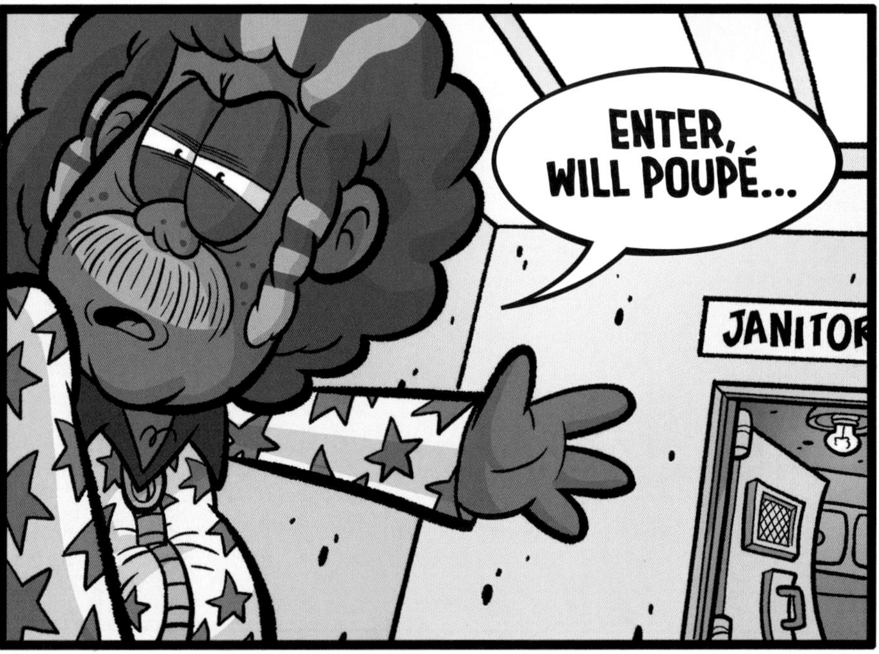
ENTER, WILL POUPÉ...
JANITOR

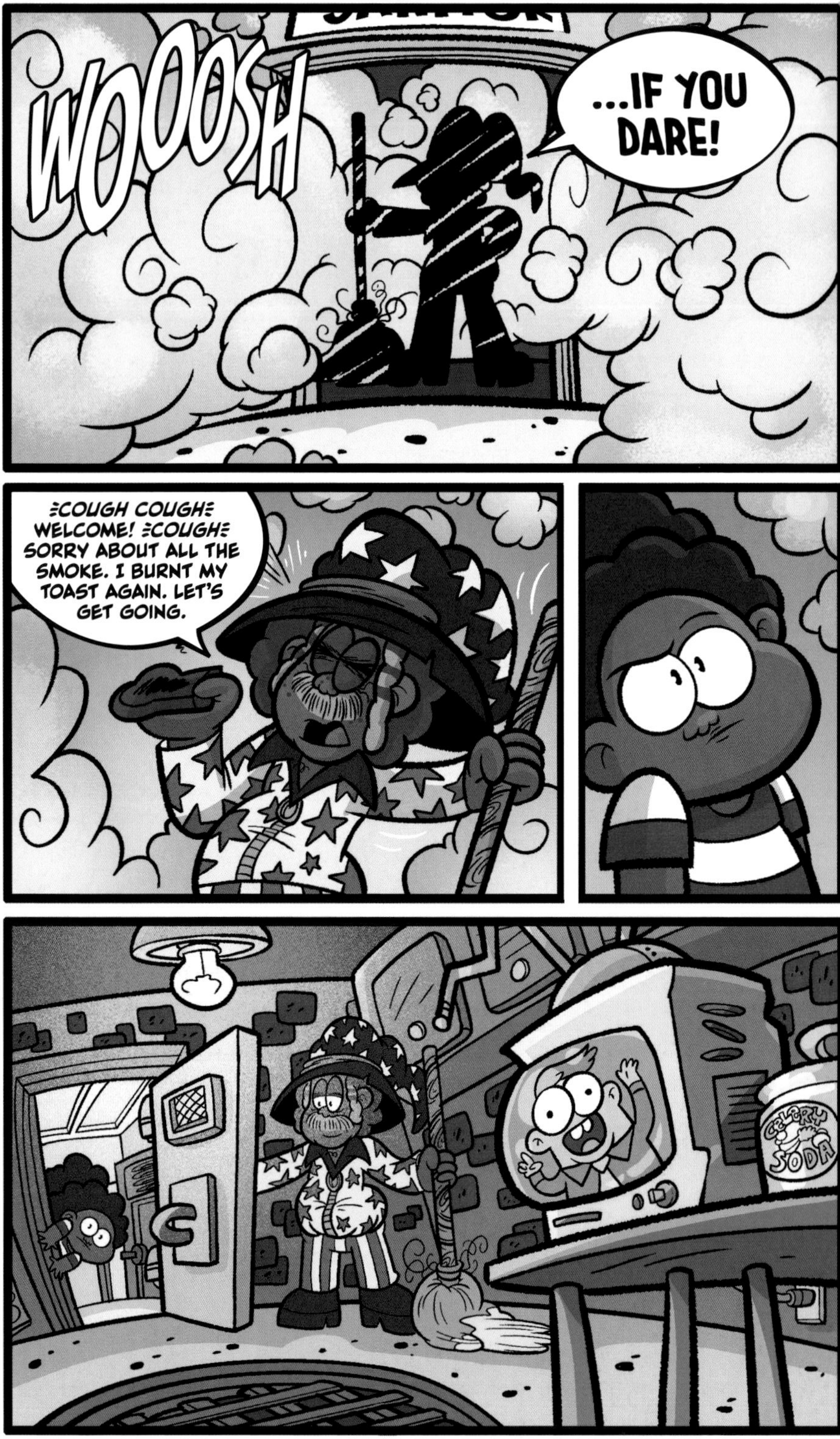
WOOOSH
...IF YOU DARE!
≡COUGH COUGH≡ WELCOME! ≡COUGH≡ SORRY ABOUT ALL THE SMOKE. I BURNT MY TOAST AGAIN. LET'S GET GOING.
CELERY SODA

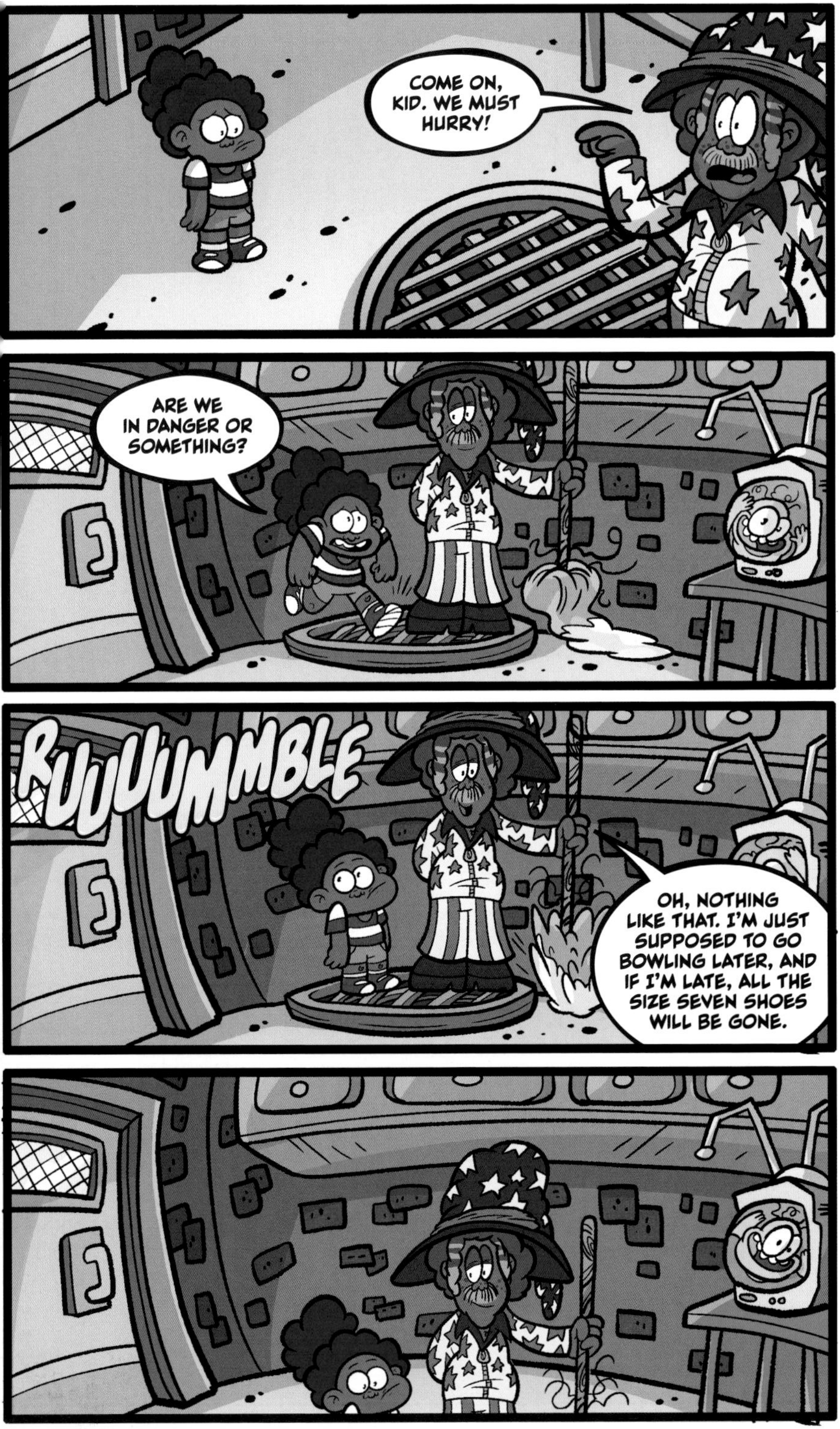
COME ON, KID. WE MUST HURRY!
ARE WE IN DANGER OR SOMETHING?
RUUUUMMBLE
OH, NOTHING LIKE THAT. I'M JUST SUPPOSED TO GO BOWLING LATER, AND IF I'M LATE, ALL THE SIZE SEVEN SHOES WILL BE GONE.

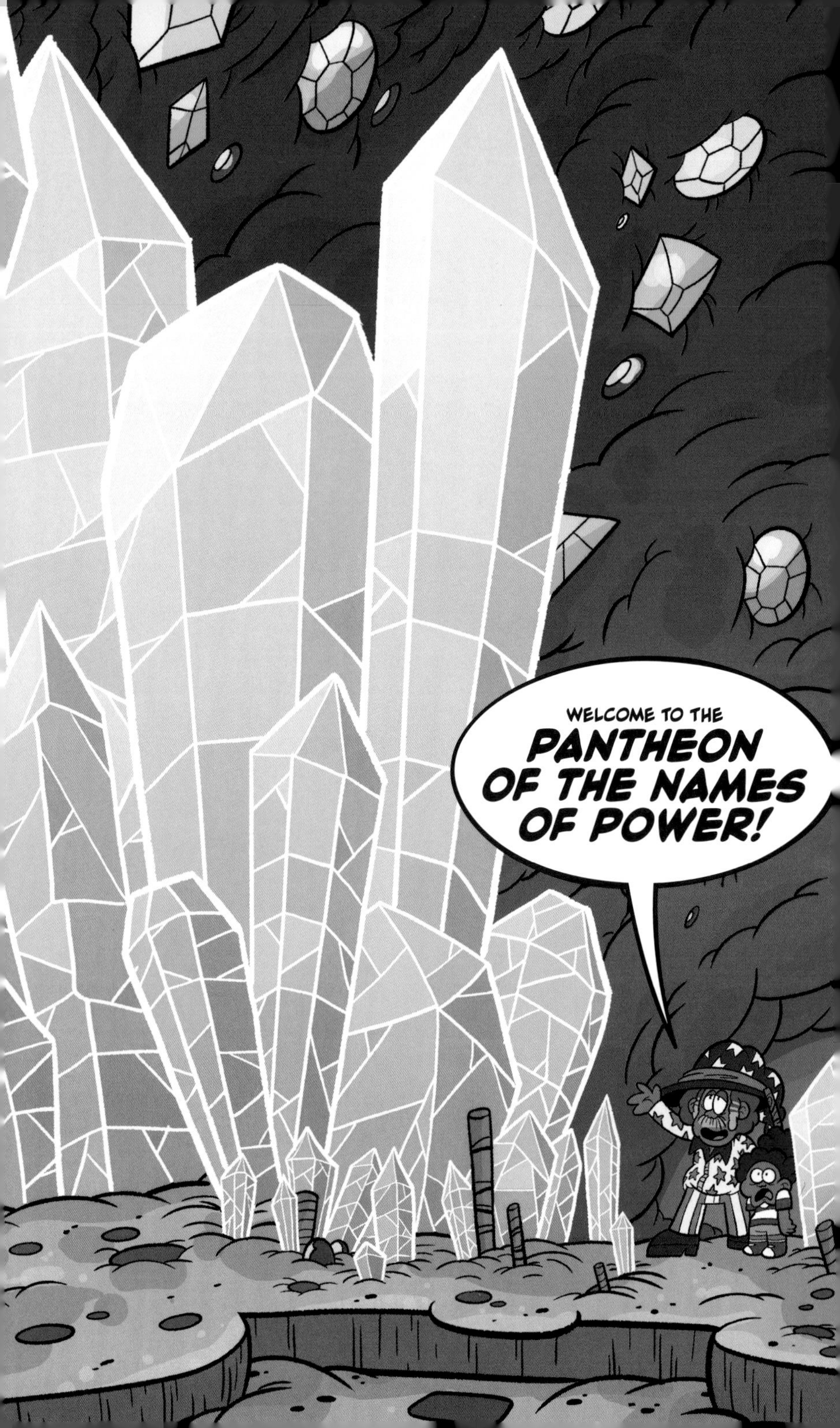
WELCOME TO THE
PANTHEON OF THE NAMES OF POWER!

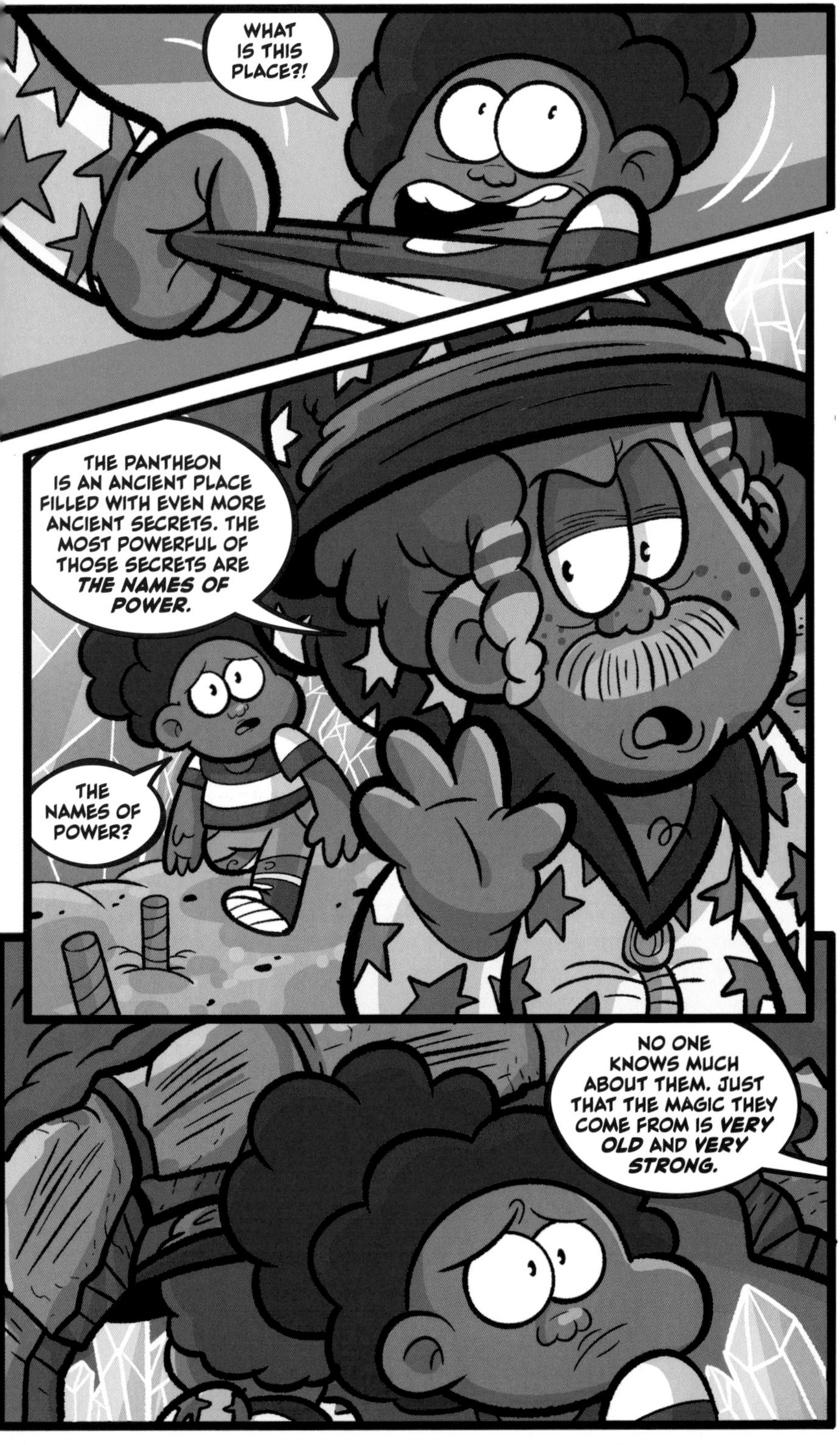
WHAT IS THIS PLACE?!
THE PANTHEON IS AN ANCIENT PLACE FILLED WITH EVEN MORE ANCIENT SECRETS. THE MOST POWERFUL OF THOSE SECRETS ARE *THE NAMES OF POWER.*
THE NAMES OF POWER?
NO ONE KNOWS MUCH ABOUT THEM. JUST THAT THE MAGIC THEY COME FROM IS *VERY OLD* AND *VERY STRONG.*

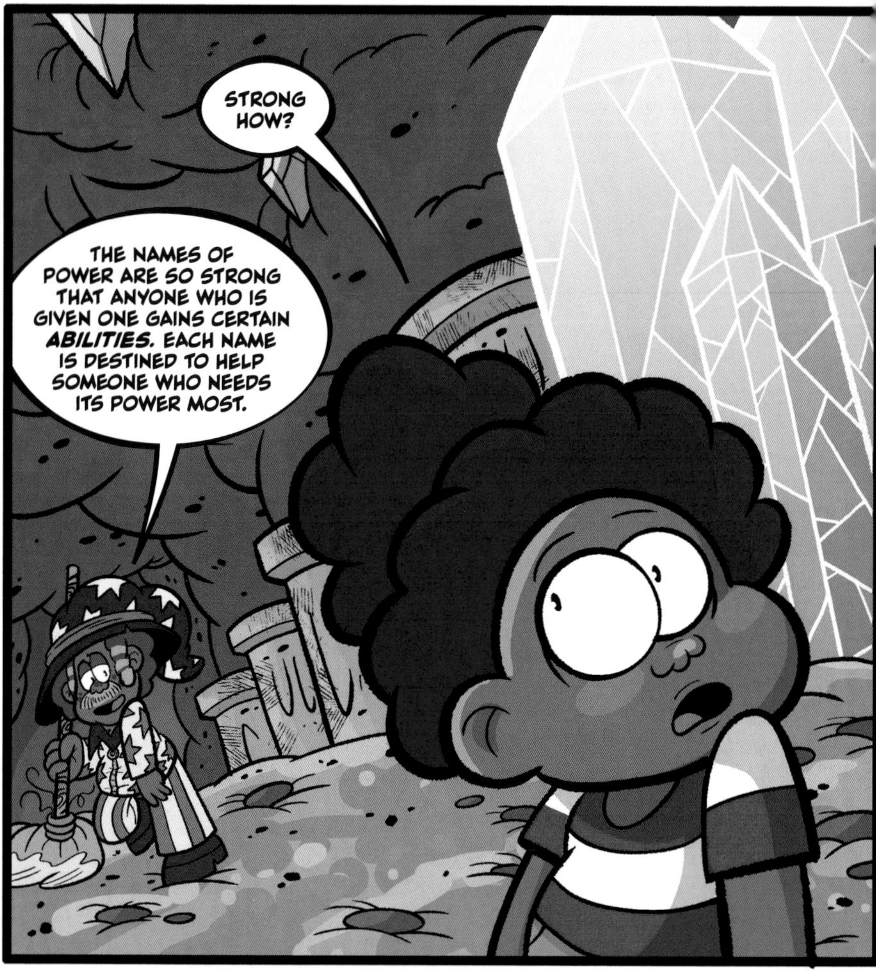
STRONG HOW?
THE NAMES OF POWER ARE SO STRONG THAT ANYONE WHO IS GIVEN ONE GAINS CERTAIN *ABILITIES.* EACH NAME IS DESTINED TO HELP SOMEONE WHO NEEDS ITS POWER MOST.

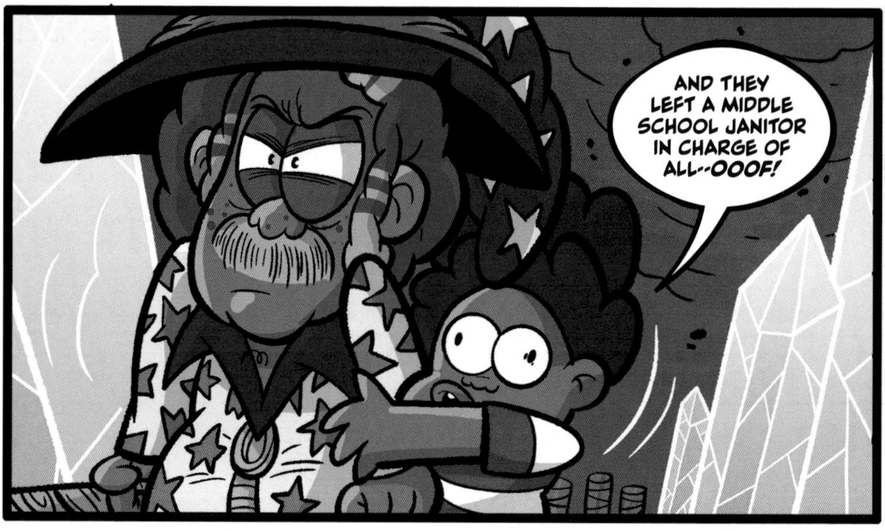
AND THEY LEFT A MIDDLE SCHOOL JANITOR IN CHARGE OF ALL--*OOOF!*

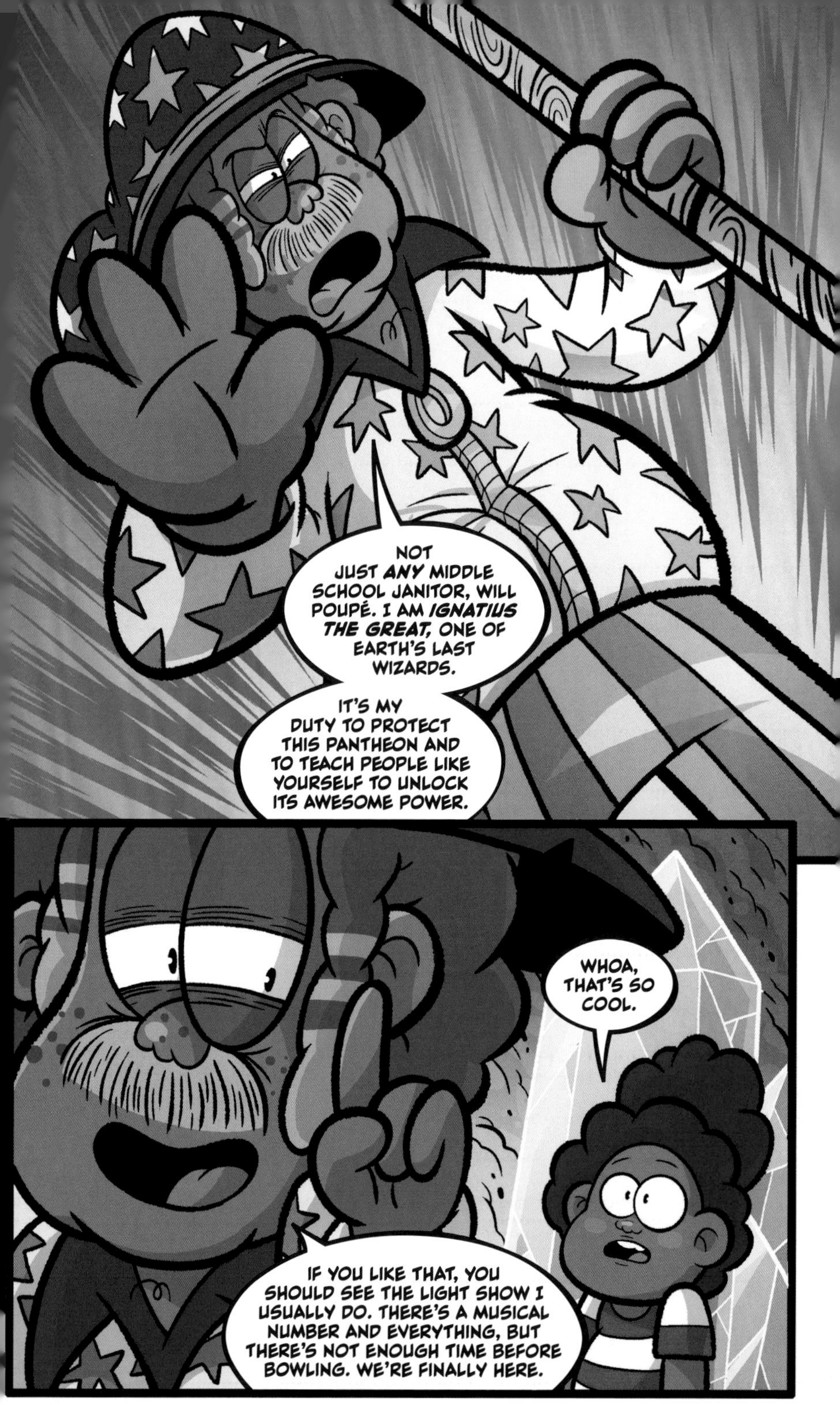
NOT JUST *ANY* MIDDLE SCHOOL JANITOR, WILL POUPÉ. I AM *IGNATIUS THE GREAT,* ONE OF EARTH'S LAST WIZARDS.
IT'S MY DUTY TO PROTECT THIS PANTHEON AND TO TEACH PEOPLE LIKE YOURSELF TO UNLOCK ITS AWESOME POWER.
WHOA, THAT'S SO COOL.
IF YOU LIKE THAT, YOU SHOULD SEE THE LIGHT SHOW I USUALLY DO. THERE'S A MUSICAL NUMBER AND EVERYTHING, BUT THERE'S NOT ENOUGH TIME BEFORE BOWLING. WE'RE FINALLY HERE.

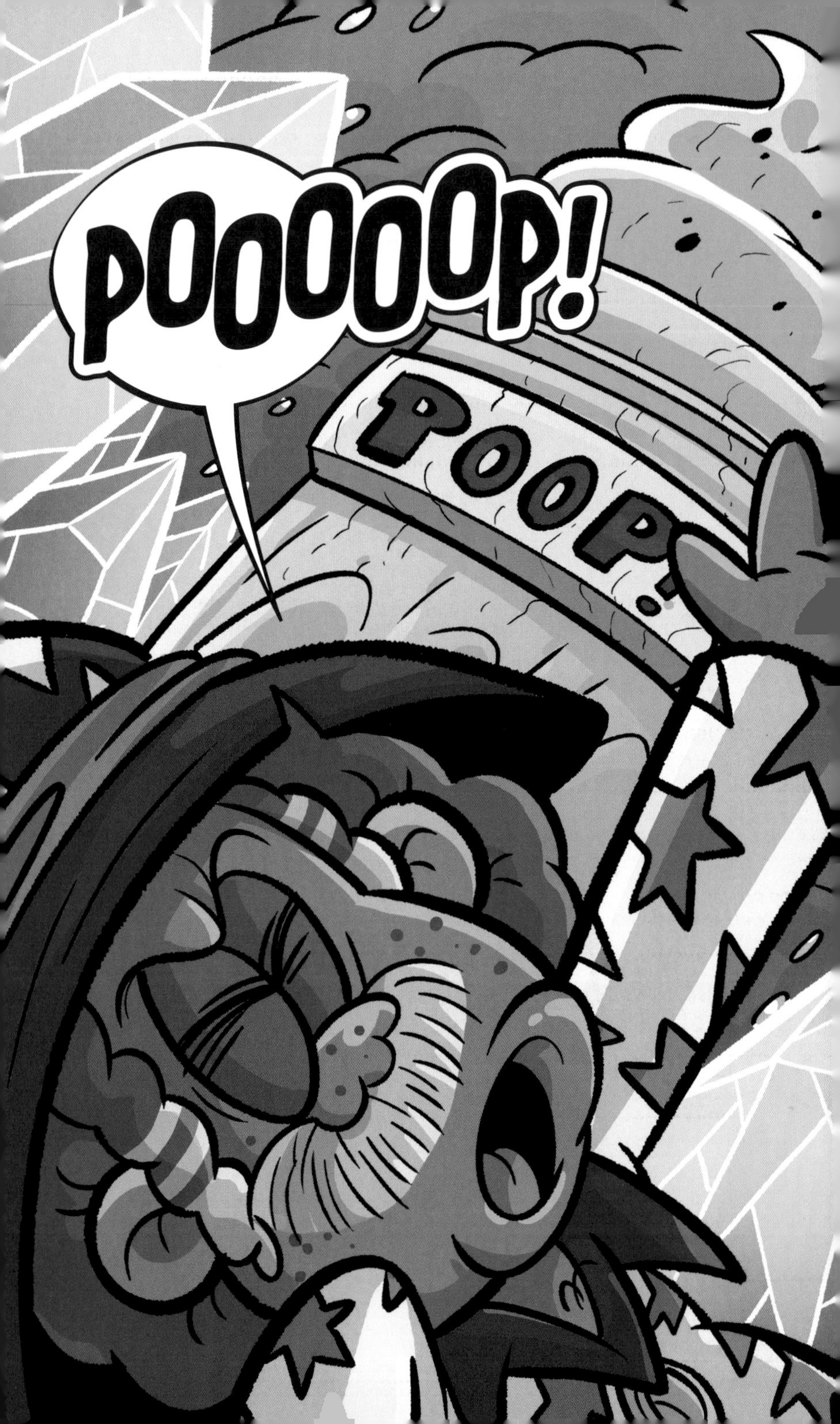
POOOOOOP!
POOP!

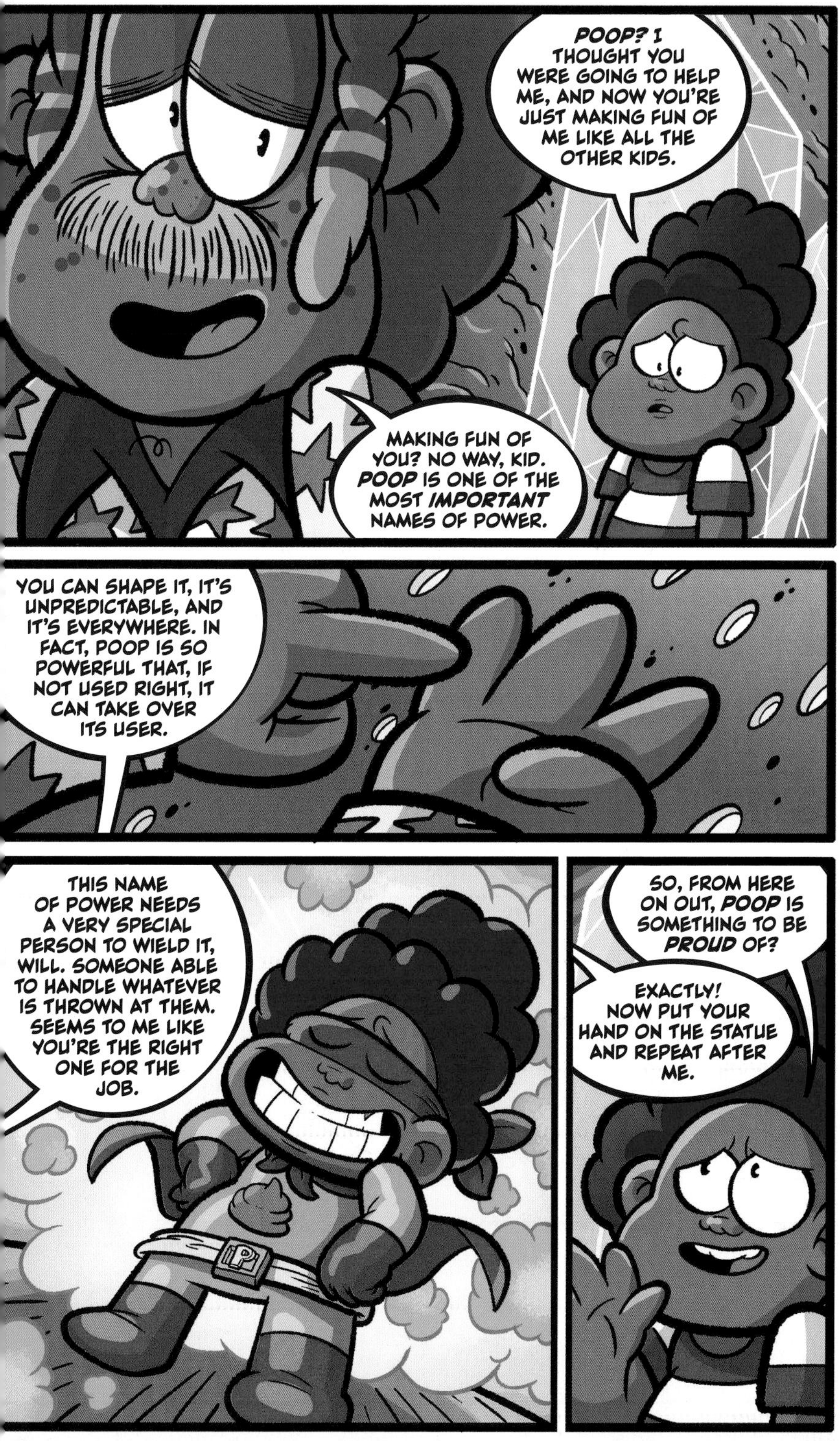
POOP? I THOUGHT YOU WERE GOING TO HELP ME, AND NOW YOU'RE JUST MAKING FUN OF ME LIKE ALL THE OTHER KIDS.
MAKING FUN OF YOU? NO WAY, KID. POOP IS ONE OF THE MOST IMPORTANT NAMES OF POWER.
YOU CAN SHAPE IT, IT'S UNPREDICTABLE, AND IT'S EVERYWHERE. IN FACT, POOP IS SO POWERFUL THAT, IF NOT USED RIGHT, IT CAN TAKE OVER ITS USER.
THIS NAME OF POWER NEEDS A VERY SPECIAL PERSON TO WIELD IT, WILL. SOMEONE ABLE TO HANDLE WHATEVER IS THROWN AT THEM. SEEMS TO ME LIKE YOU'RE THE RIGHT ONE FOR THE JOB.
SO, FROM HERE ON OUT, POOP IS SOMETHING TO BE PROUD OF?
EXACTLY! NOW PUT YOUR HAND ON THE STATUE AND REPEAT AFTER ME.

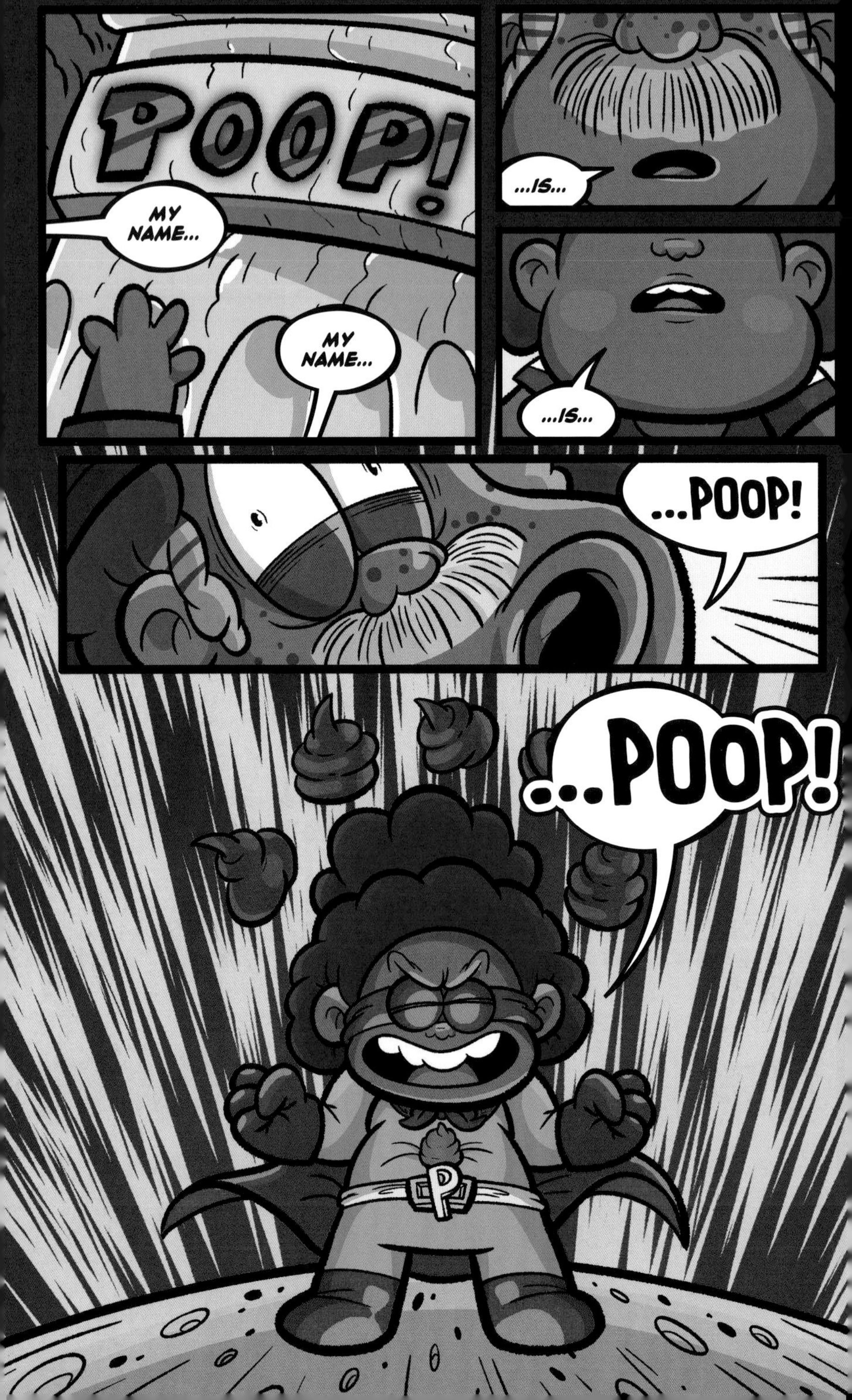
POOP!
MY NAME...
MY NAME...
...IS...
...IS...
...POOP!
...POOP!

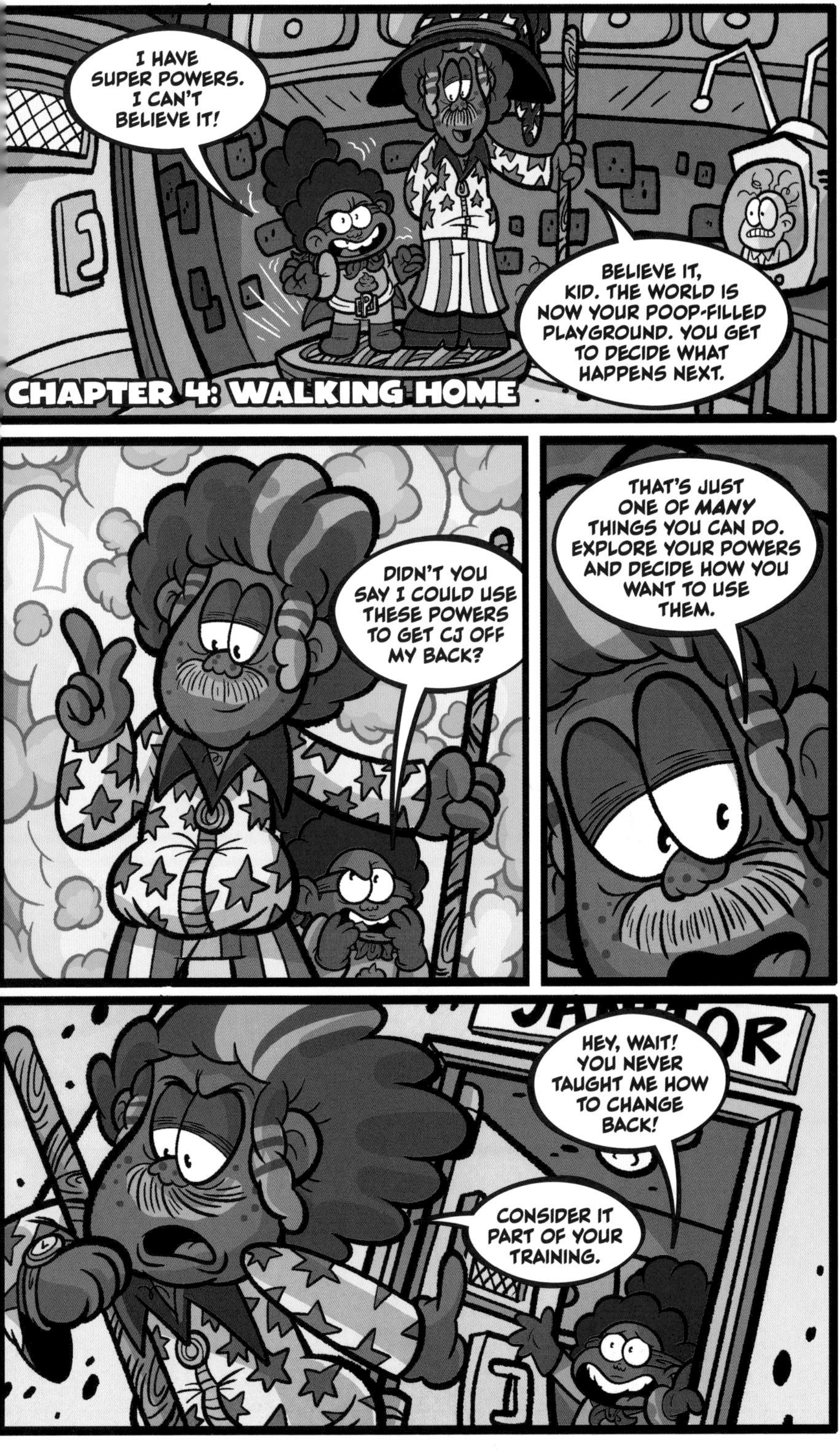
I HAVE SUPER POWERS. I CAN'T BELIEVE IT!
BELIEVE IT, KID. THE WORLD IS NOW YOUR POOP-FILLED PLAYGROUND. YOU GET TO DECIDE WHAT HAPPENS NEXT.
CHAPTER 4: WALKING HOME
DIDN'T YOU SAY I COULD USE THESE POWERS TO GET CJ OFF MY BACK?
THAT'S JUST ONE OF MANY THINGS YOU CAN DO. EXPLORE YOUR POWERS AND DECIDE HOW YOU WANT TO USE THEM.
HEY, WAIT! YOU NEVER TAUGHT ME HOW TO CHANGE BACK!
CONSIDER IT PART OF YOUR TRAINING.

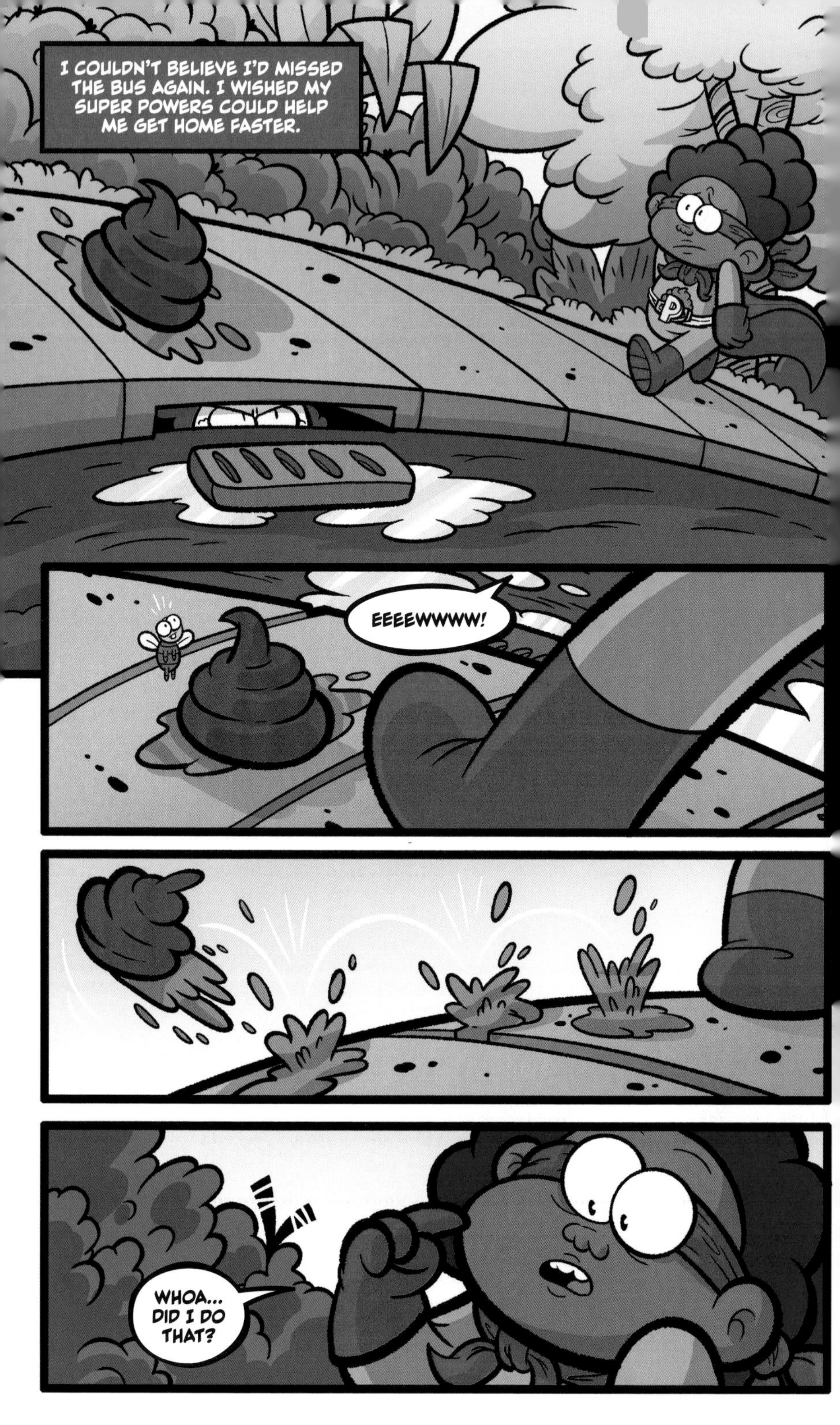
I COULDN'T BELIEVE I'D MISSED THE BUS AGAIN. I WISHED MY SUPER POWERS COULD HELP ME GET HOME FASTER.
EEEEWWWW!
WHOA... DID I DO THAT?

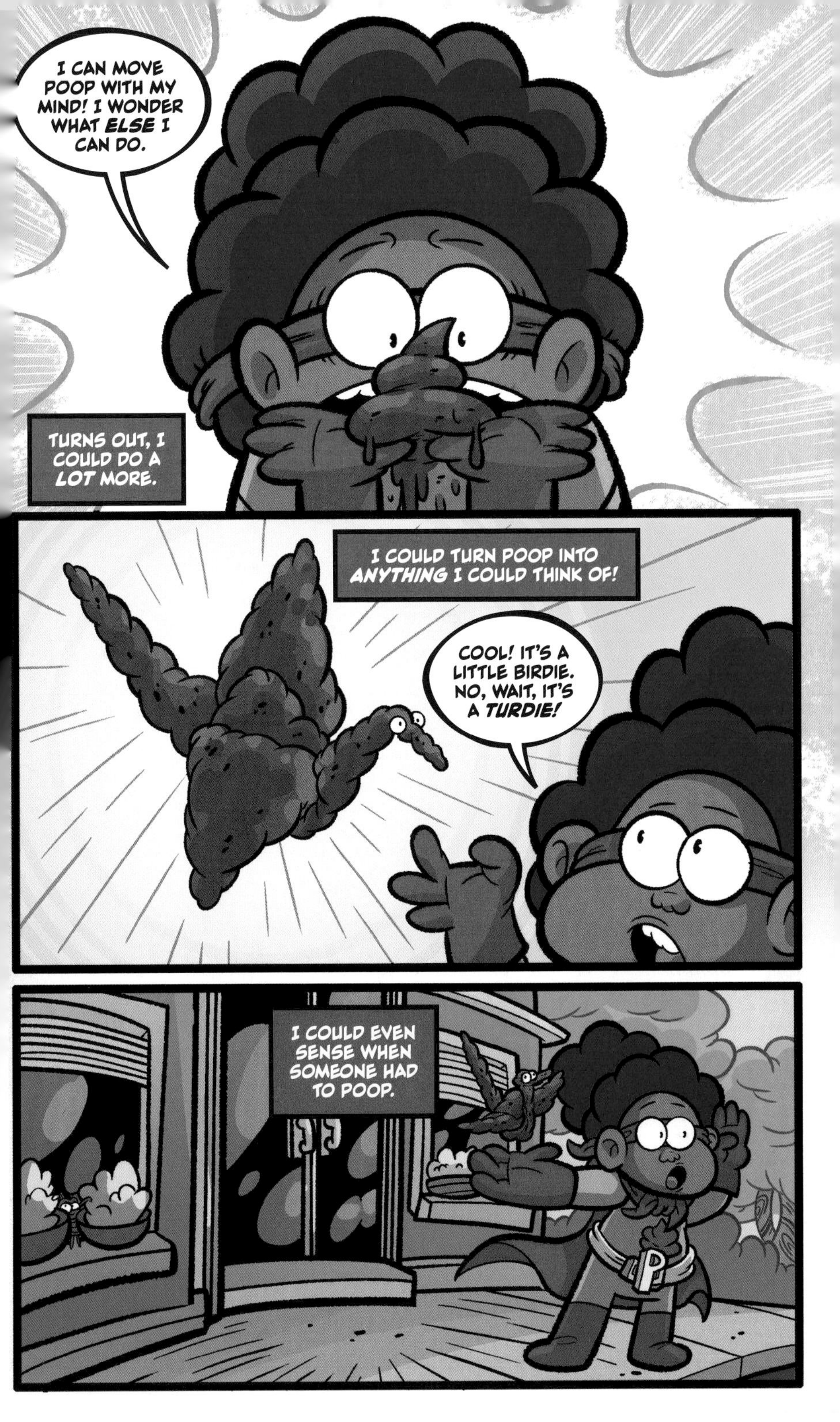
I CAN MOVE POOP WITH MY MIND! I WONDER WHAT ELSE I CAN DO.
TURNS OUT, I COULD DO A LOT MORE.
I COULD TURN POOP INTO ANYTHING I COULD THINK OF!
COOL! IT'S A LITTLE BIRDIE. NO, WAIT, IT'S A TURDIE!
I COULD EVEN SENSE WHEN SOMEONE HAD TO POOP.

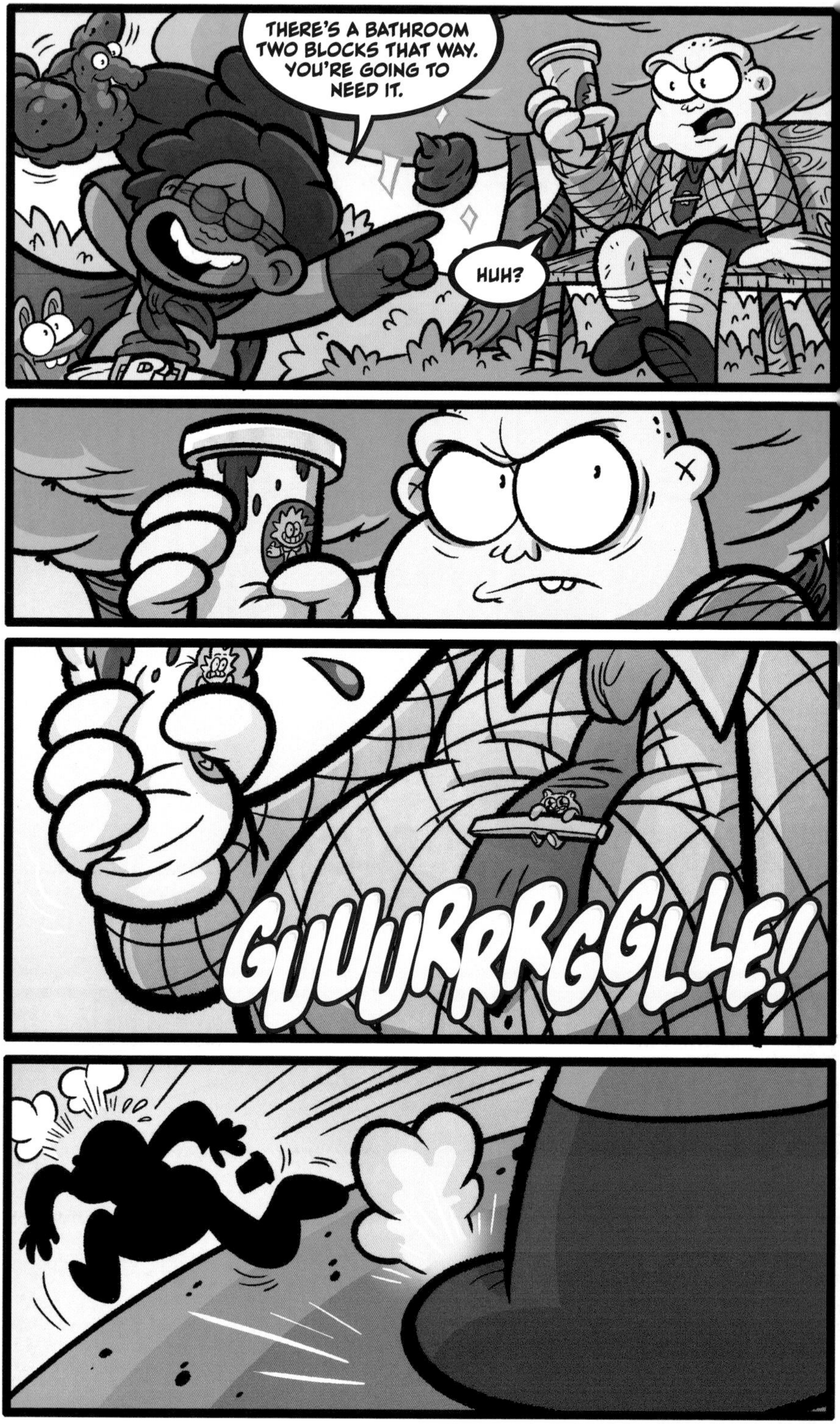
THERE'S A BATHROOM TWO BLOCKS THAT WAY. YOU'RE GOING TO NEED IT.
HUH?
GUUURRRGGLLE!

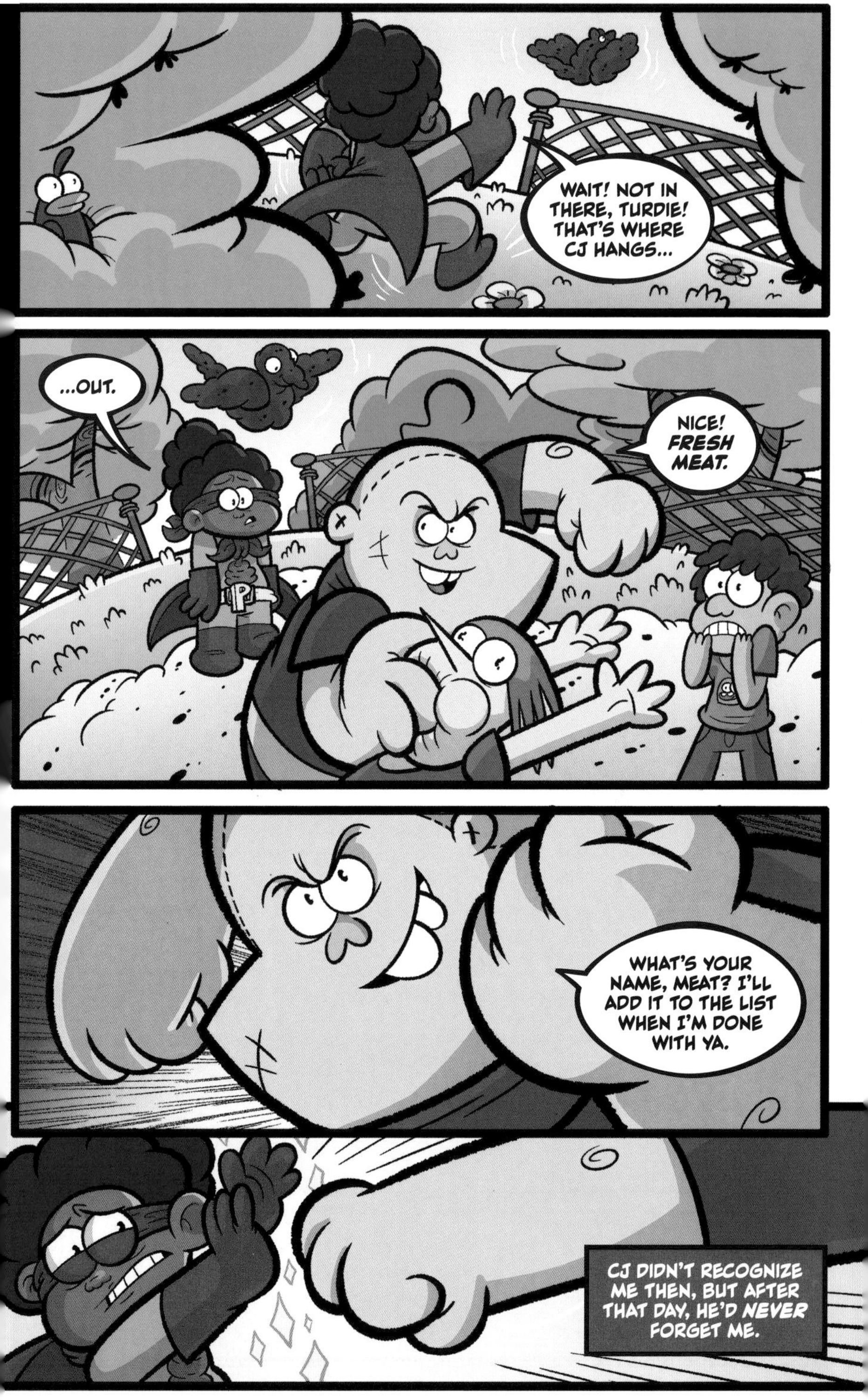
WAIT! NOT IN THERE, TURDIE! THAT'S WHERE CJ HANGS...
...OUT.
NICE! FRESH MEAT.
WHAT'S YOUR NAME, MEAT? I'LL ADD IT TO THE LIST WHEN I'M DONE WITH YA.
CJ DIDN'T RECOGNIZE ME THEN, BUT AFTER THAT DAY, HE'D NEVER FORGET ME.

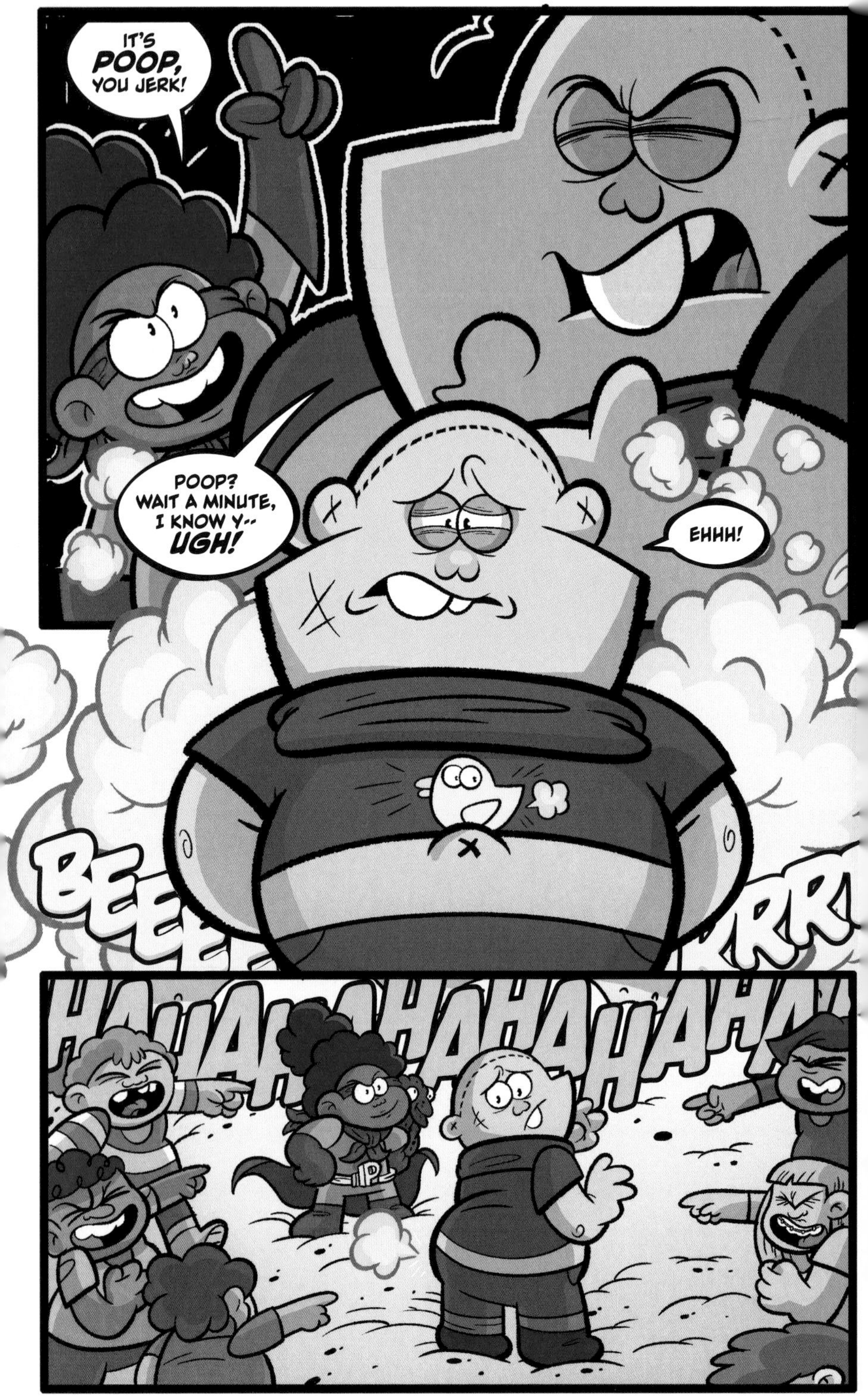
IT'S POOP, YOU JERK!
POOP? WAIT A MINUTE, I KNOW Y-- UGH!
EHHH!
HAHAHAHAHAHAHAHA

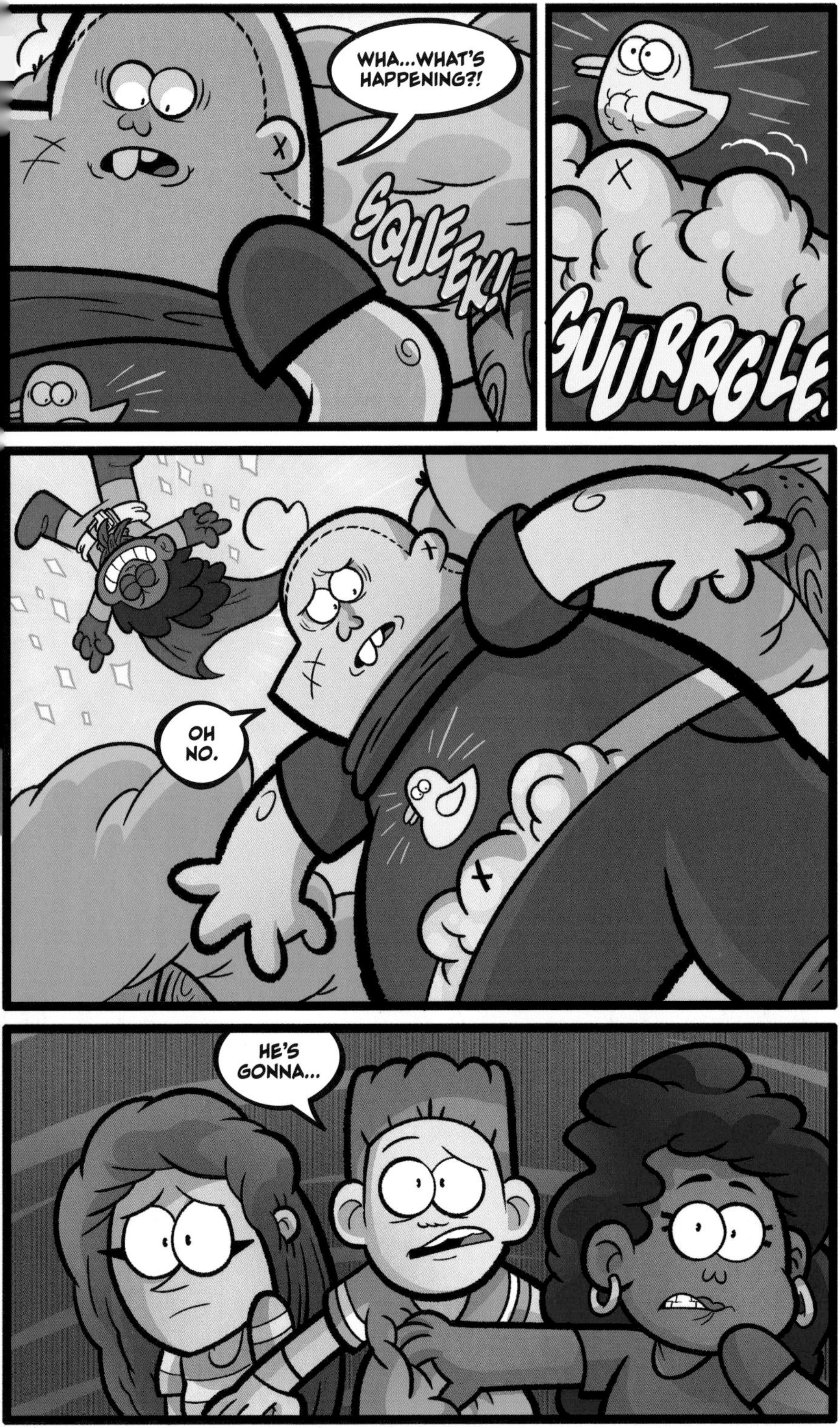
WHA...WHAT'S HAPPENING?!
SQUEEEK!
GUURRGLE.
OH NO.
HE'S GONNA...

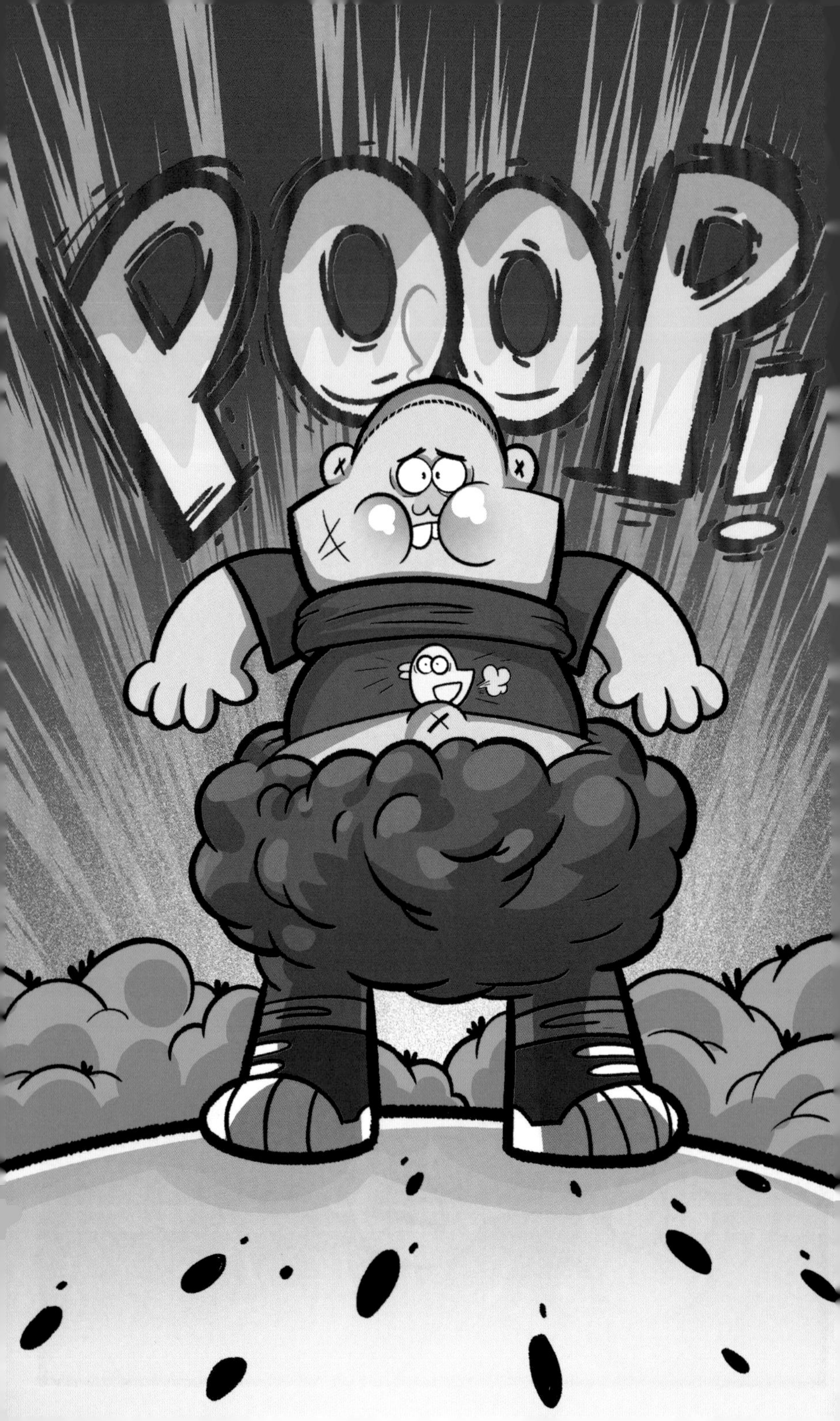
POOP!

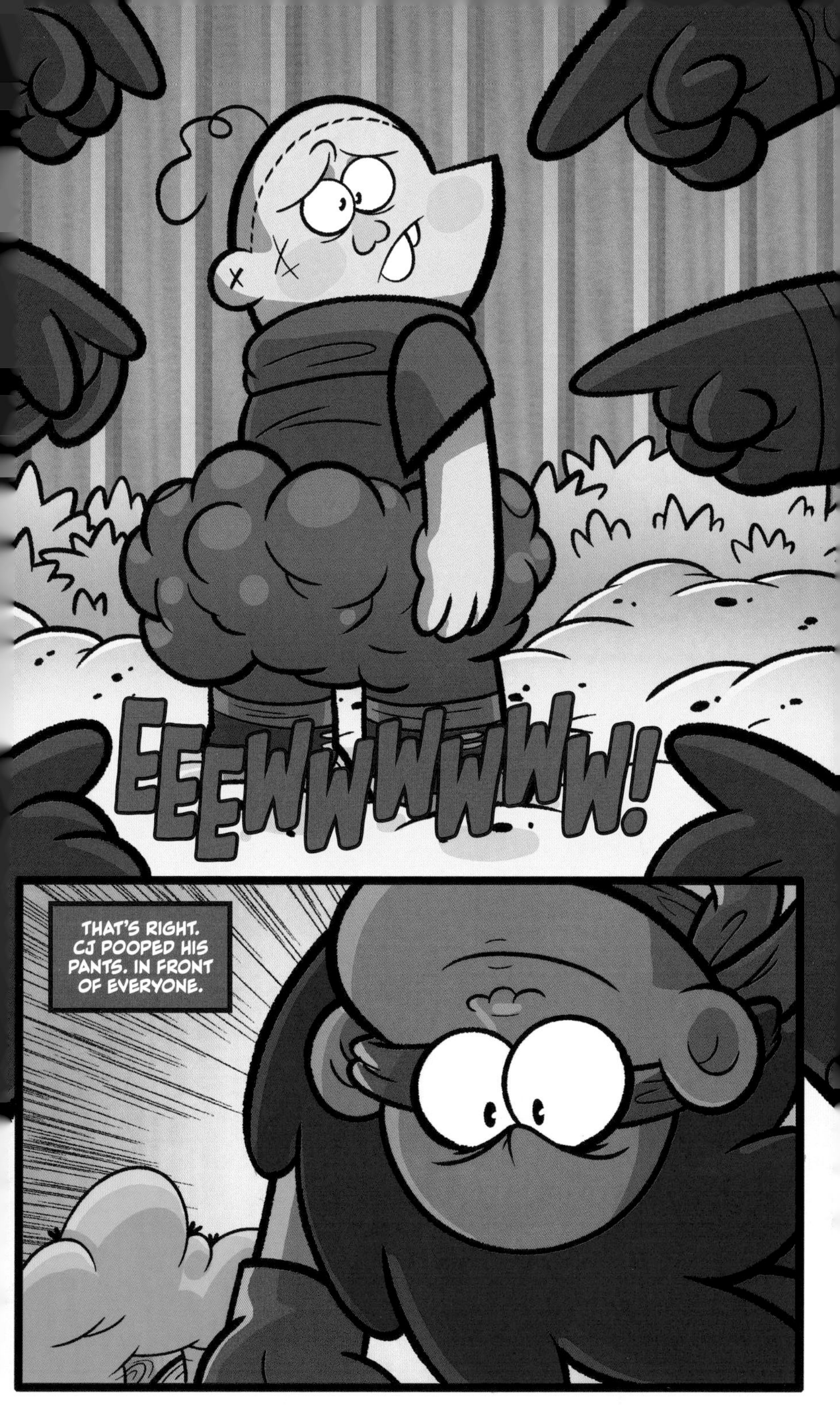
EEEWWWWWWWW!
THAT'S RIGHT. CJ POOPED HIS PANTS. IN FRONT OF EVERYONE.

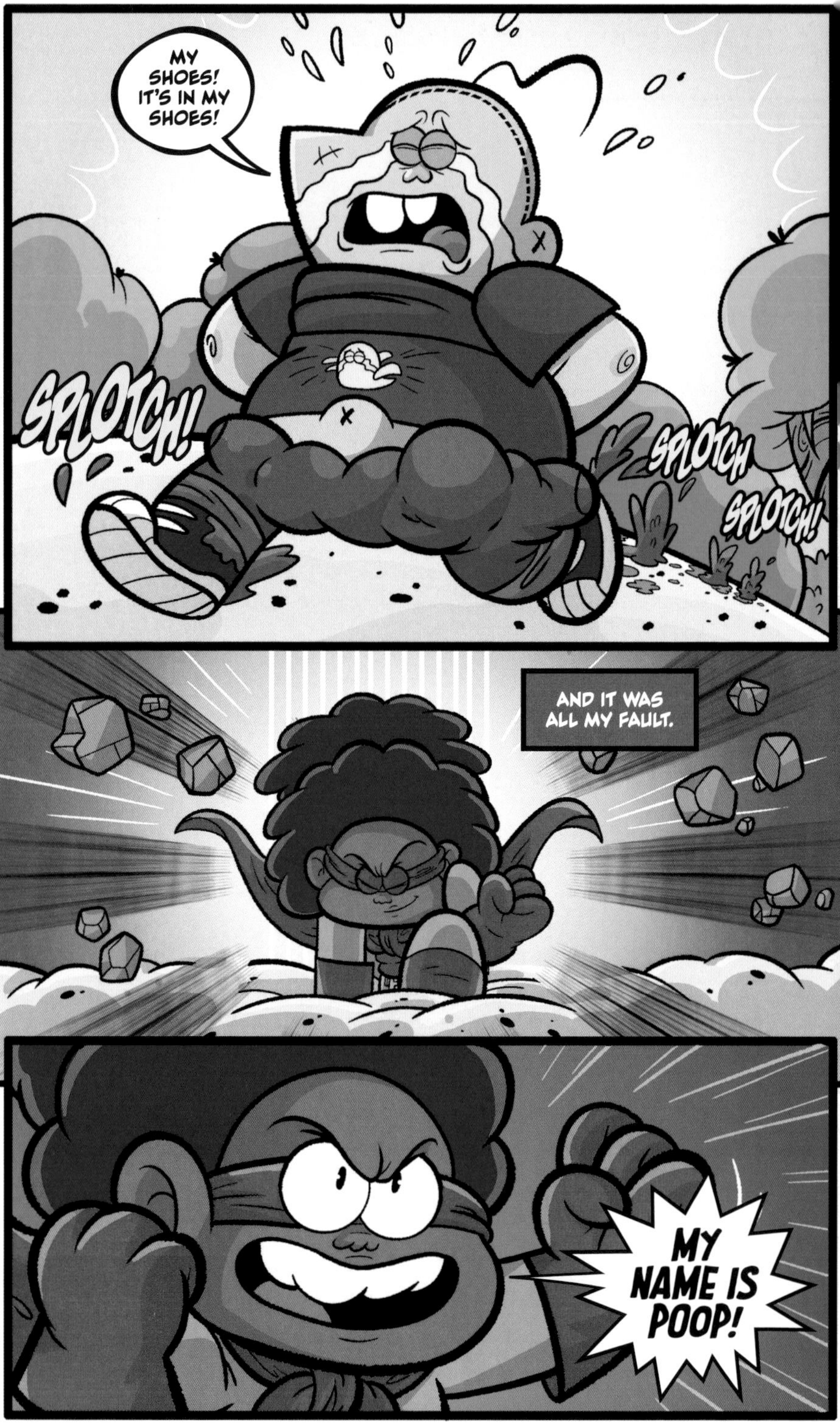

MY SHOES! IT'S IN MY SHOES!
SPLOTCH!
SPLOTCH
SPLOTCH!
AND IT WAS ALL MY FAULT.
MY NAME IS POOP!

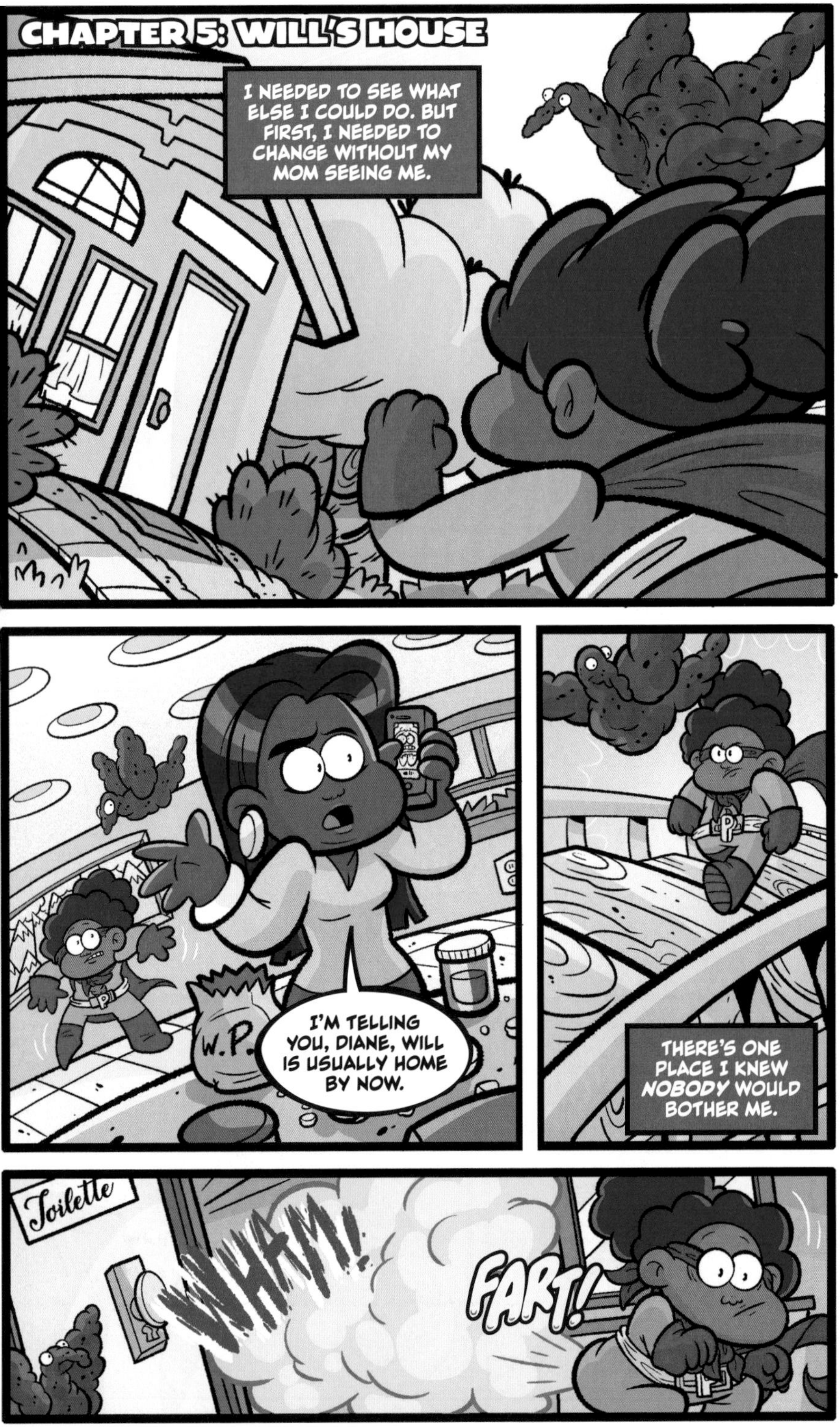
CHAPTER 5: WILL'S HOUSE
I NEEDED TO SEE WHAT ELSE I COULD DO. BUT FIRST, I NEEDED TO CHANGE WITHOUT MY MOM SEEING ME.
W.P.
I'M TELLING YOU, DIANE, WILL IS USUALLY HOME BY NOW.
THERE'S ONE PLACE I KNEW *NOBODY* WOULD BOTHER ME.
Toilette
WHAM!!
FART!

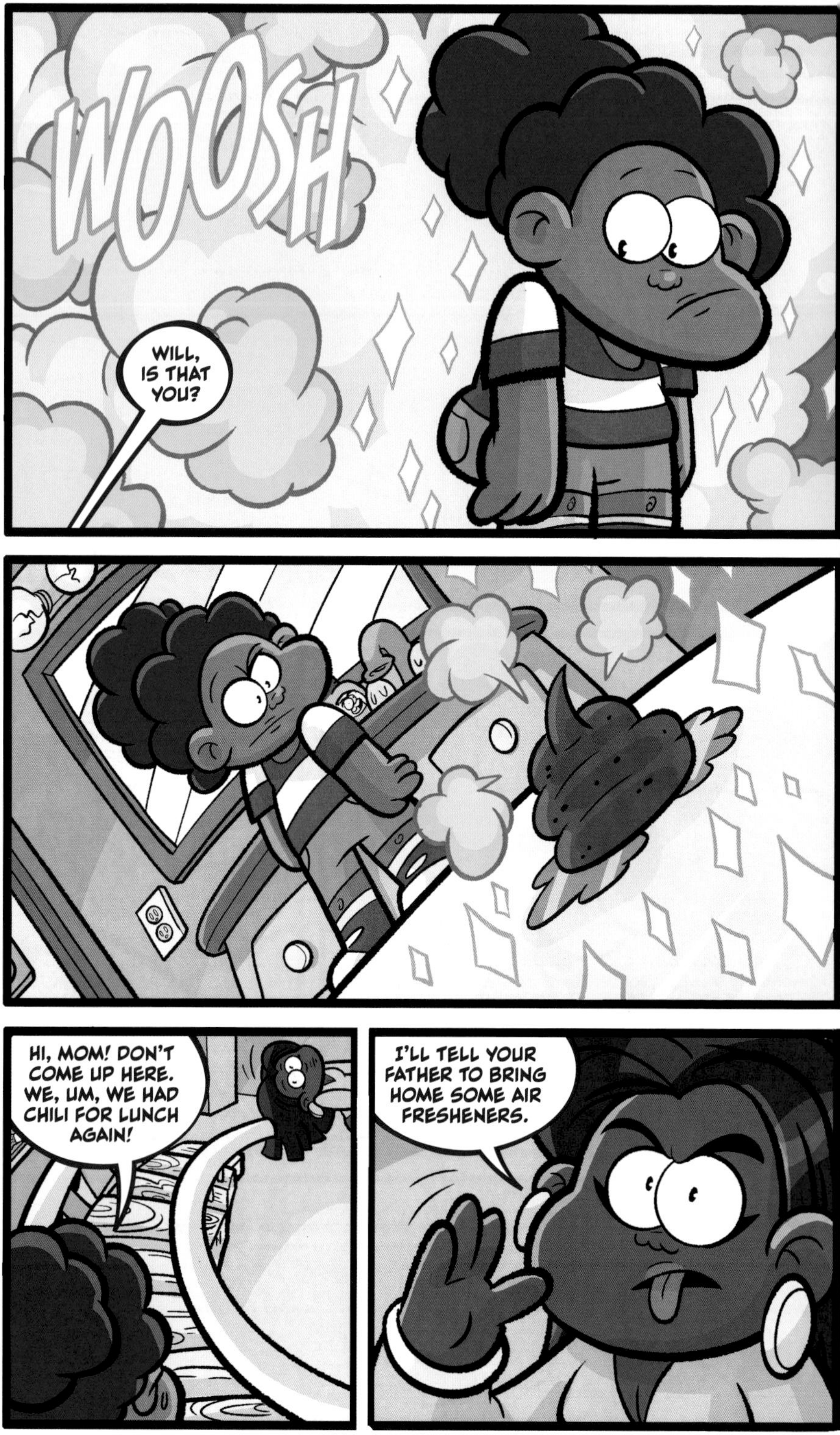
WOOSH
WILL, IS THAT YOU?
HI, MOM! DON'T COME UP HERE. WE, UM, WE HAD CHILI FOR LUNCH AGAIN!
I'LL TELL YOUR FATHER TO BRING HOME SOME AIR FRESHENERS.

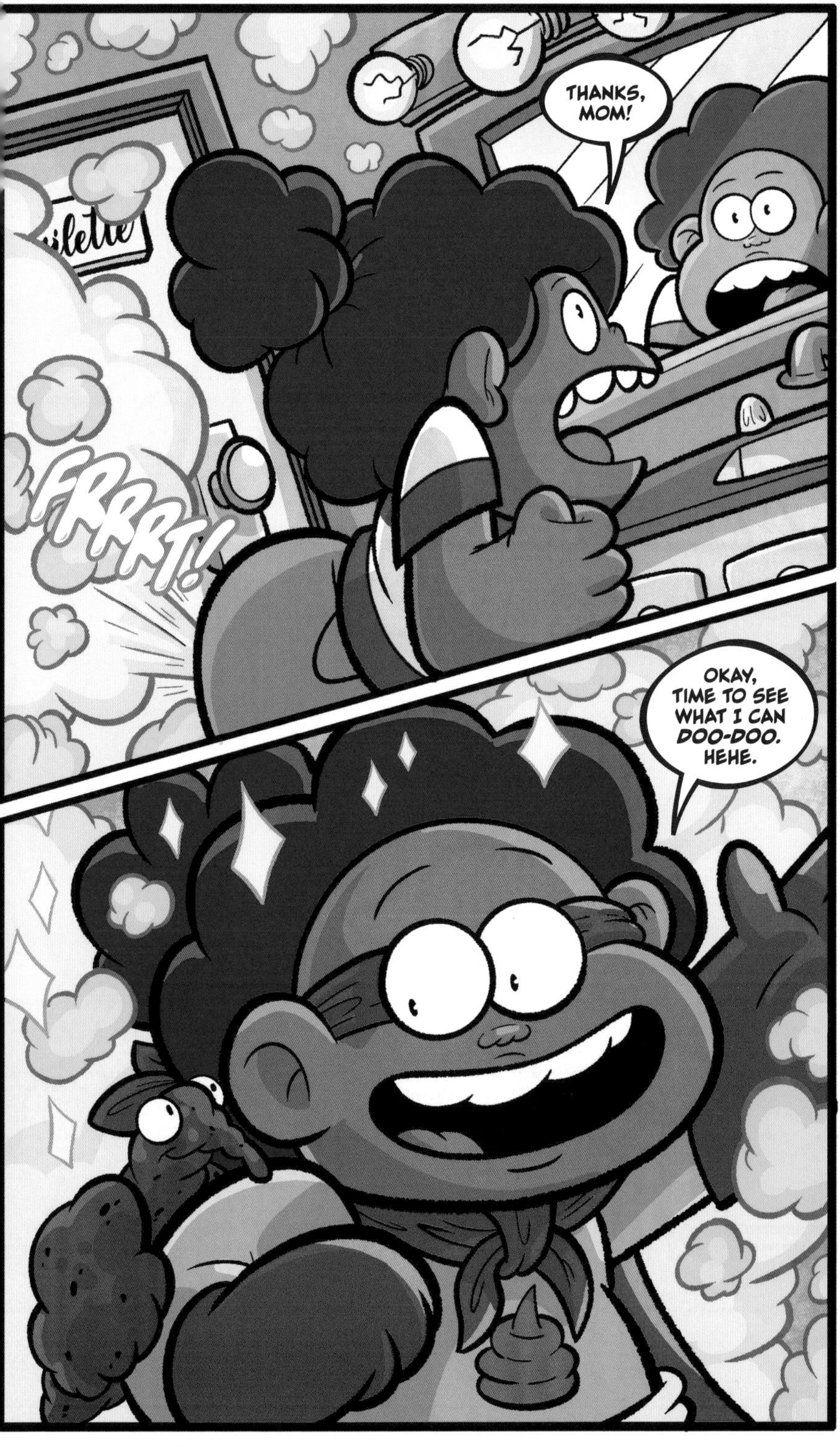
THANKS, MOM!
FRRRT!
OKAY, TIME TO SEE WHAT I CAN DOO-DOO. HEHE.

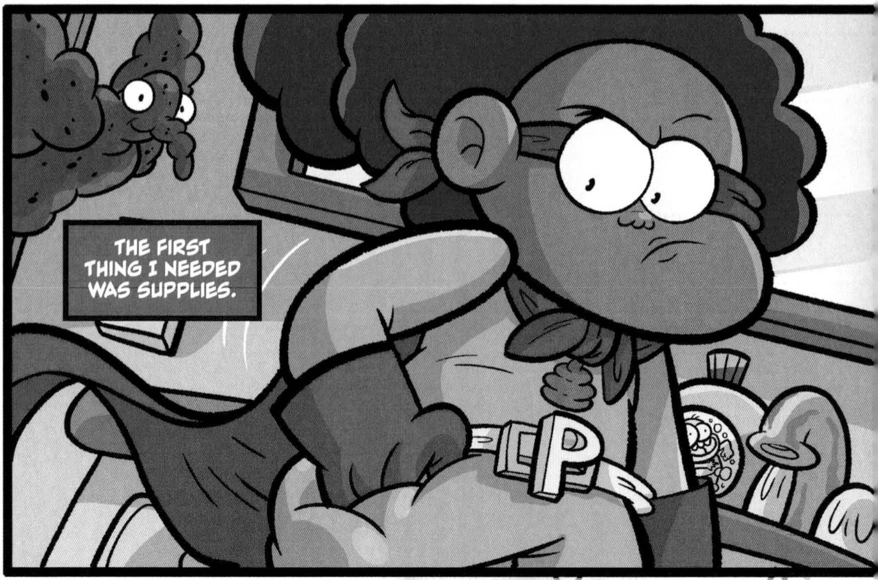
THE FIRST THING I NEEDED WAS SUPPLIES.

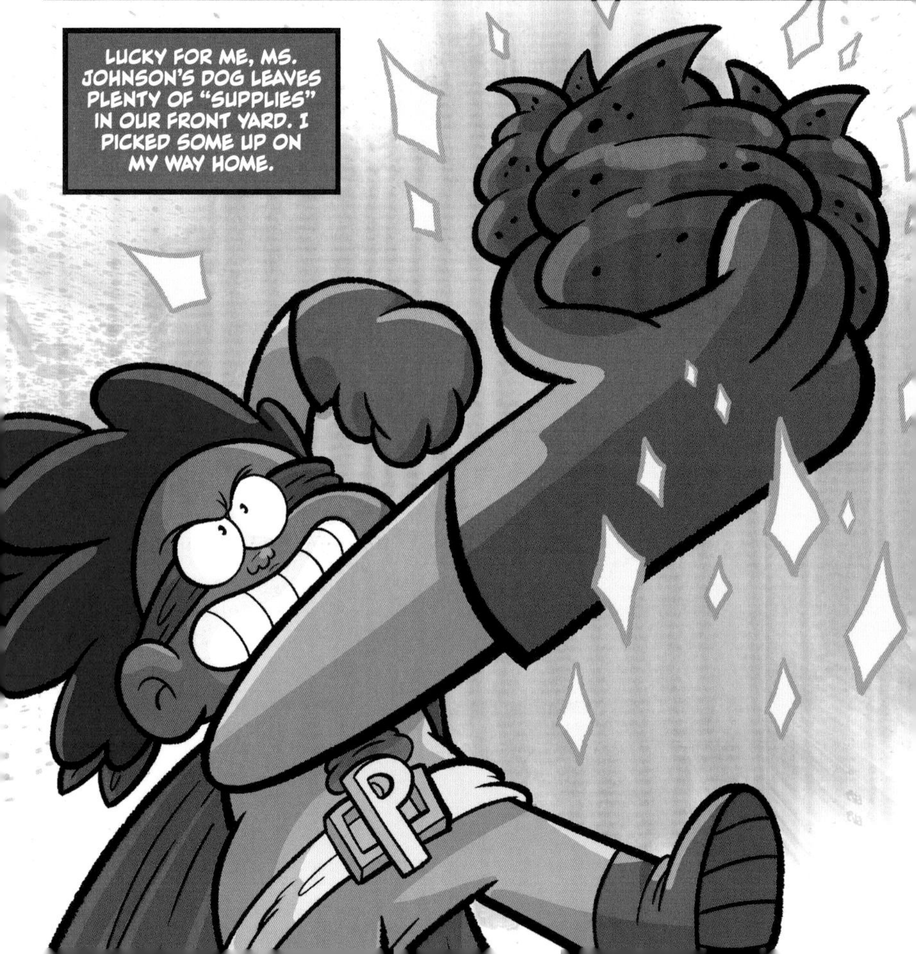
LUCKY FOR ME, MS. JOHNSON'S DOG LEAVES PLENTY OF "SUPPLIES" IN OUR FRONT YARD. I PICKED SOME UP ON MY WAY HOME.

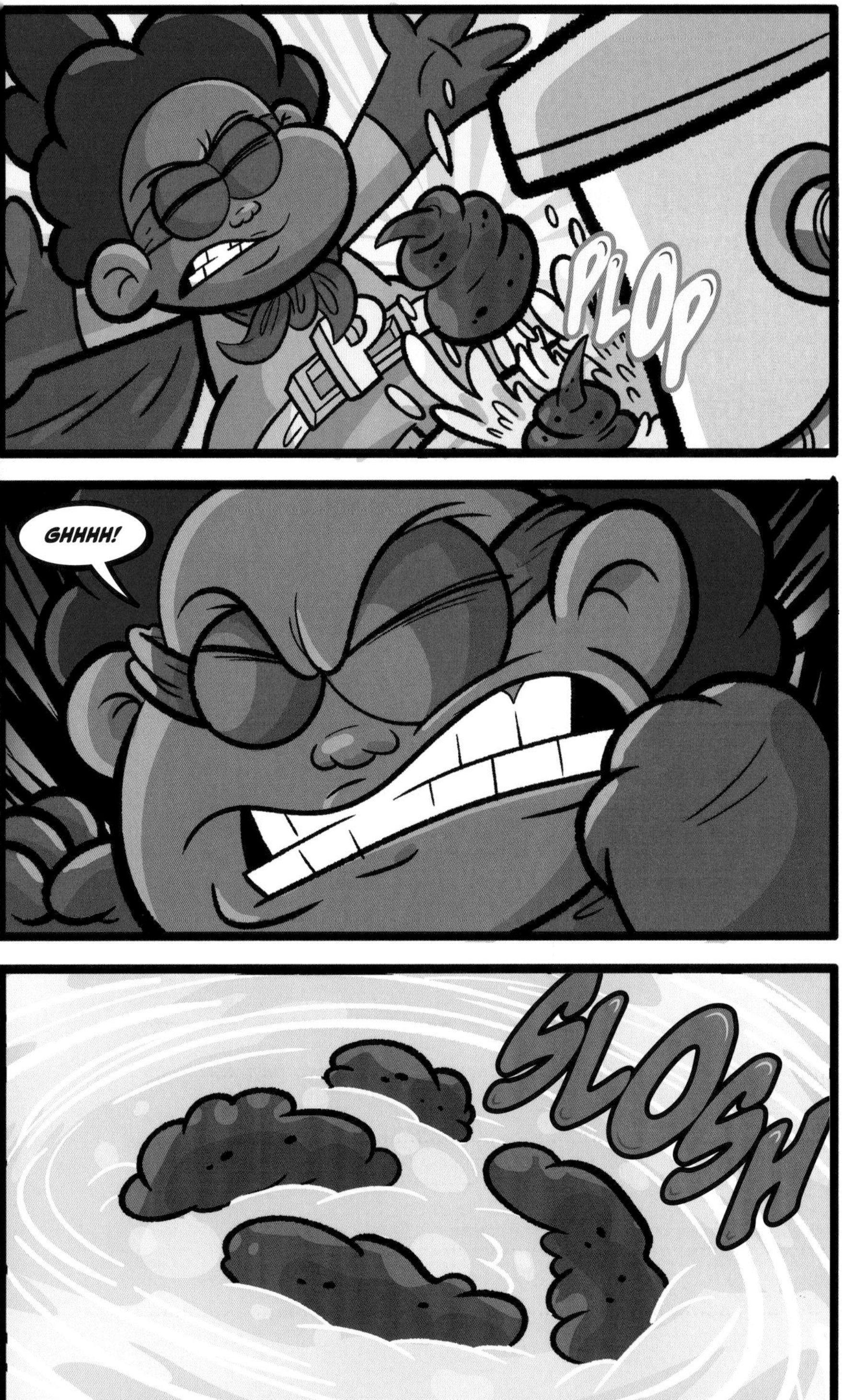
PLOP
GHHHH!
SLOSH

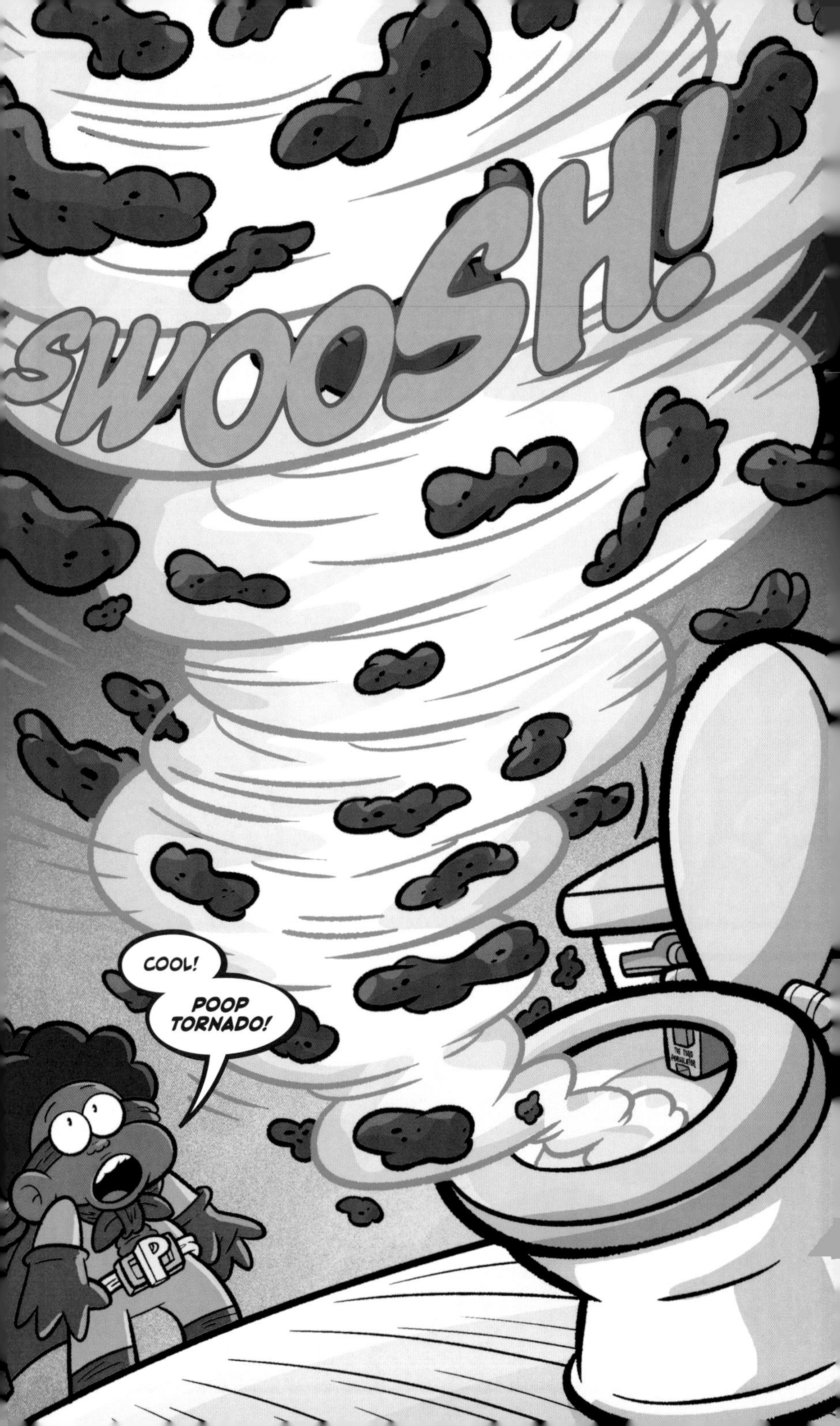
SWOOSH!
COOL!
POOP TORNADO!

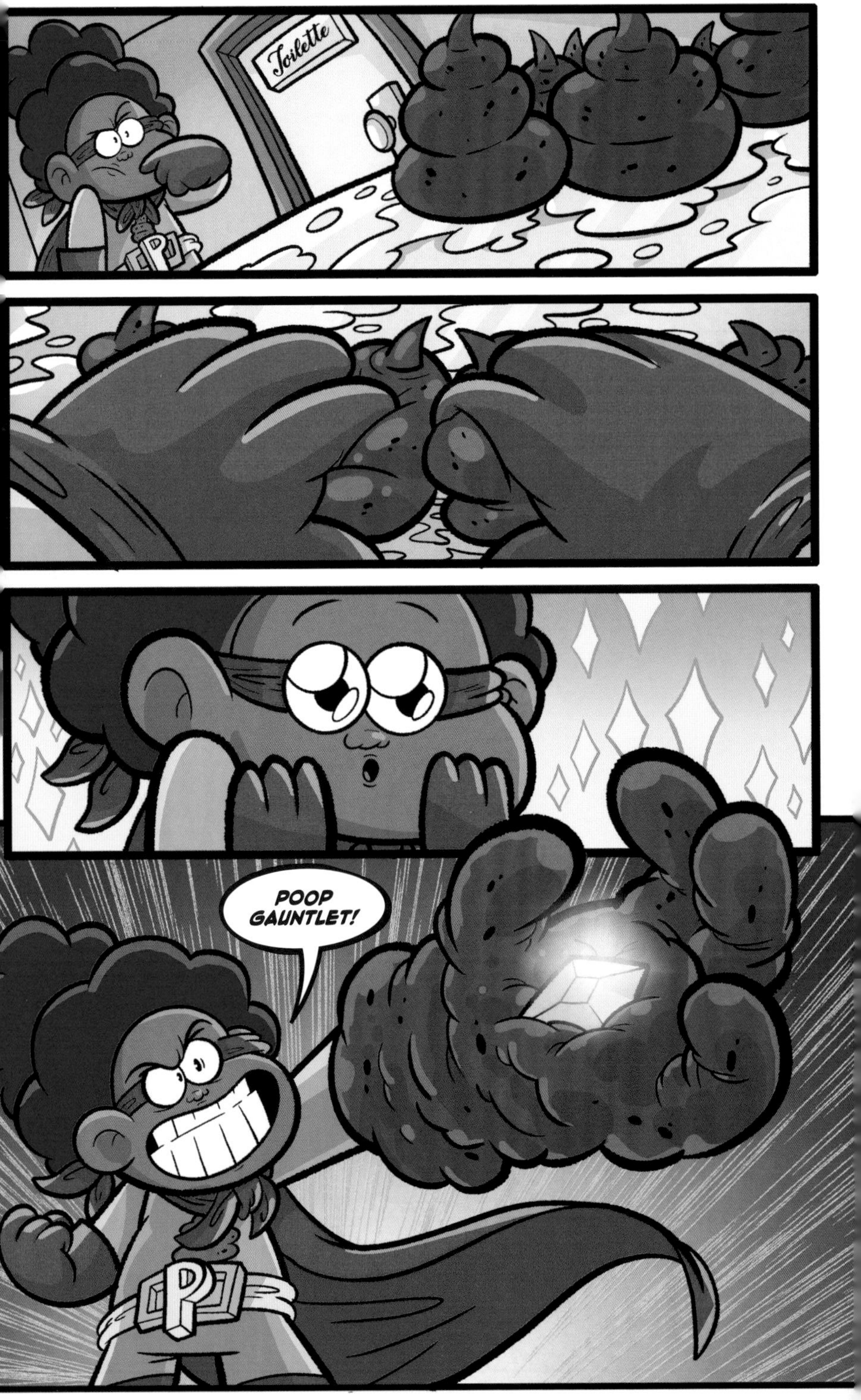
Toilette
POOP GAUNTLET!

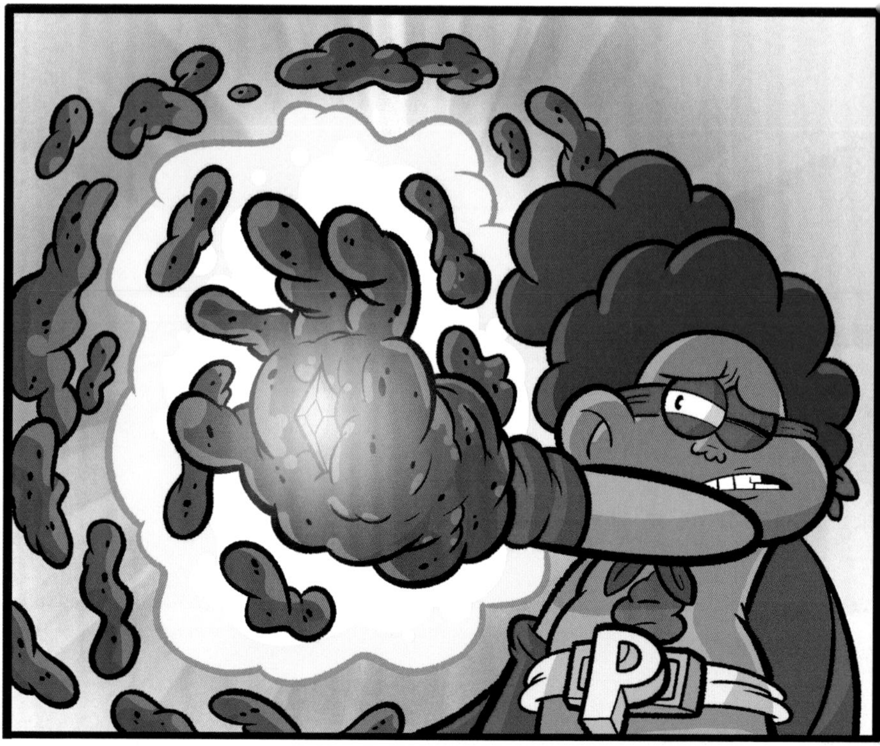

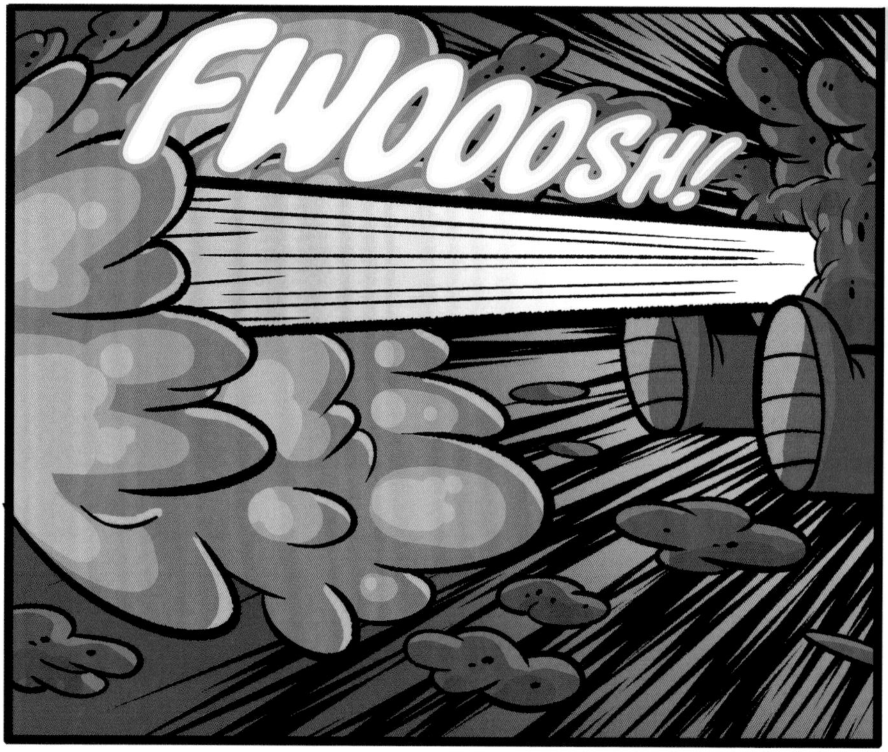
FWOOOSH!

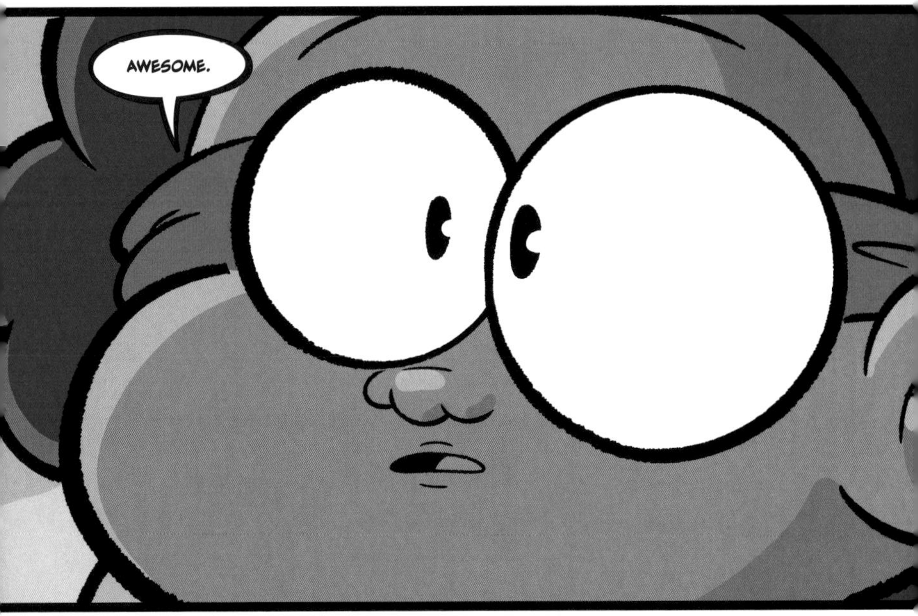
AWESOME.

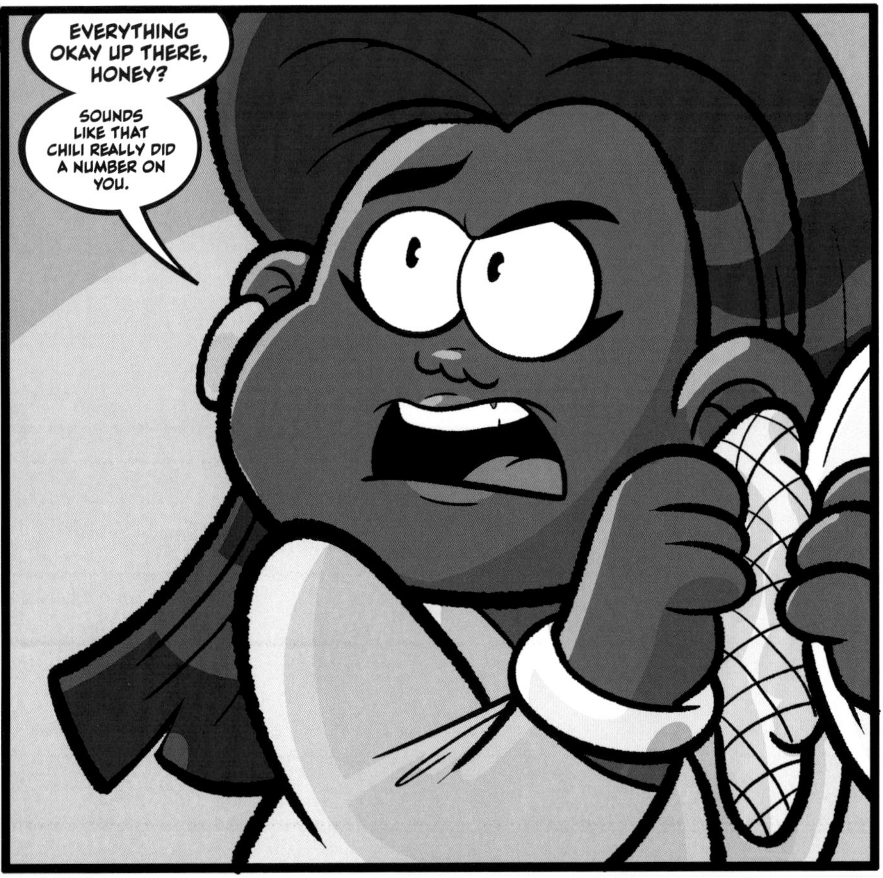
EVERYTHING OKAY UP THERE, HONEY?
SOUNDS LIKE THAT CHILI REALLY DID A NUMBER ON YOU.

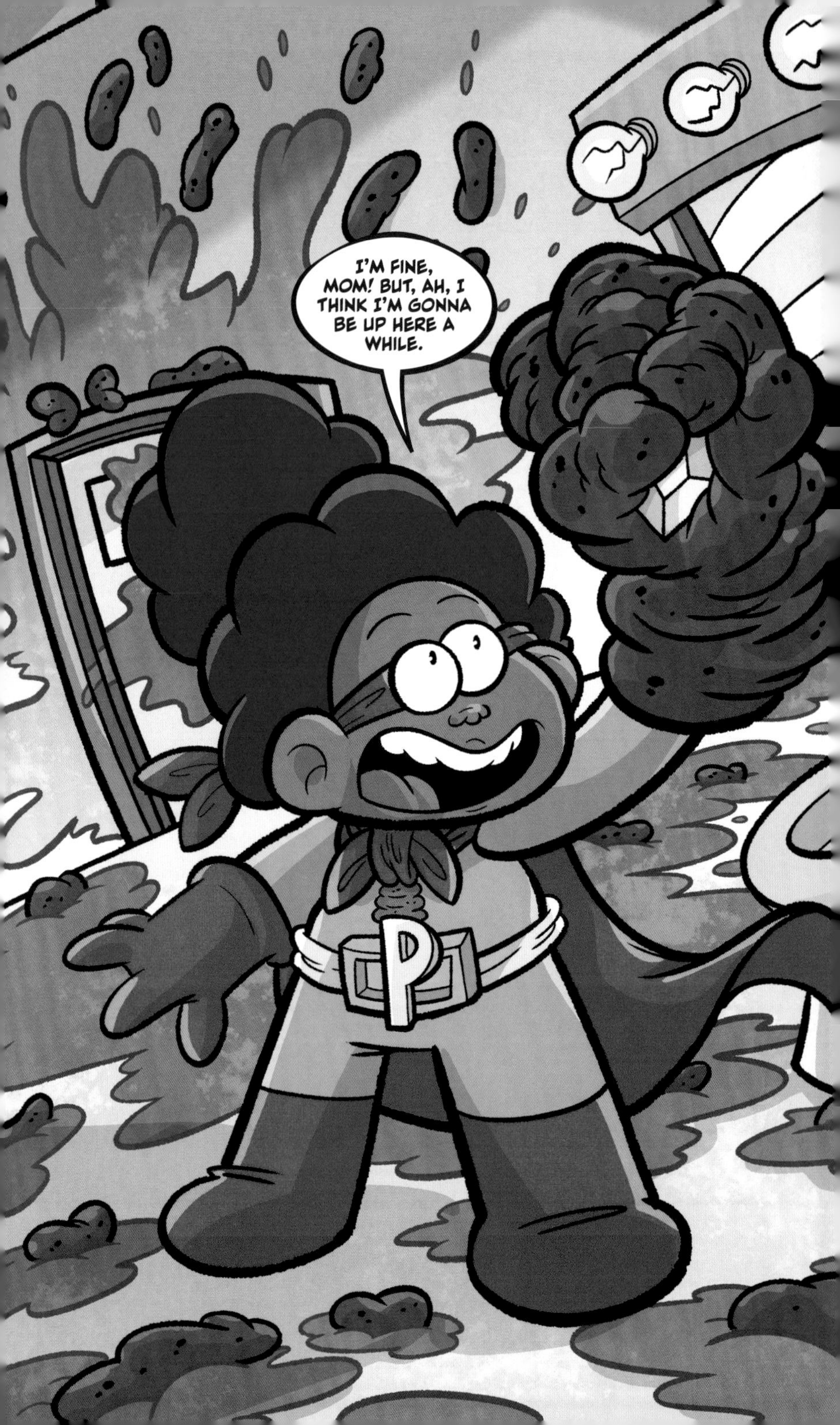
I'M FINE, MOM! BUT, AH, I THINK I'M GONNA BE UP HERE A WHILE.

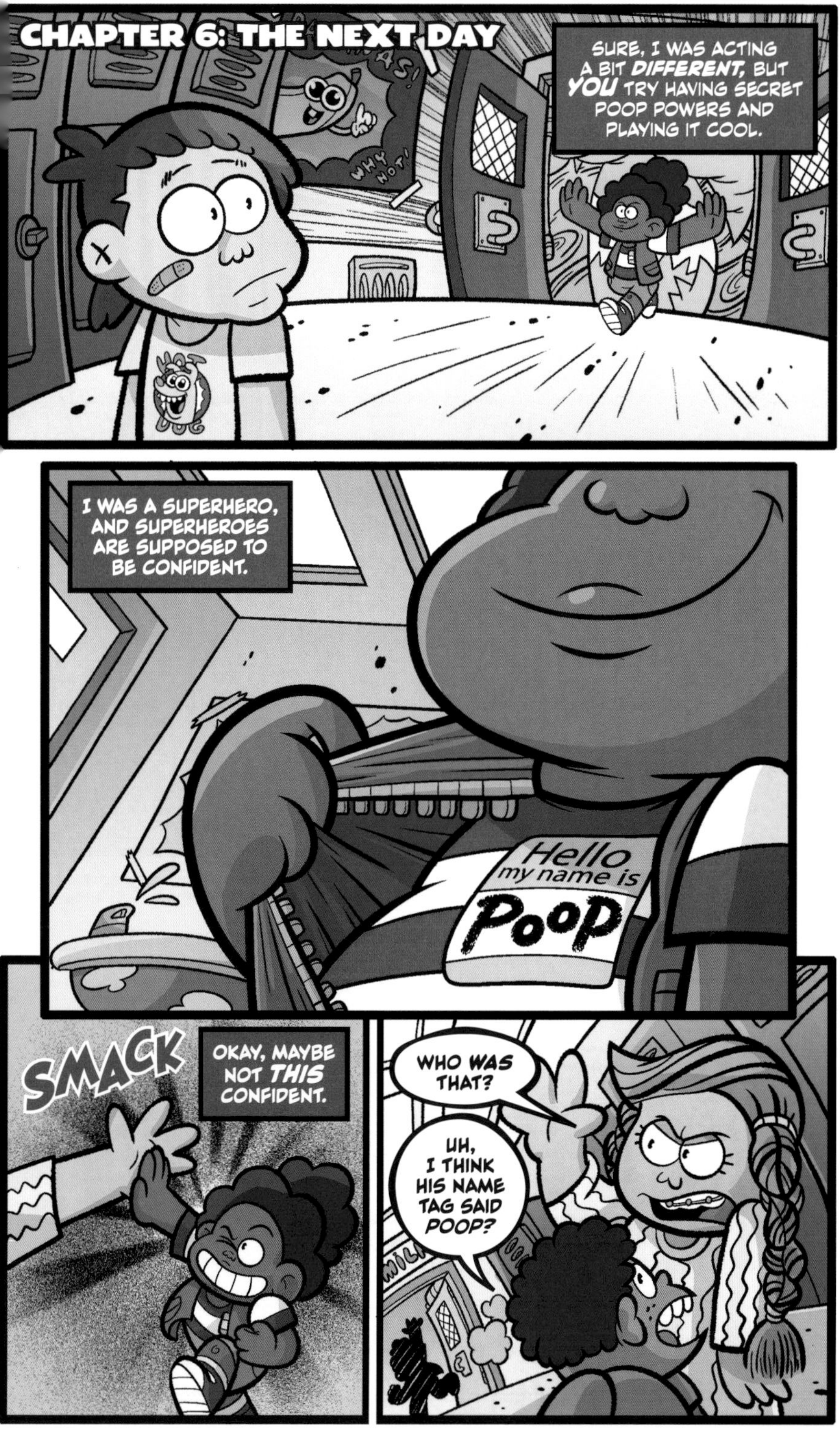
CHAPTER 6: THE NEXT DAY
SURE, I WAS ACTING A BIT DIFFERENT, BUT YOU TRY HAVING SECRET POOP POWERS AND PLAYING IT COOL.
WHY NOT!
DOG
I WAS A SUPERHERO, AND SUPERHEROES ARE SUPPOSED TO BE CONFIDENT.
Hello my name is
POOP
SMACK
OKAY, MAYBE NOT THIS CONFIDENT.
WHO WAS THAT?
UH, I THINK HIS NAME TAG SAID POOP?

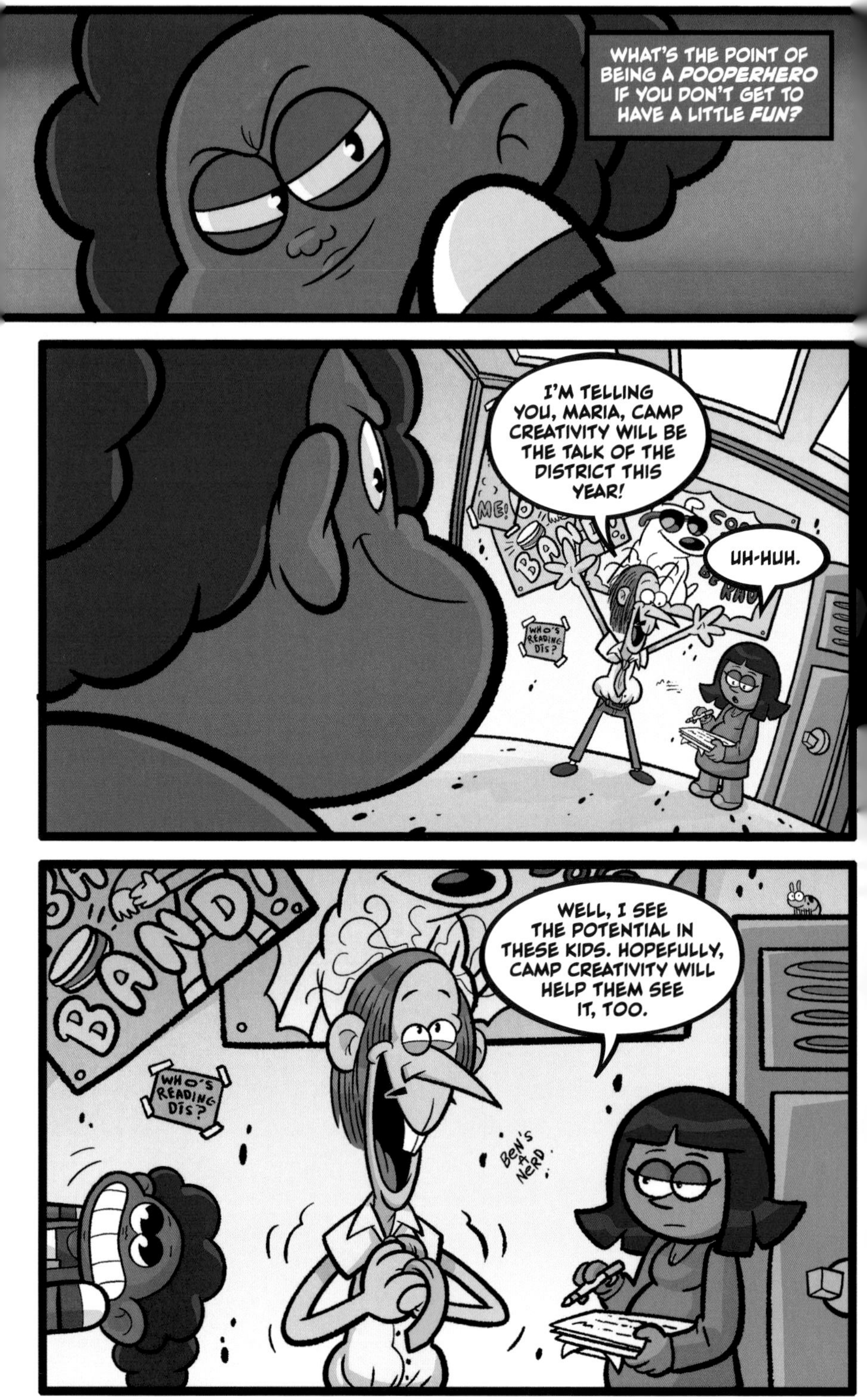
WHAT'S THE POINT OF BEING A POOPERHERO IF YOU DON'T GET TO HAVE A LITTLE FUN?
I'M TELLING YOU, MARIA, CAMP CREATIVITY WILL BE THE TALK OF THE DISTRICT THIS YEAR!
UH-HUH.
WHO'S READING DIS?
WELL, I SEE THE POTENTIAL IN THESE KIDS. HOPEFULLY, CAMP CREATIVITY WILL HELP THEM SEE IT, TOO.
WHO'S READING DIS?
BEN'S A NERD

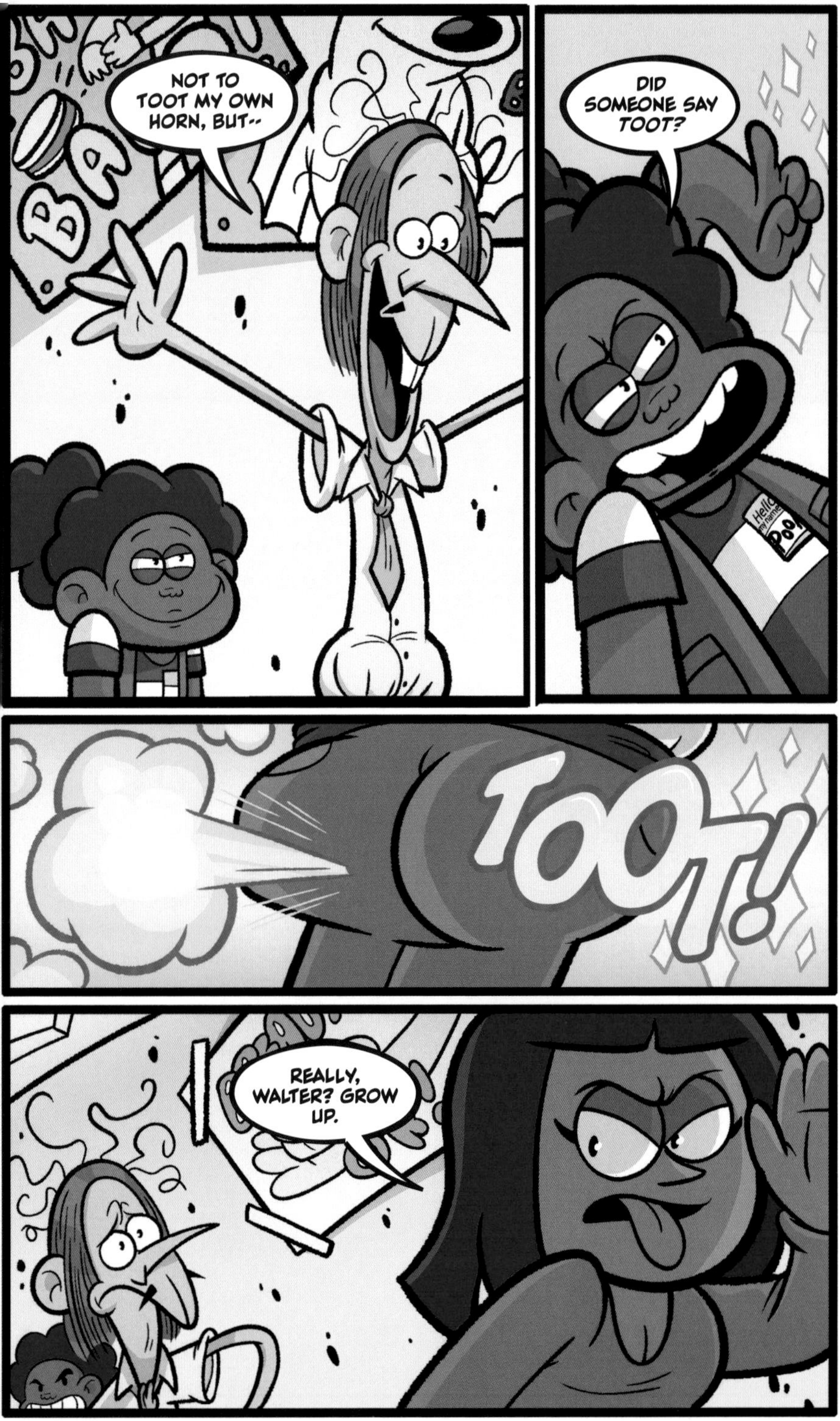
NOT TO TOOT MY OWN HORN, BUT--
DID SOMEONE SAY TOOT?
TOOT!
REALLY, WALTER? GROW UP.

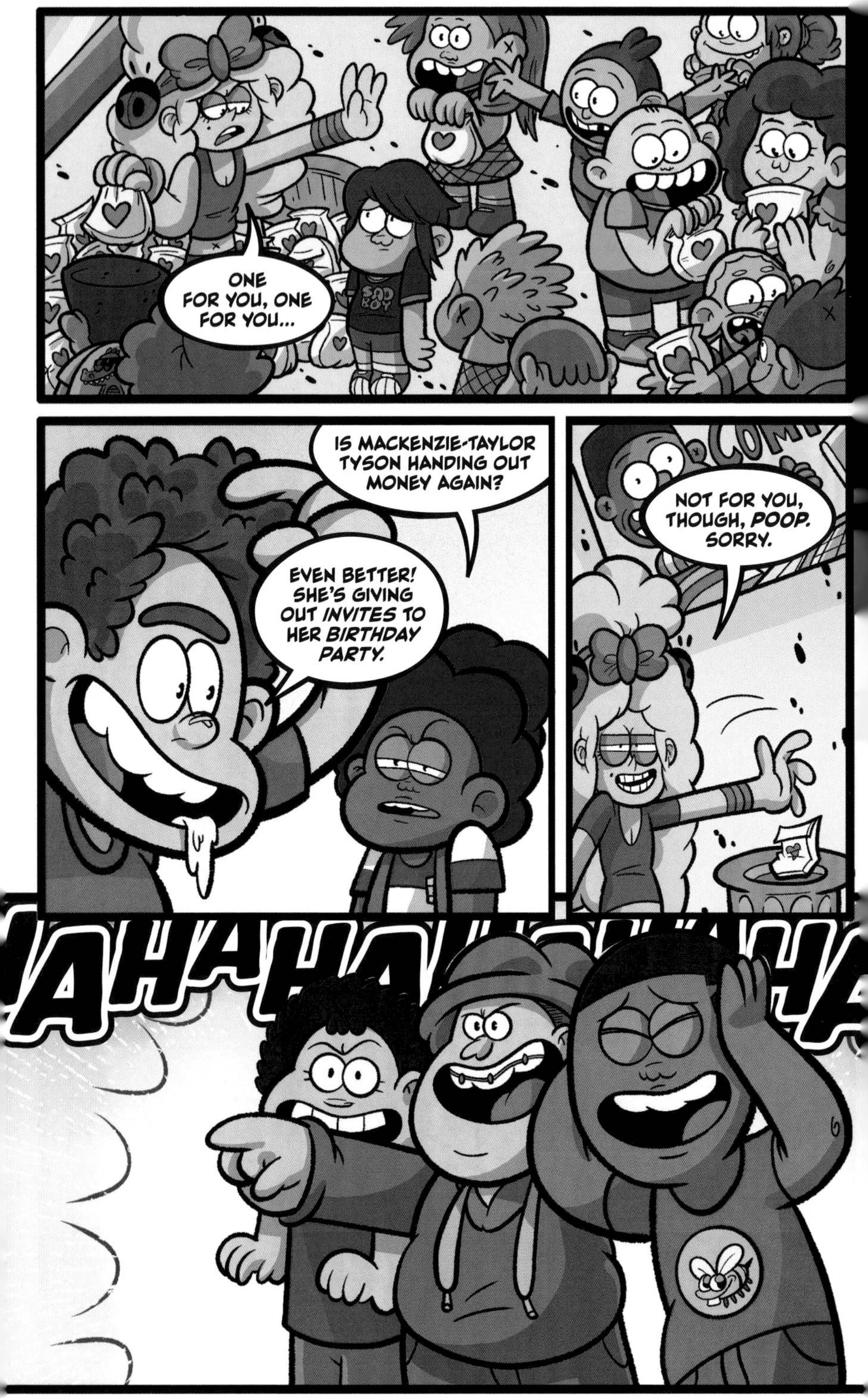
SAD BOY
ONE FOR YOU, ONE FOR YOU...
IS MACKENZIE-TAYLOR TYSON HANDING OUT MONEY AGAIN?
EVEN BETTER! SHE'S GIVING OUT *INVITES* TO HER *BIRTHDAY* PARTY.
NOT FOR YOU, THOUGH, *POOP*. SORRY.
AHAHAHAHAHA

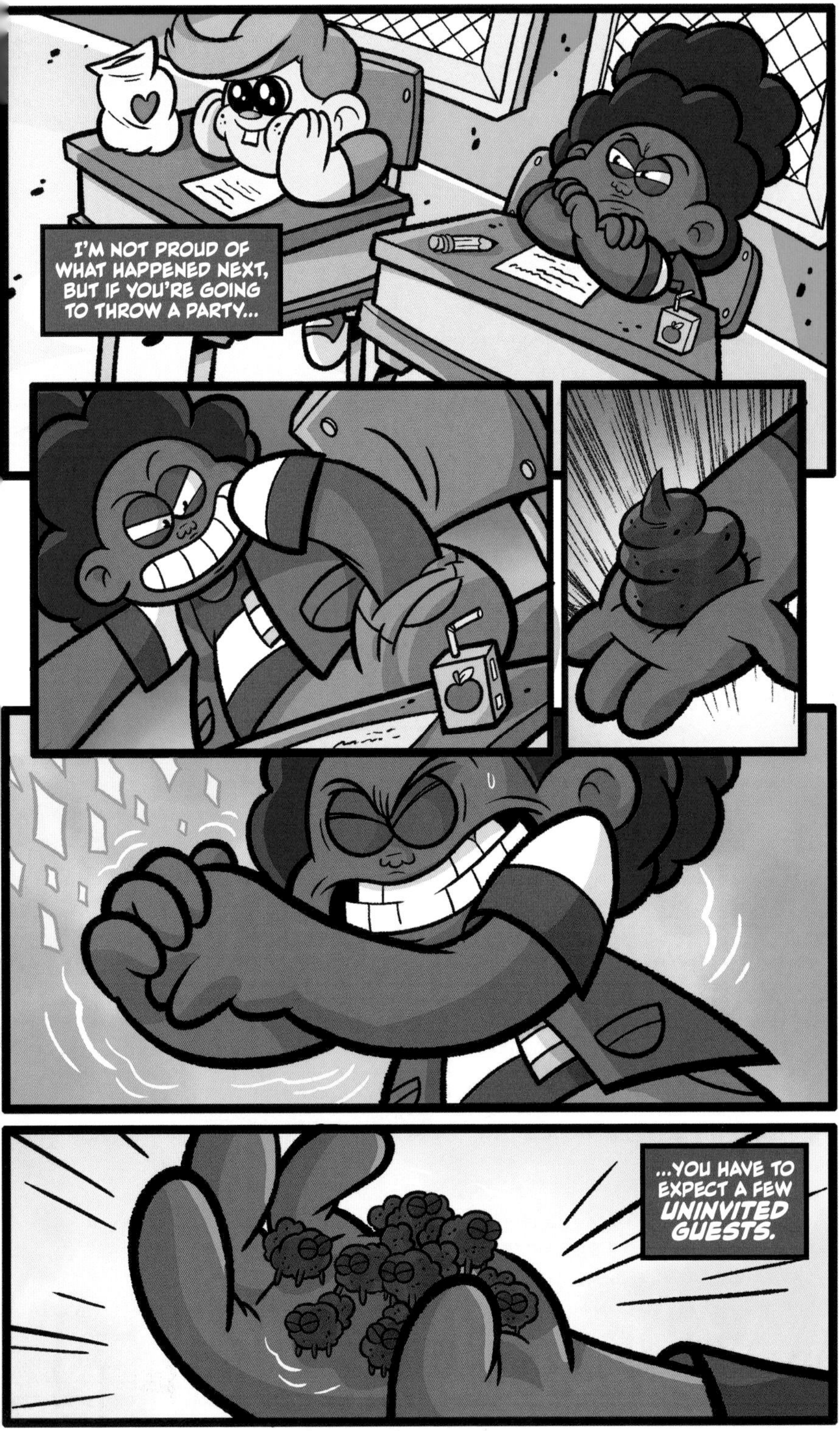
I'M NOT PROUD OF WHAT HAPPENED NEXT, BUT IF YOU'RE GOING TO THROW A PARTY...
...YOU HAVE TO EXPECT A FEW UNINVITED GUESTS.

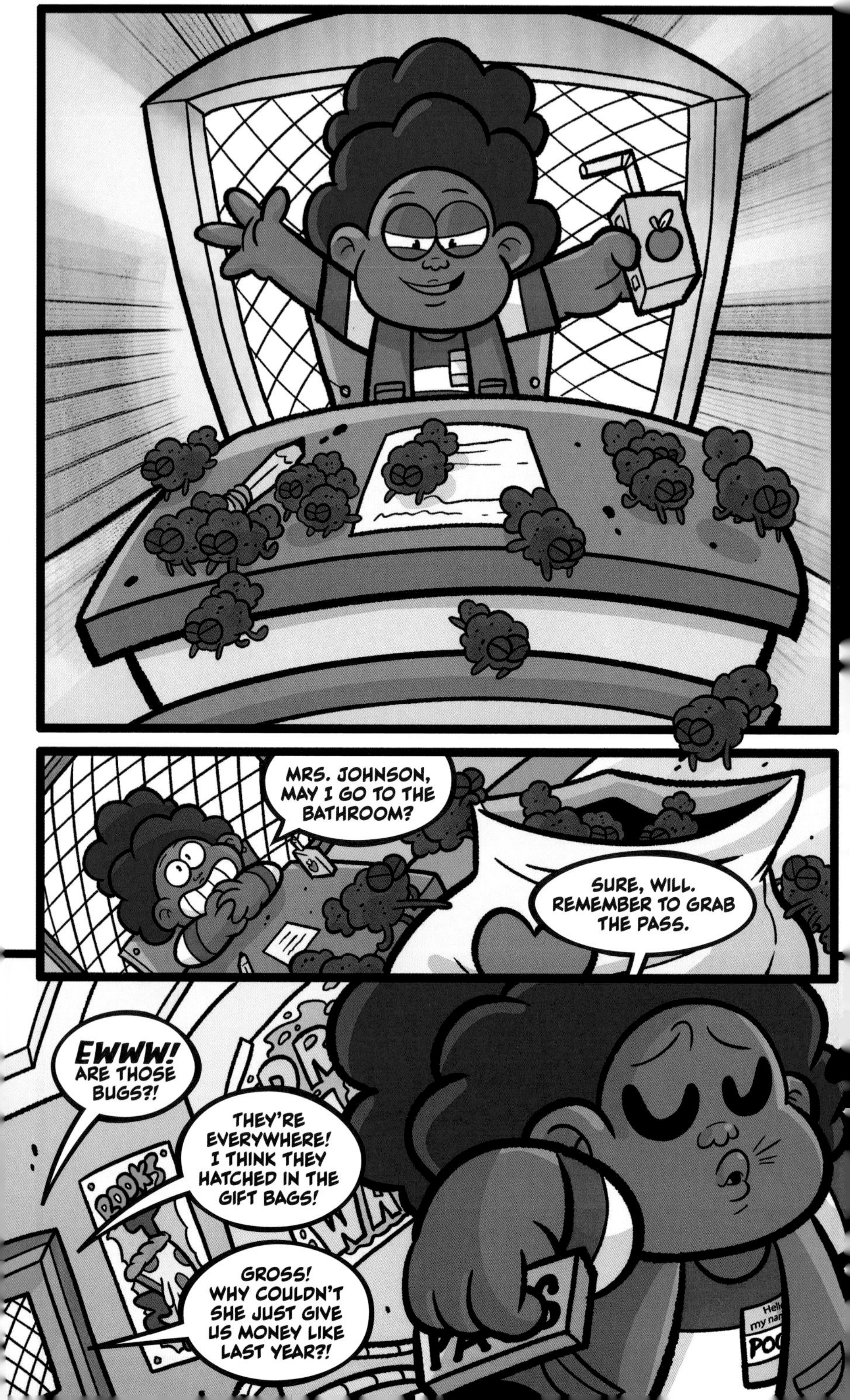
MRS. JOHNSON, MAY I GO TO THE BATHROOM?
SURE, WILL. REMEMBER TO GRAB THE PASS.
EWWW! ARE THOSE BUGS?!
THEY'RE EVERYWHERE! I THINK THEY HATCHED IN THE GIFT BAGS!
GROSS! WHY COULDN'T SHE JUST GIVE US MONEY LIKE LAST YEAR?!

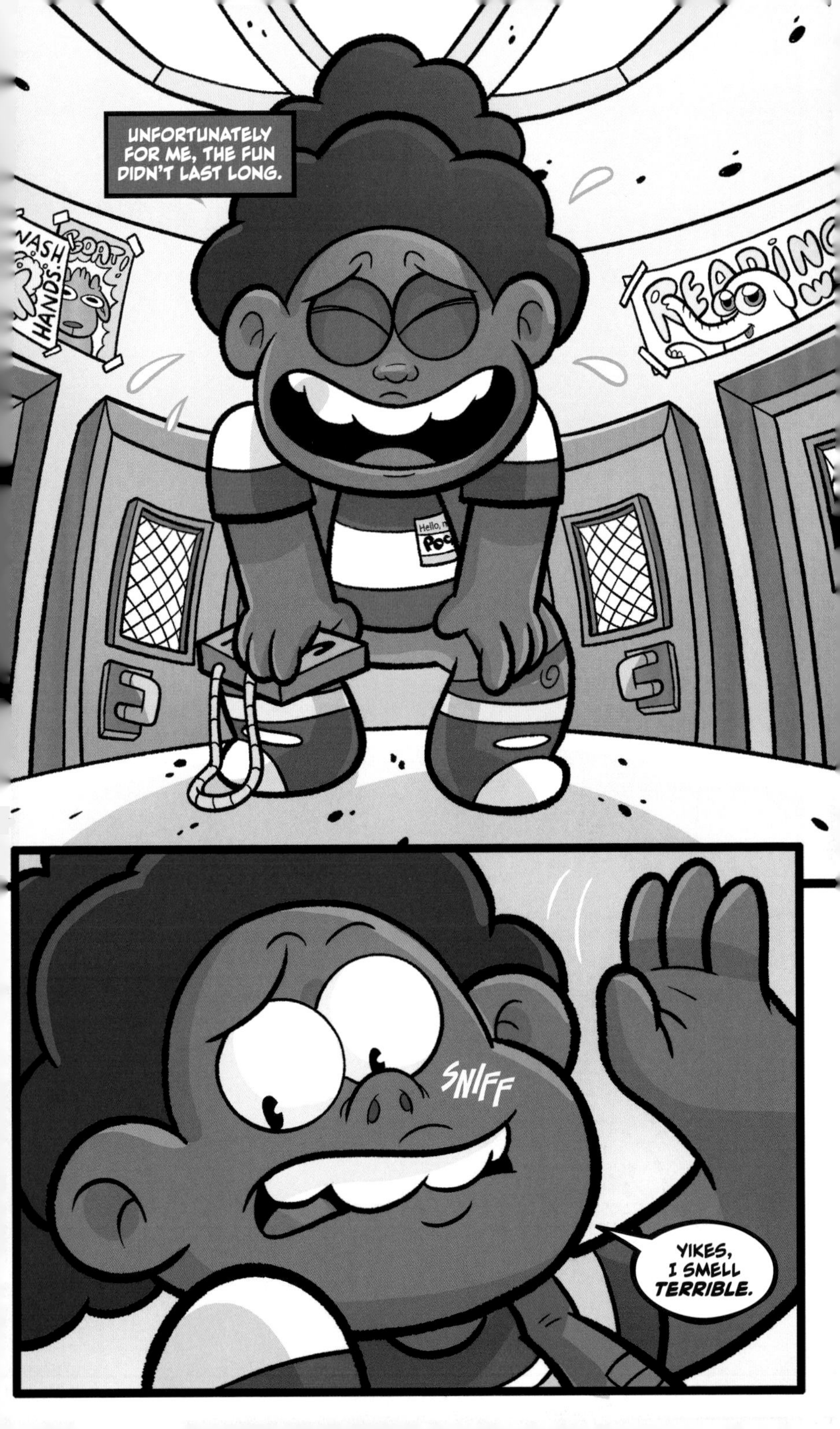
UNFORTUNATELY FOR ME, THE FUN DIDN'T LAST LONG.
WASH HANDS!
BOAT!
READING
SNIFF
YIKES, I SMELL *TERRIBLE.*

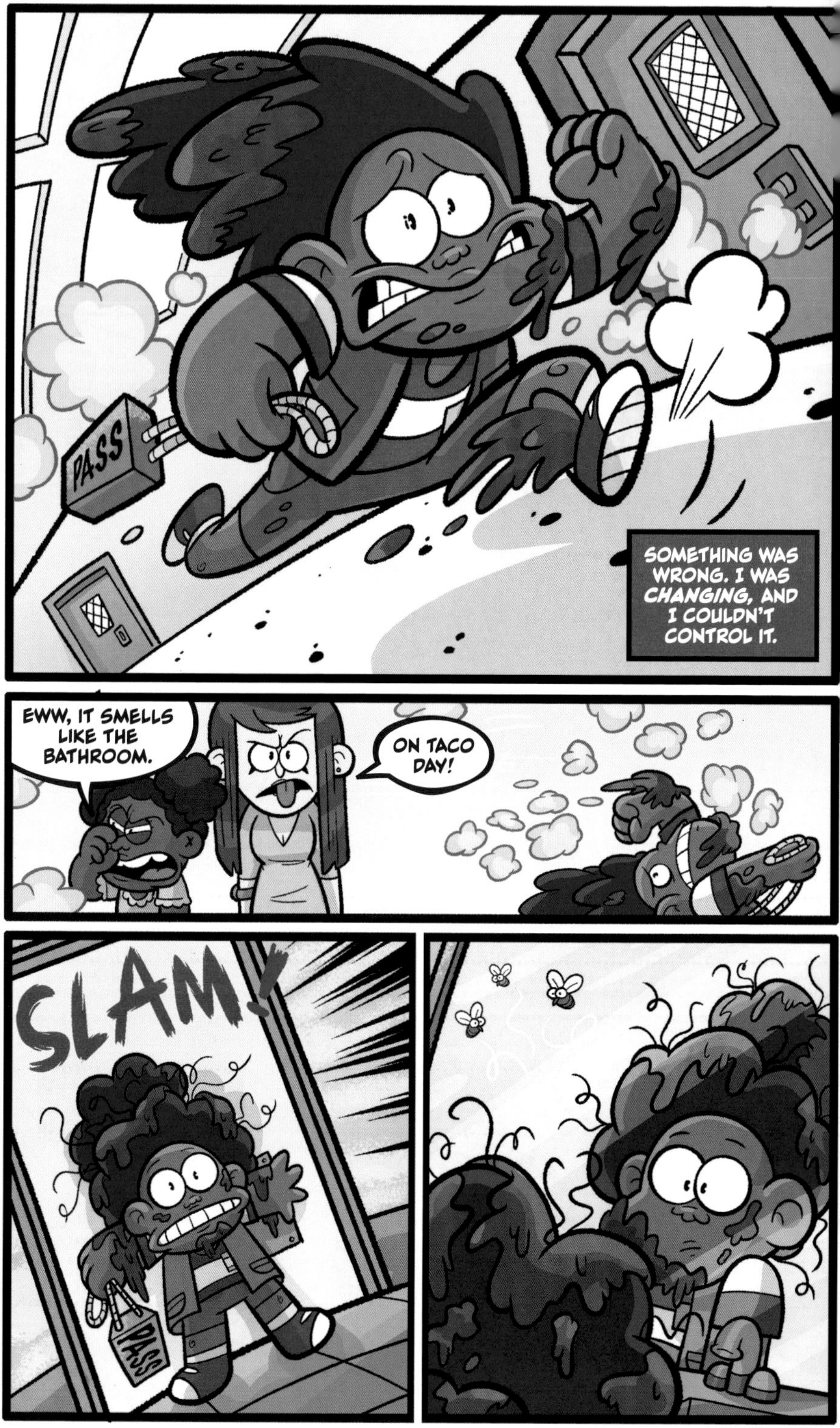
SOMETHING WAS WRONG. I WAS *CHANGING*, AND I COULDN'T CONTROL IT.
PASS
EWW, IT SMELLS LIKE THE BATHROOM.
ON TACO DAY!
SLAM!
PASS

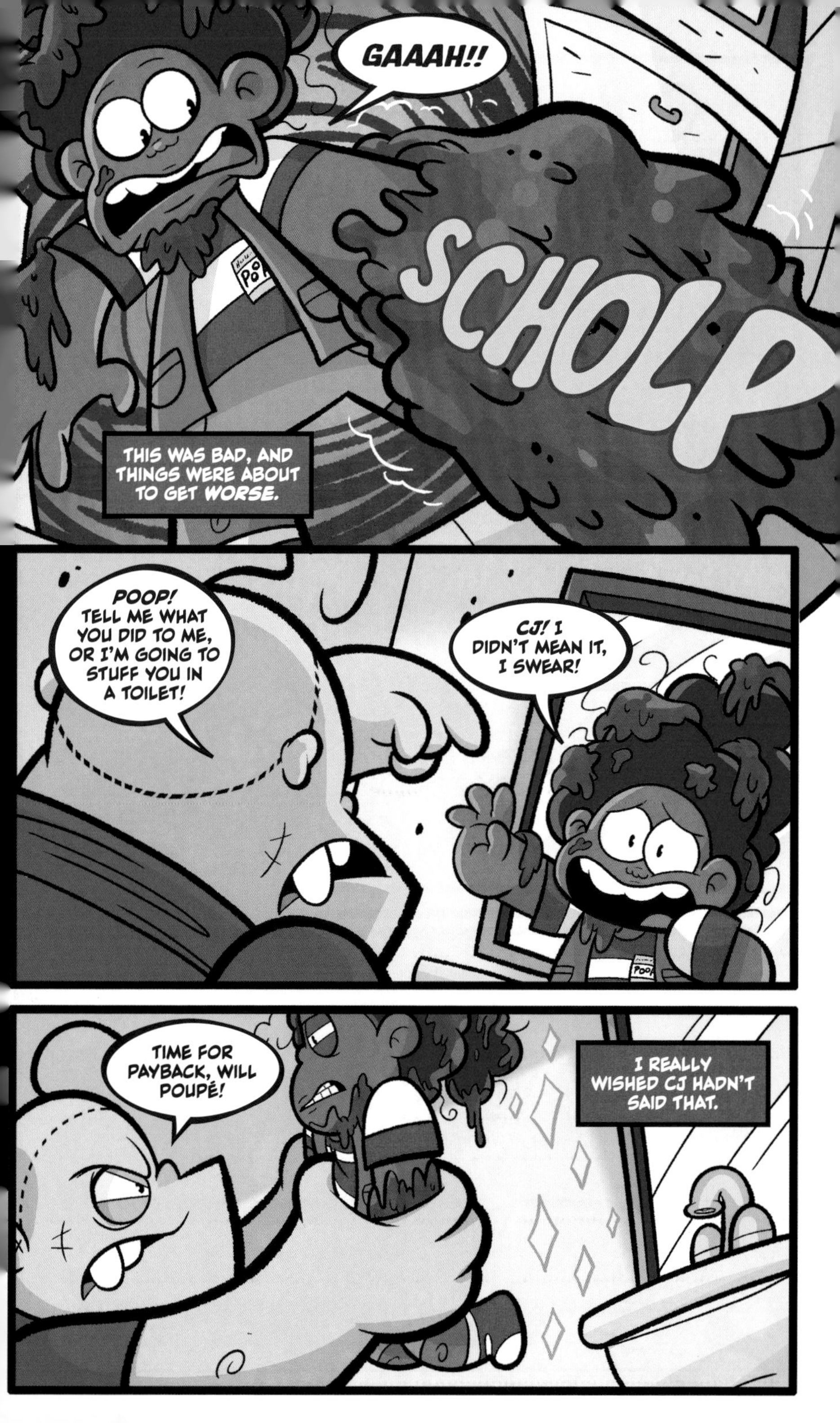
GAAAH!!
SCHOLP
THIS WAS BAD, AND THINGS WERE ABOUT TO GET WORSE.
POOP! TELL ME WHAT YOU DID TO ME, OR I'M GOING TO STUFF YOU IN A TOILET!
CJ! I DIDN'T MEAN IT, I SWEAR!
TIME FOR PAYBACK, WILL POUPÉ!
I REALLY WISHED CJ HADN'T SAID THAT.

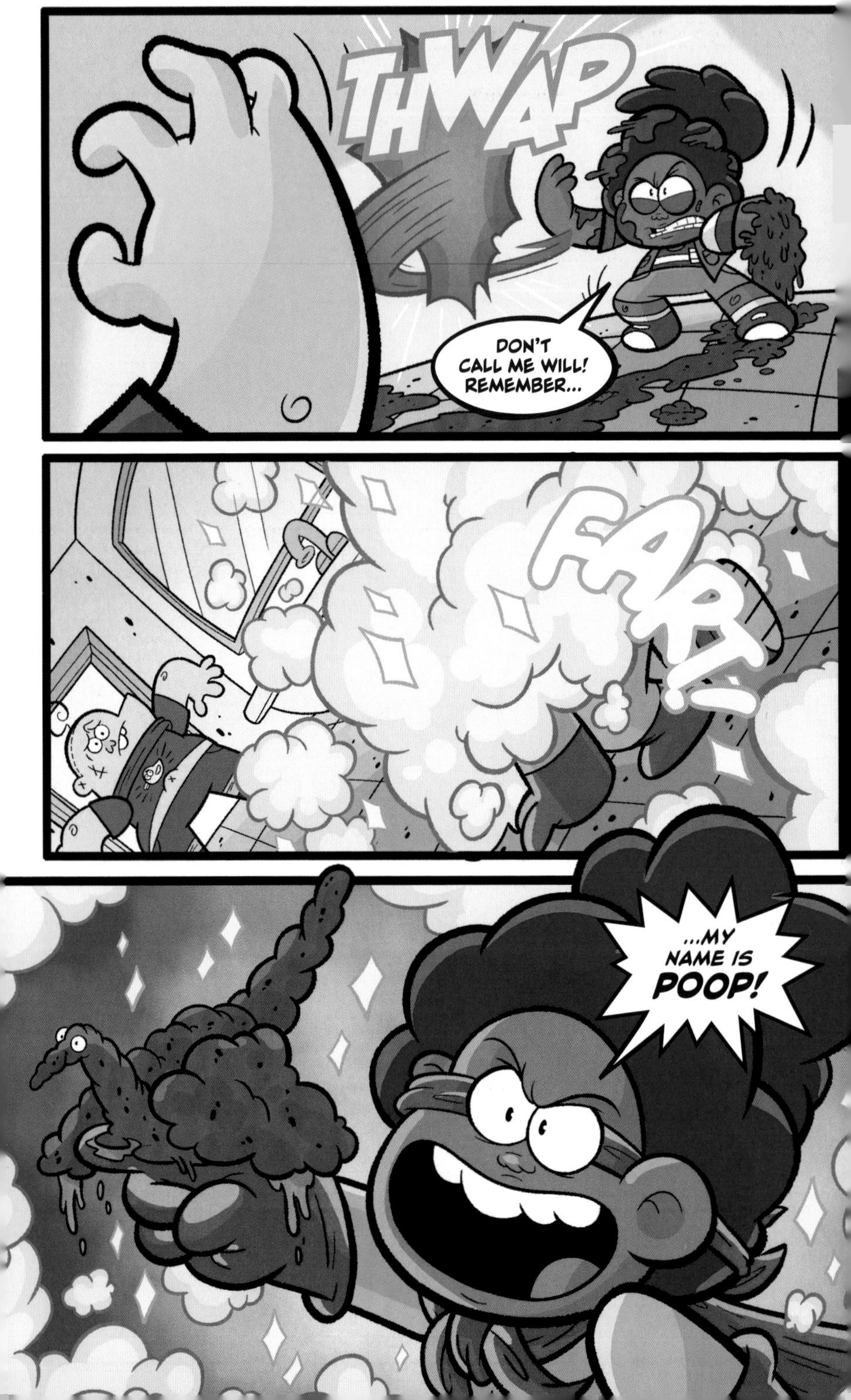
THWAP
DON'T CALL ME WILL! REMEMBER...
FART
...MY NAME IS POOP!

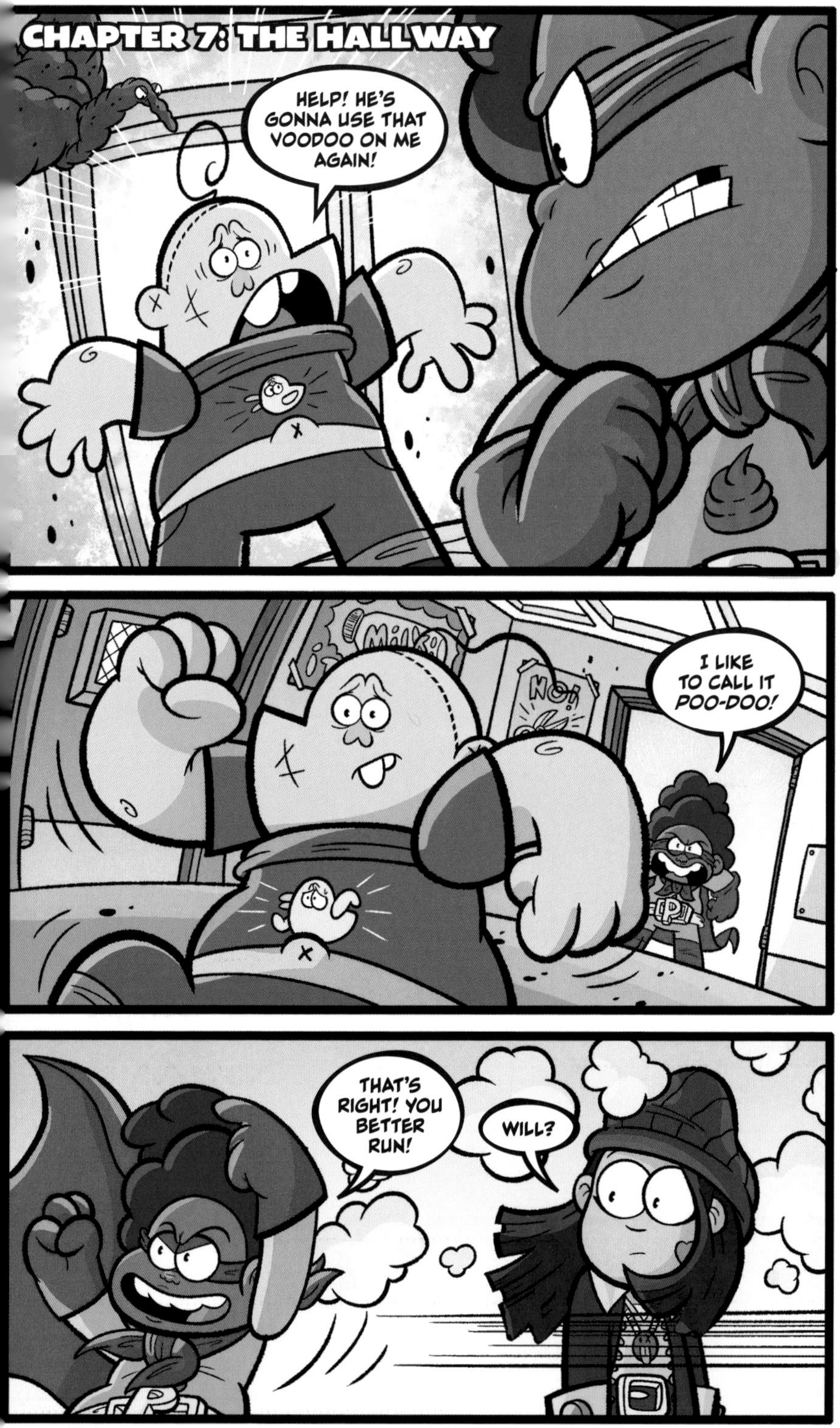
CHAPTER 7: THE HALLWAY
HELP! HE'S GONNA USE THAT VOODOO ON ME AGAIN!
I LIKE TO CALL IT POO-DOO!
THAT'S RIGHT! YOU BETTER RUN!
WILL?

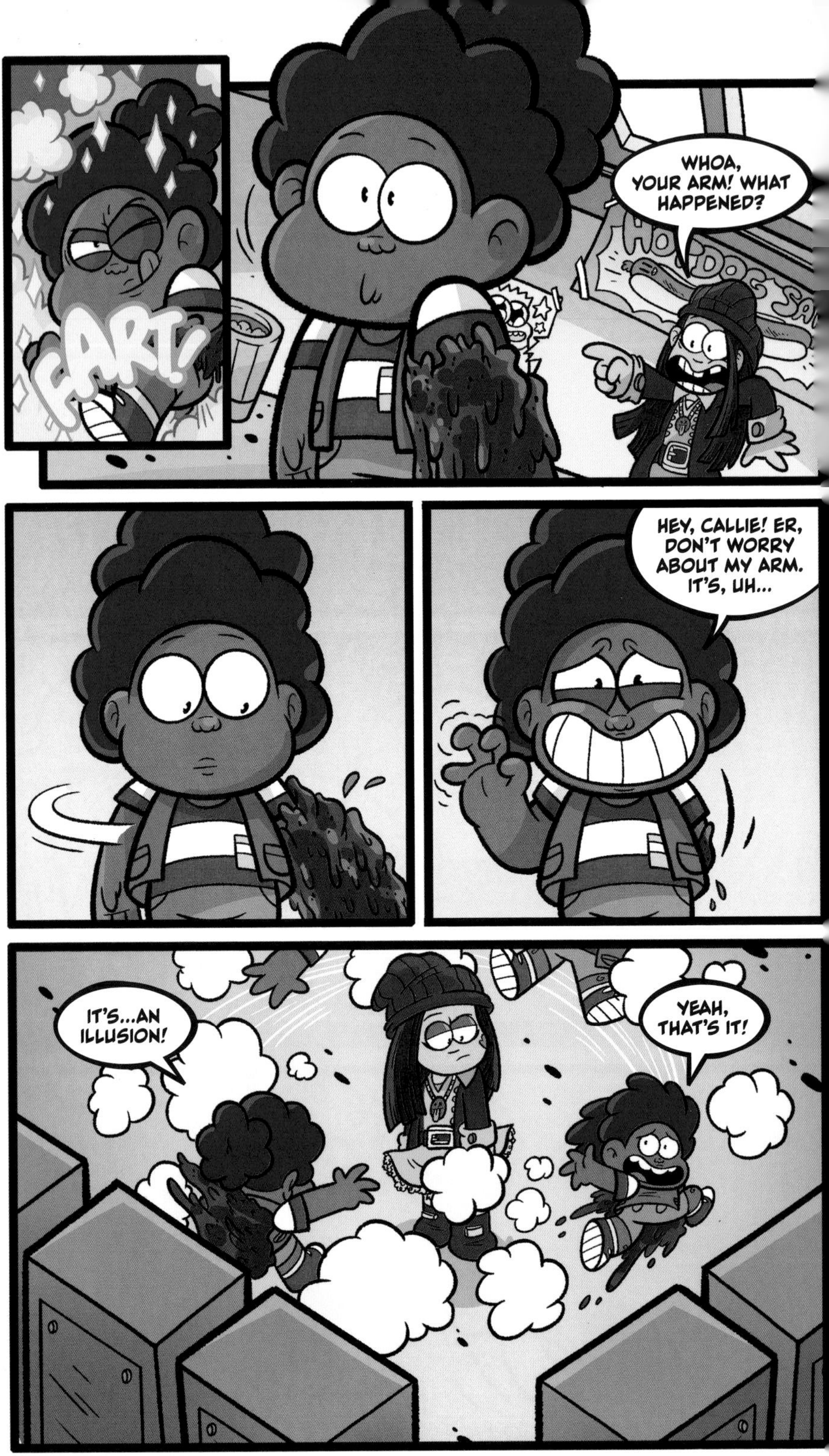
FART!
WHOA, YOUR ARM! WHAT HAPPENED?
HEY, CALLIE! ER, DON'T WORRY ABOUT MY ARM. IT'S, UH...
IT'S...AN ILLUSION!
YEAH, THAT'S IT!

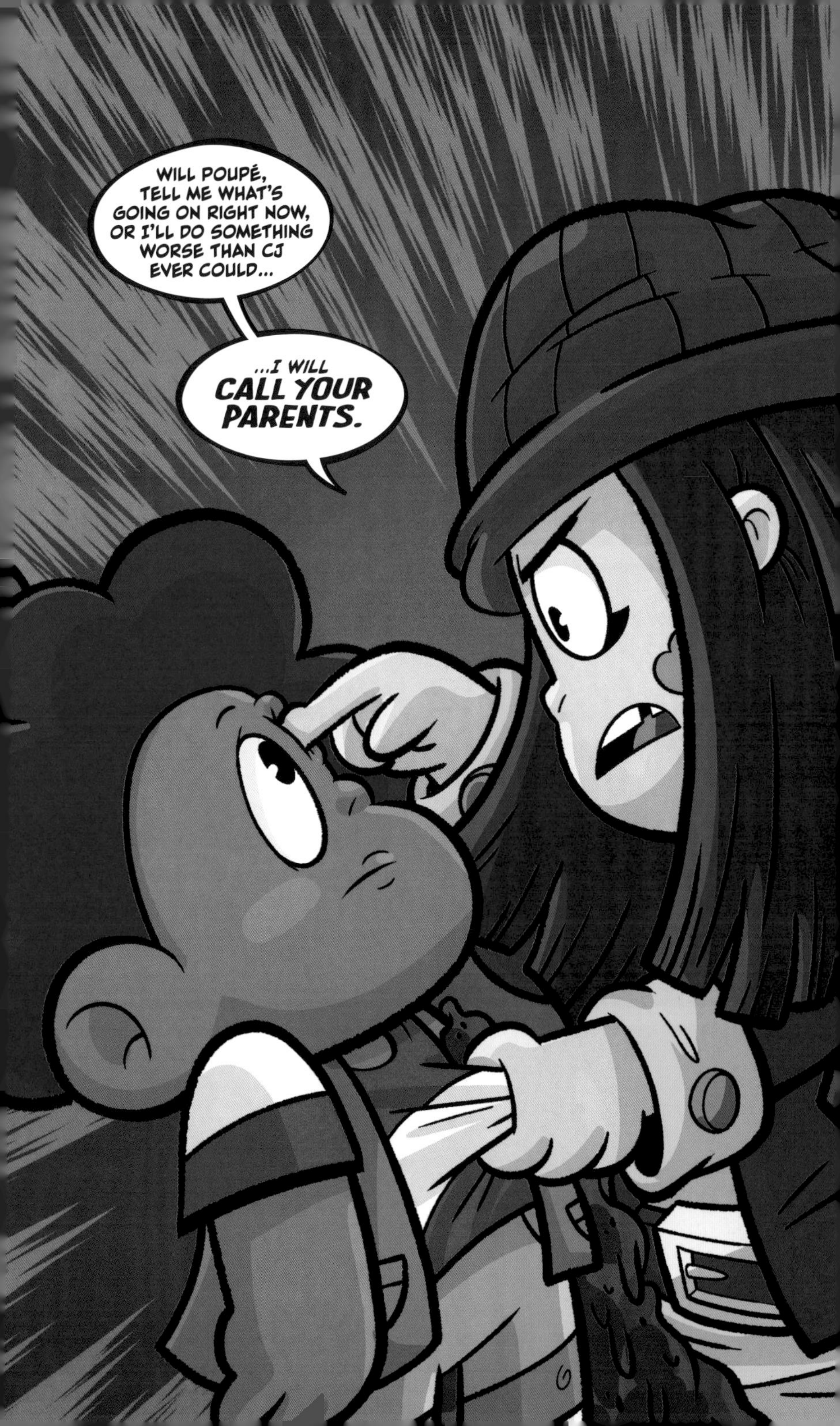
WILL POUPÉ, TELL ME WHAT'S GOING ON RIGHT NOW, OR I'LL DO SOMETHING WORSE THAN CJ EVER COULD...
...I WILL CALL YOUR PARENTS.

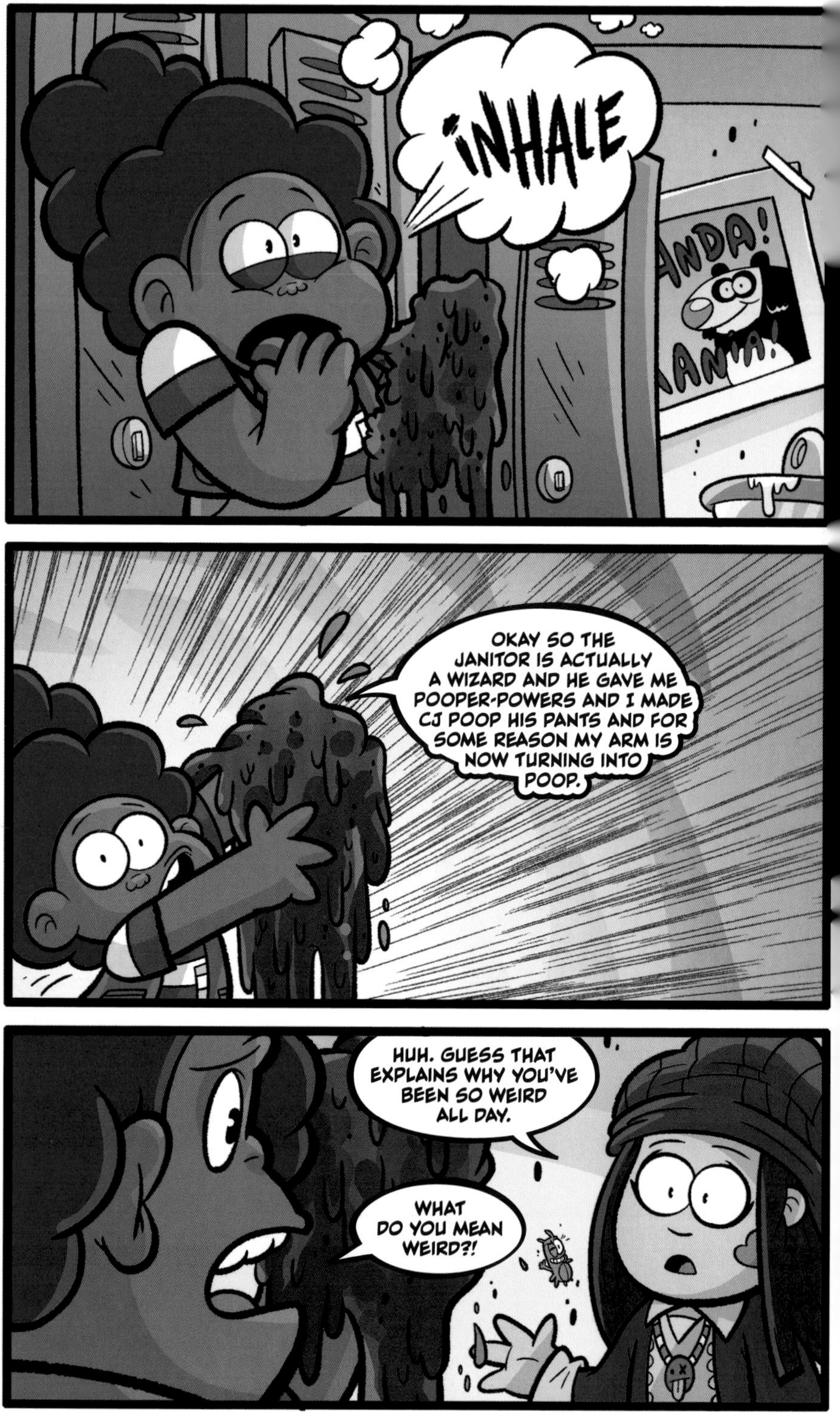
INHALE
OKAY SO THE JANITOR IS ACTUALLY A WIZARD AND HE GAVE ME POOPER-POWERS AND I MADE CJ POOP HIS PANTS AND FOR SOME REASON MY ARM IS NOW TURNING INTO POOP.
HUH. GUESS THAT EXPLAINS WHY YOU'VE BEEN SO WEIRD ALL DAY.
WHAT DO YOU MEAN WEIRD?!

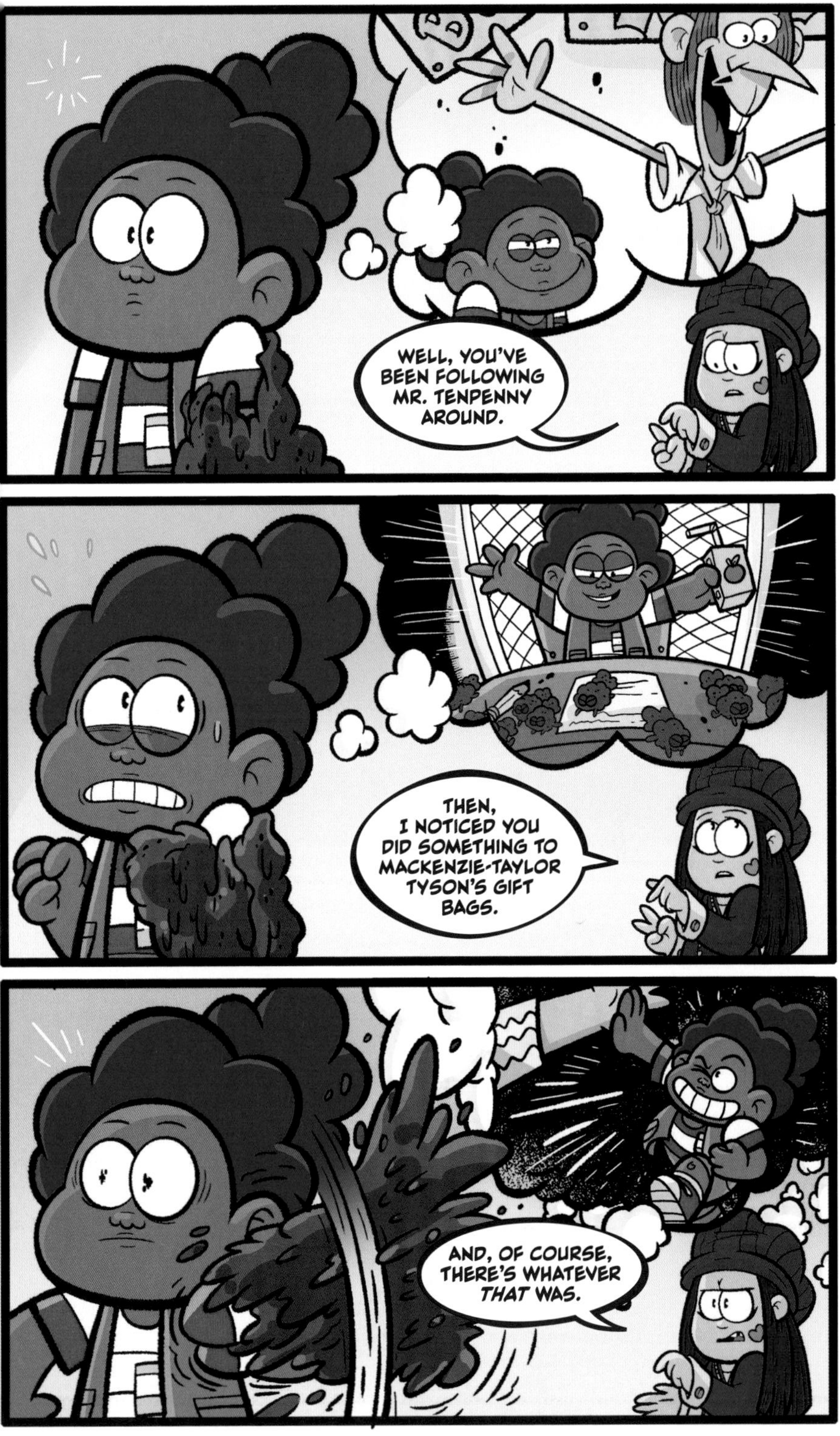
WELL, YOU'VE BEEN FOLLOWING MR. TENPENNY AROUND.
THEN, I NOTICED YOU DID SOMETHING TO MACKENZIE-TAYLOR TYSON'S GIFT BAGS.
AND, OF COURSE, THERE'S WHATEVER *THAT* WAS.

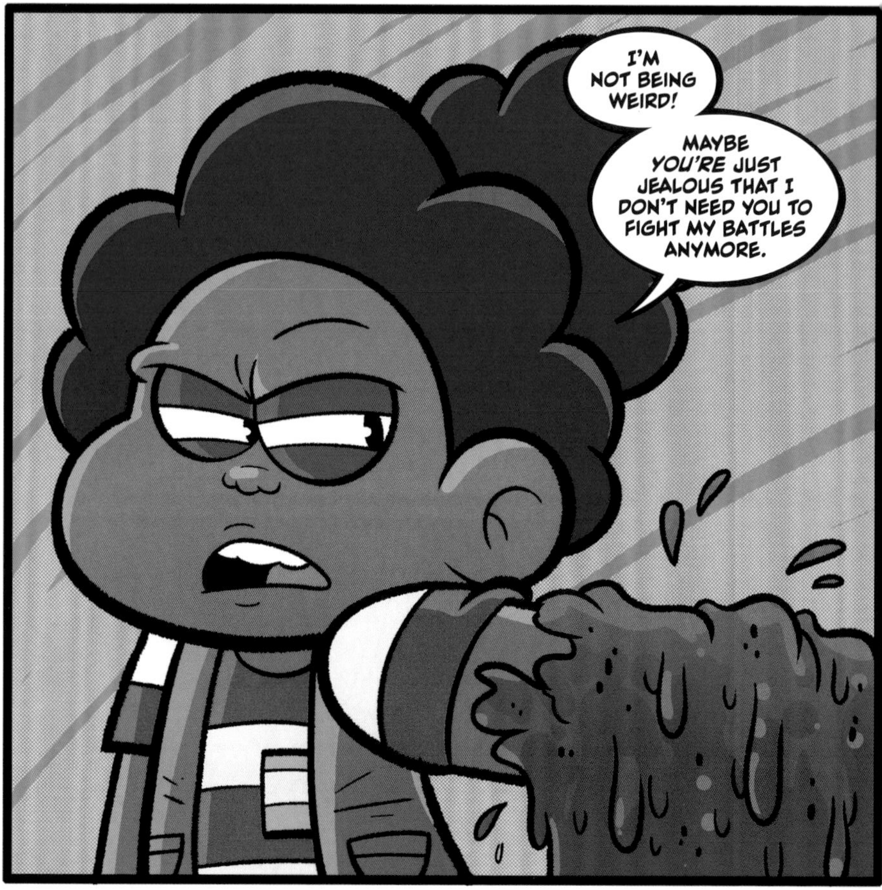
I'M NOT BEING WEIRD!
MAYBE YOU'RE JUST JEALOUS THAT I DON'T NEED YOU TO FIGHT MY BATTLES ANYMORE.

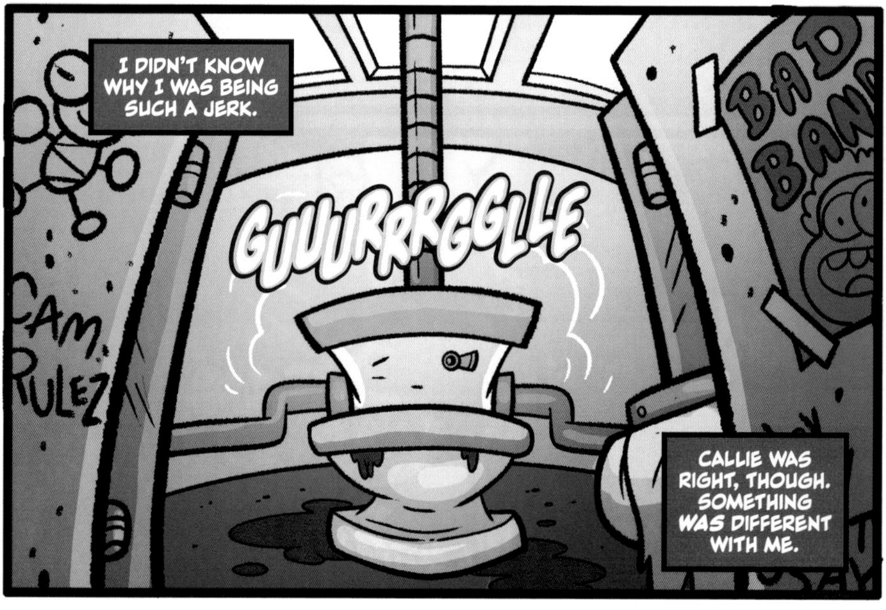
I DIDN'T KNOW WHY I WAS BEING SUCH A JERK.
GUUURRRGGLLE
CAM RULEZ
CALLIE WAS RIGHT, THOUGH. SOMETHING WAS DIFFERENT WITH ME.

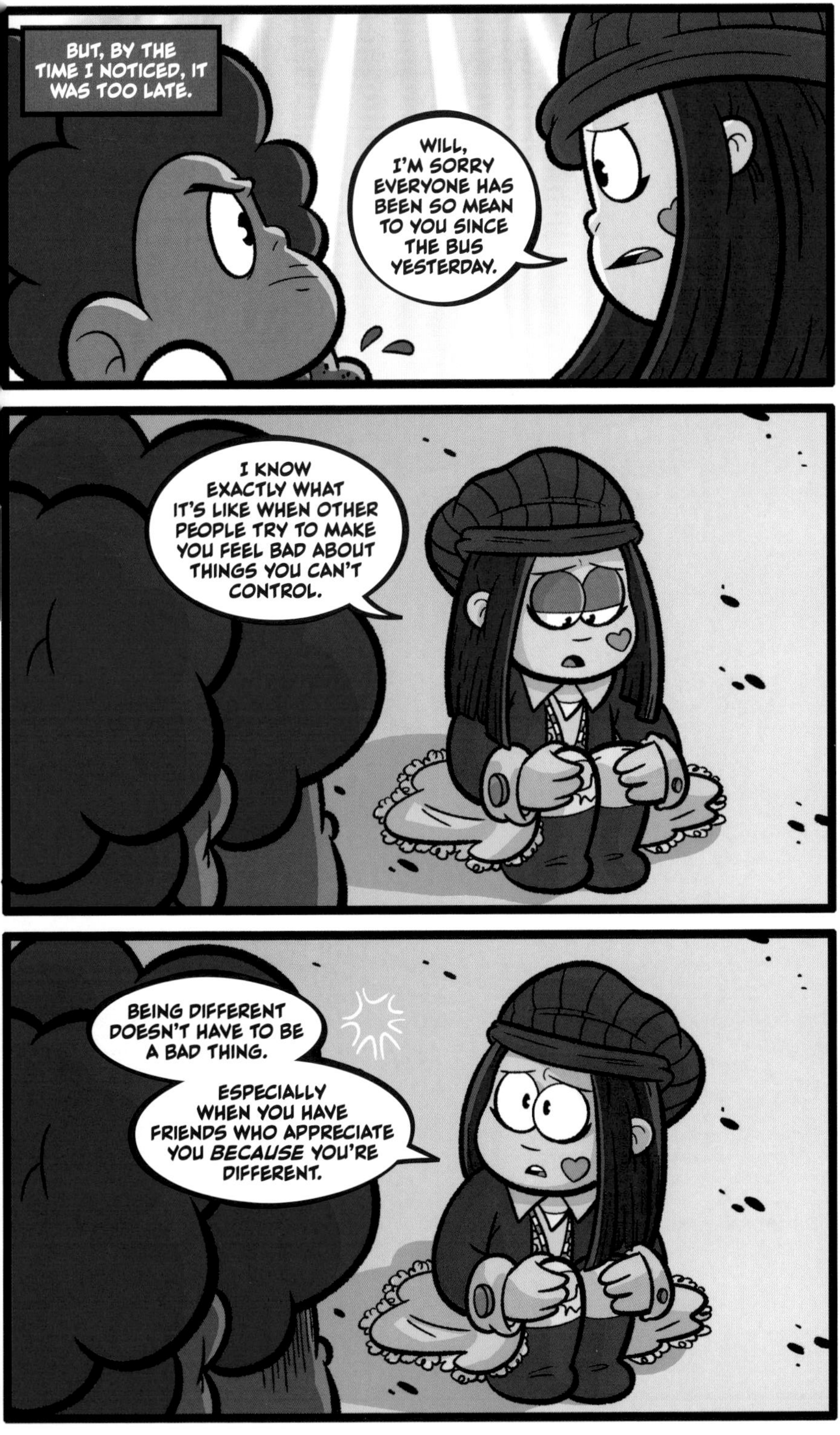
BUT, BY THE TIME I NOTICED, IT WAS TOO LATE.
WILL, I'M SORRY EVERYONE HAS BEEN SO MEAN TO YOU SINCE THE BUS YESTERDAY.
I KNOW EXACTLY WHAT IT'S LIKE WHEN OTHER PEOPLE TRY TO MAKE YOU FEEL BAD ABOUT THINGS YOU CAN'T CONTROL.
BEING DIFFERENT DOESN'T HAVE TO BE A BAD THING.
ESPECIALLY WHEN YOU HAVE FRIENDS WHO APPRECIATE YOU *BECAUSE* YOU'RE DIFFERENT.

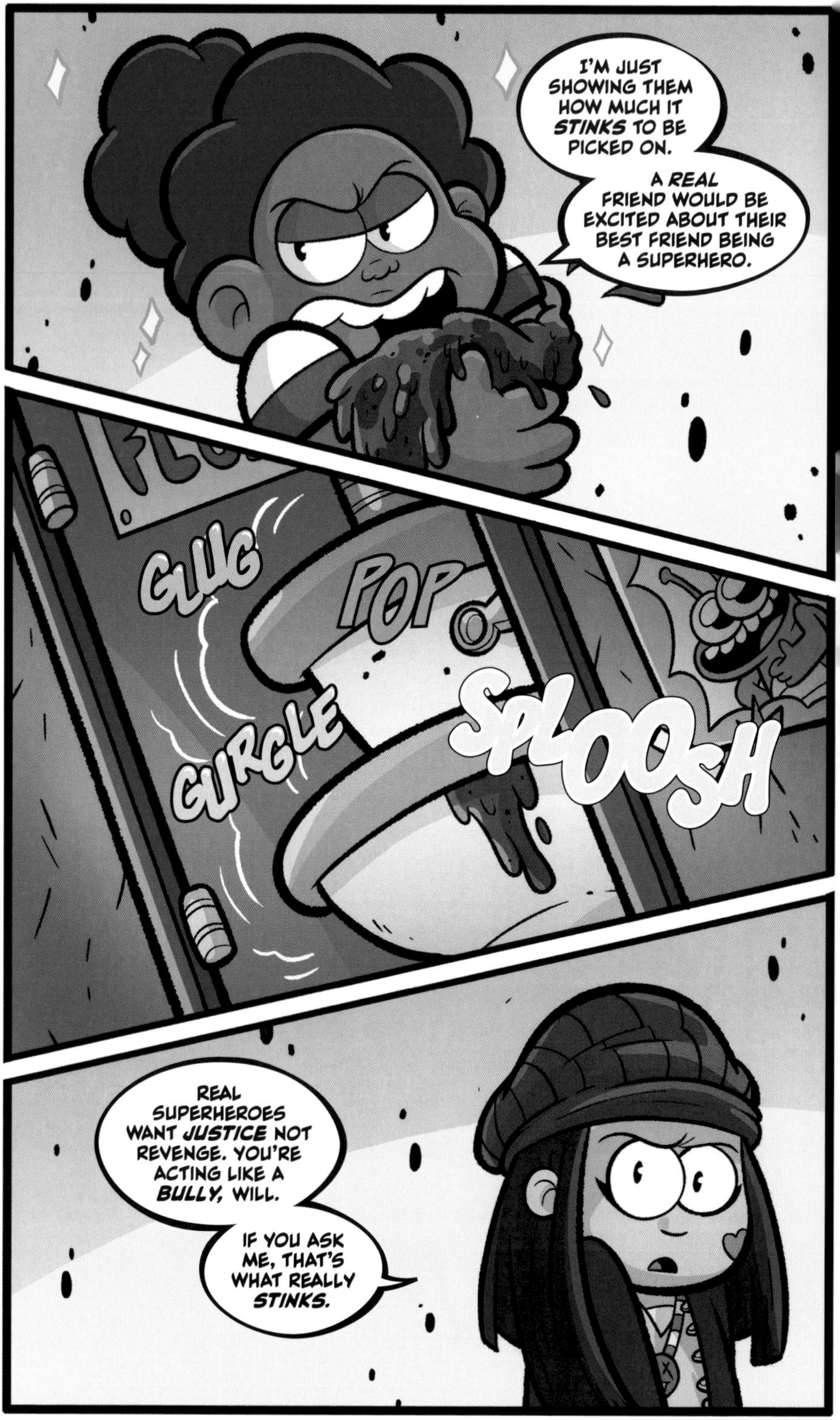
I'M JUST SHOWING THEM HOW MUCH IT STINKS TO BE PICKED ON.
A REAL FRIEND WOULD BE EXCITED ABOUT THEIR BEST FRIEND BEING A SUPERHERO.
GLUG
POP
GURGLE
SPLOOSH
REAL SUPERHEROES WANT JUSTICE NOT REVENGE. YOU'RE ACTING LIKE A BULLY, WILL.
IF YOU ASK ME, THAT'S WHAT REALLY STINKS.

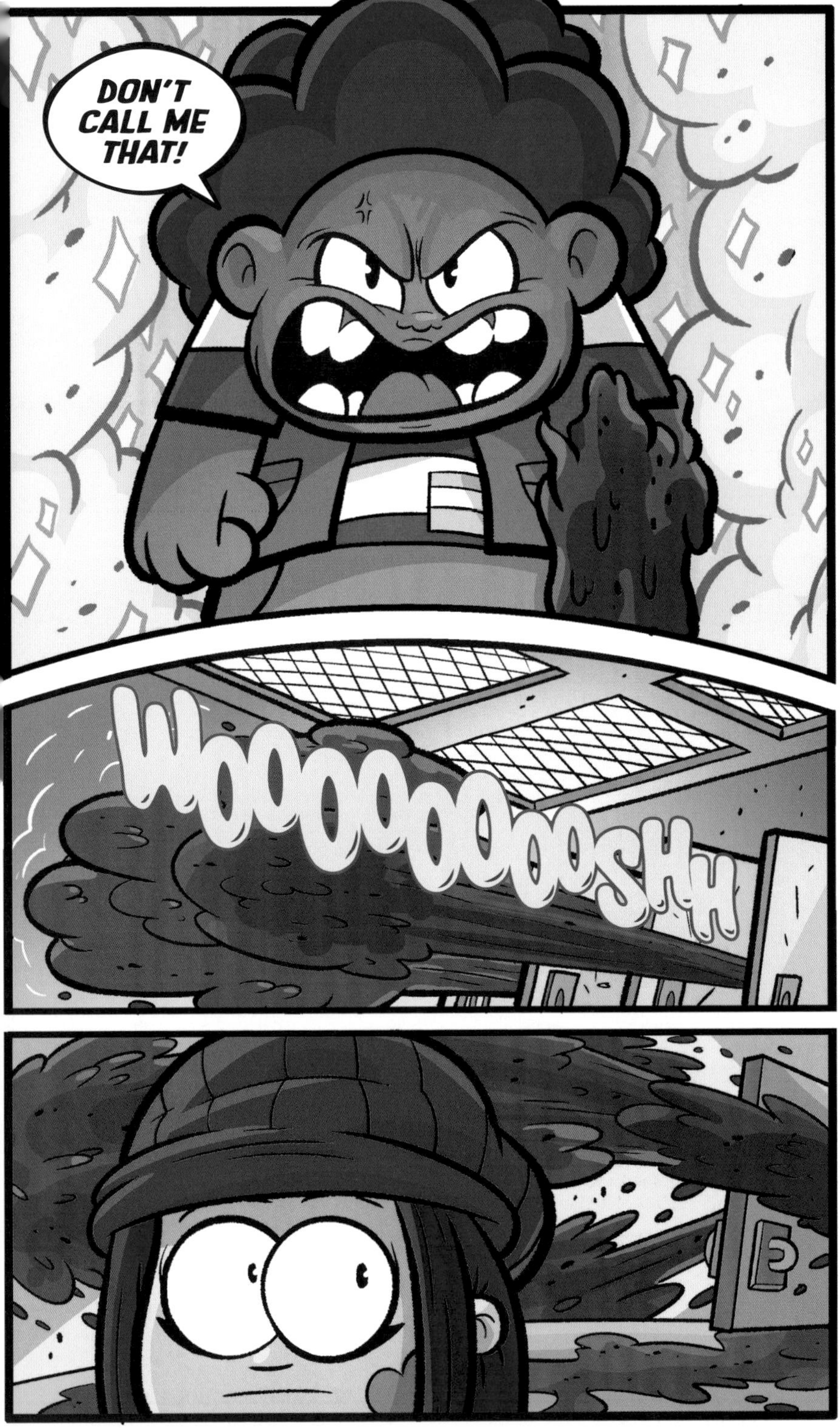
DON'T CALL ME THAT!
WOOOOOOOOSHH

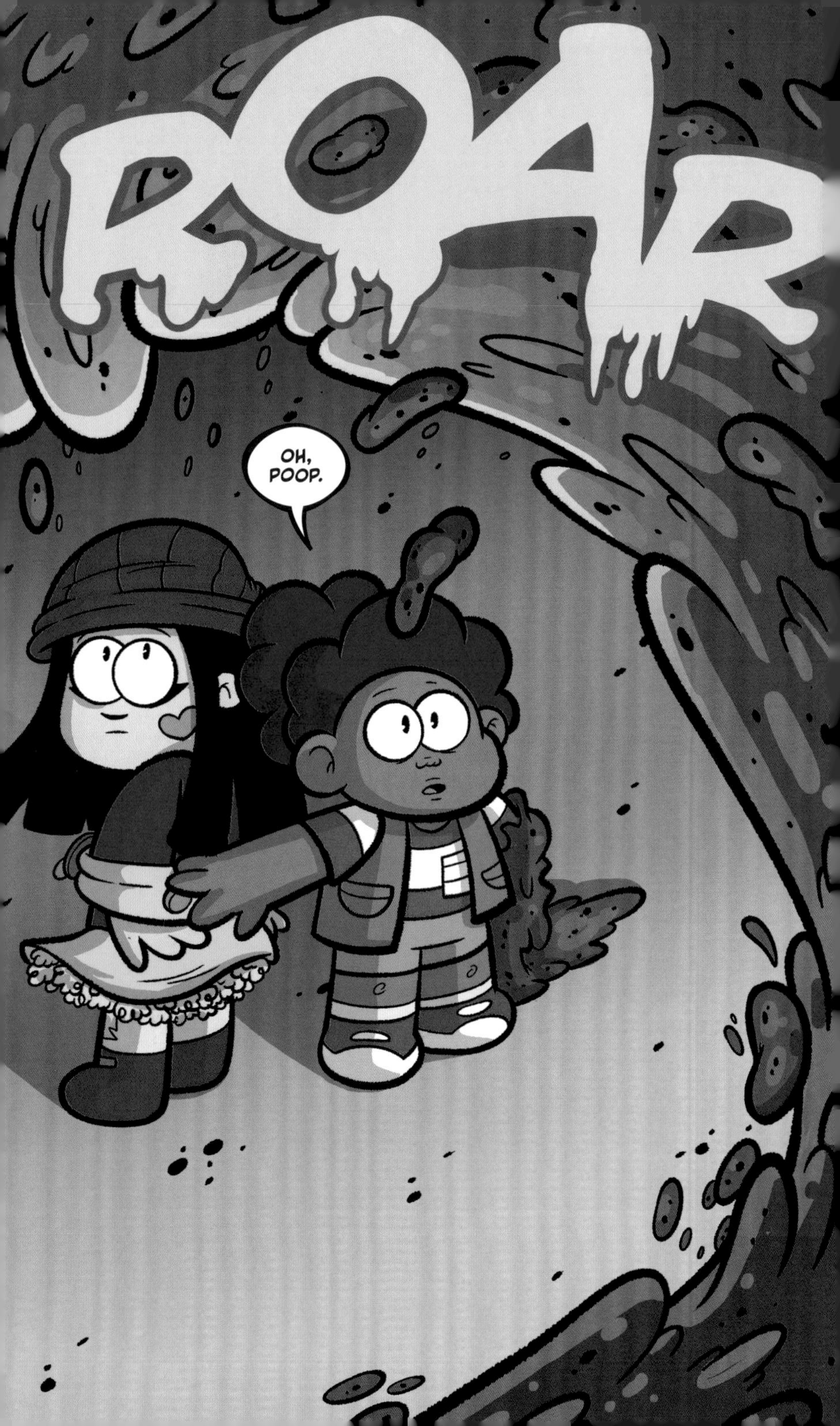
ROAR
OH, POOP.

CHAPTER 8: THE AFTERMATH

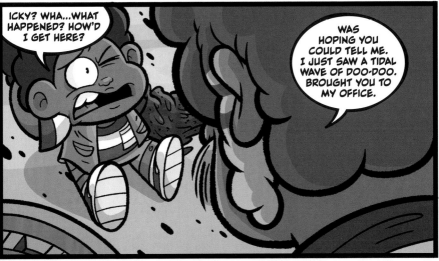

ICKY? WHA...WHAT HAPPENED? HOW'D I GET HERE?

WAS HOPING YOU COULD TELL ME. I JUST SAW A TIDAL WAVE OF DOO-DOO. BROUGHT YOU TO MY OFFICE.

OH NO! CALLIE! IS SHE OKAY?

IT'S GONNA TAKE MORE THAN A POOP TSUNAMI TO TAKE HER OUT. SHE'S A TOUGH ONE.

I DIDN'T MEAN TO HURT HER. ICKY, WHAT'S HAPPENING TO ME?!

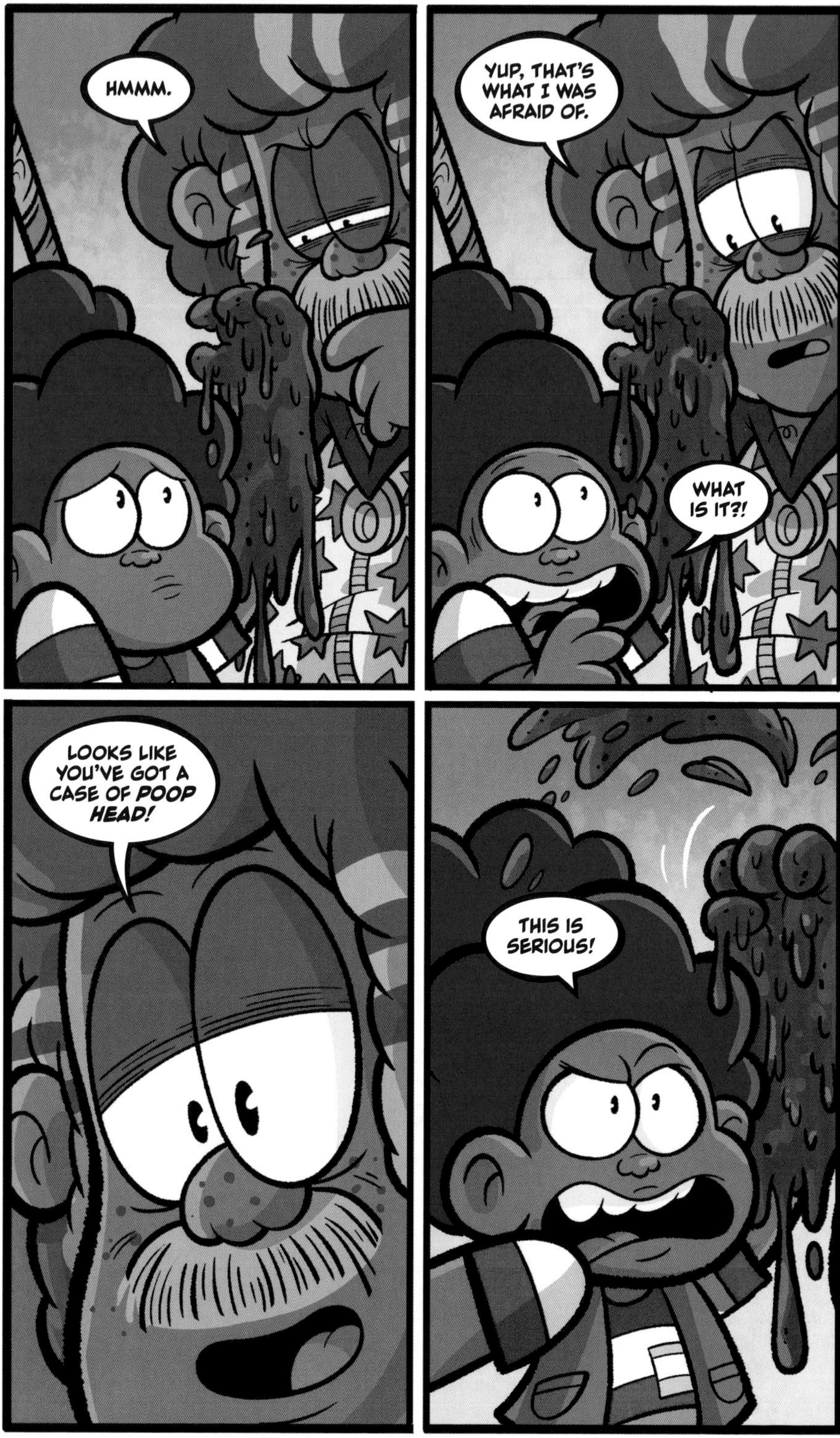
HMMM.
YUP, THAT'S WHAT I WAS AFRAID OF.
WHAT IS IT?!
LOOKS LIKE YOU'VE GOT A CASE OF *POOP HEAD!*
THIS IS SERIOUS!

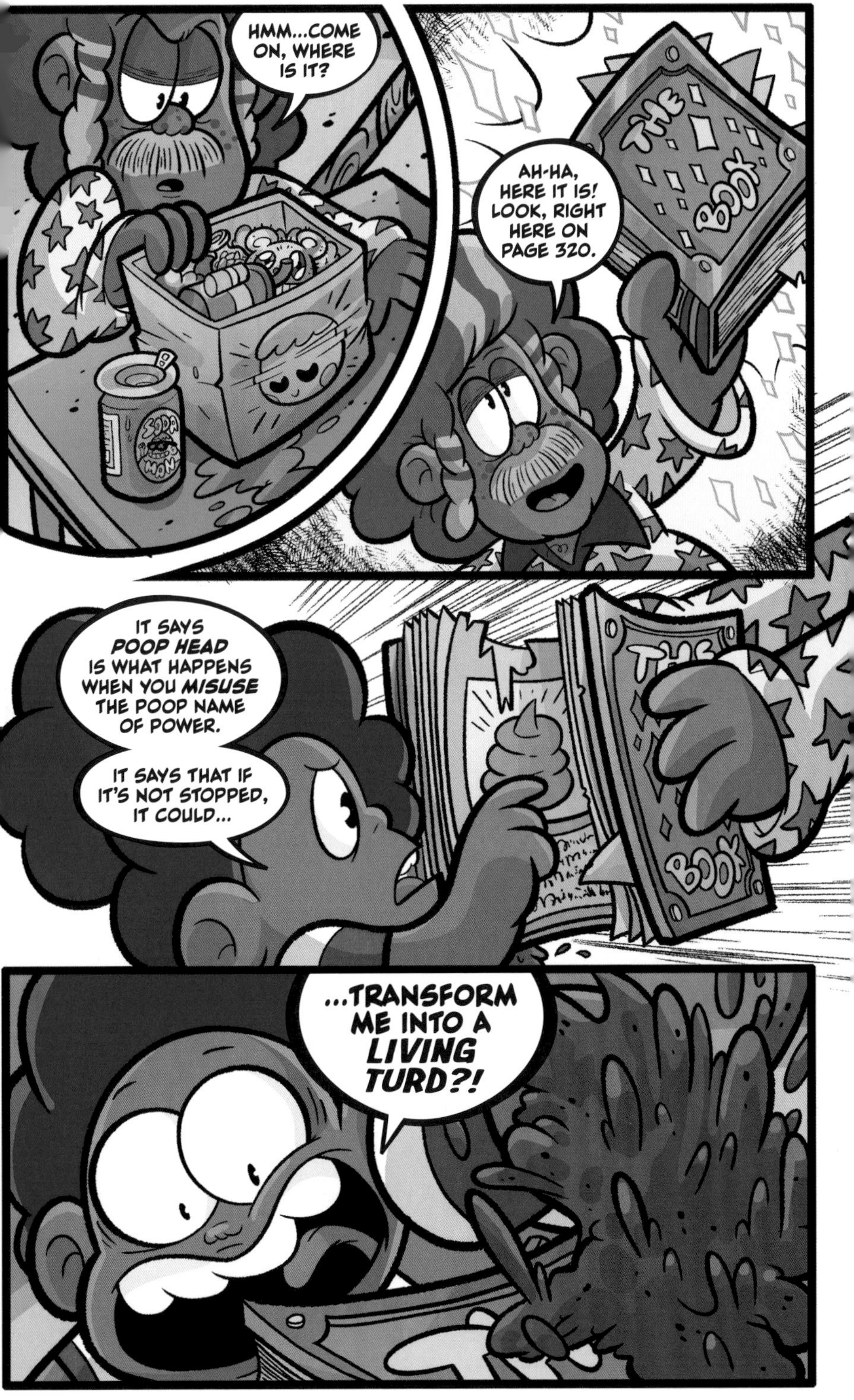
HMM...COME ON, WHERE IS IT?
AH-HA, HERE IT IS! LOOK, RIGHT HERE ON PAGE 320.
THE BOOK
IT SAYS *POOP HEAD* IS WHAT HAPPENS WHEN YOU *MISUSE* THE POOP NAME OF POWER.
IT SAYS THAT IF IT'S NOT STOPPED, IT COULD...
...TRANSFORM ME INTO A *LIVING TURD?!*

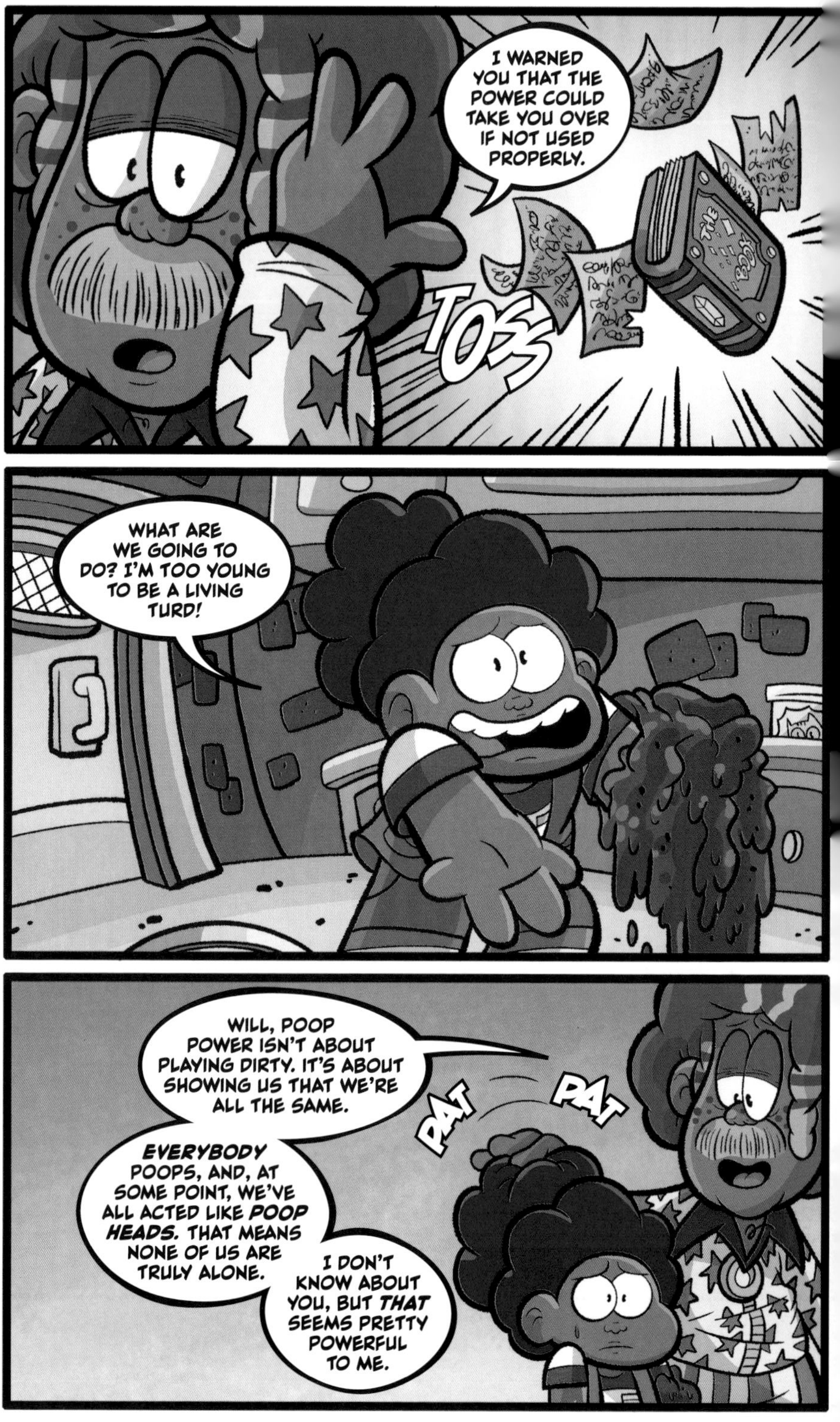
I WARNED YOU THAT THE POWER COULD TAKE YOU OVER IF NOT USED PROPERLY.
TOSS
THE BOOK
WHAT ARE WE GOING TO DO? I'M TOO YOUNG TO BE A LIVING TURD!
WILL, POOP POWER ISN'T ABOUT PLAYING DIRTY. IT'S ABOUT SHOWING US THAT WE'RE ALL THE SAME.
PAT
PAT
EVERYBODY POOPS, AND, AT SOME POINT, WE'VE ALL ACTED LIKE POOP HEADS. THAT MEANS NONE OF US ARE TRULY ALONE.
I DON'T KNOW ABOUT YOU, BUT THAT SEEMS PRETTY POWERFUL TO ME.

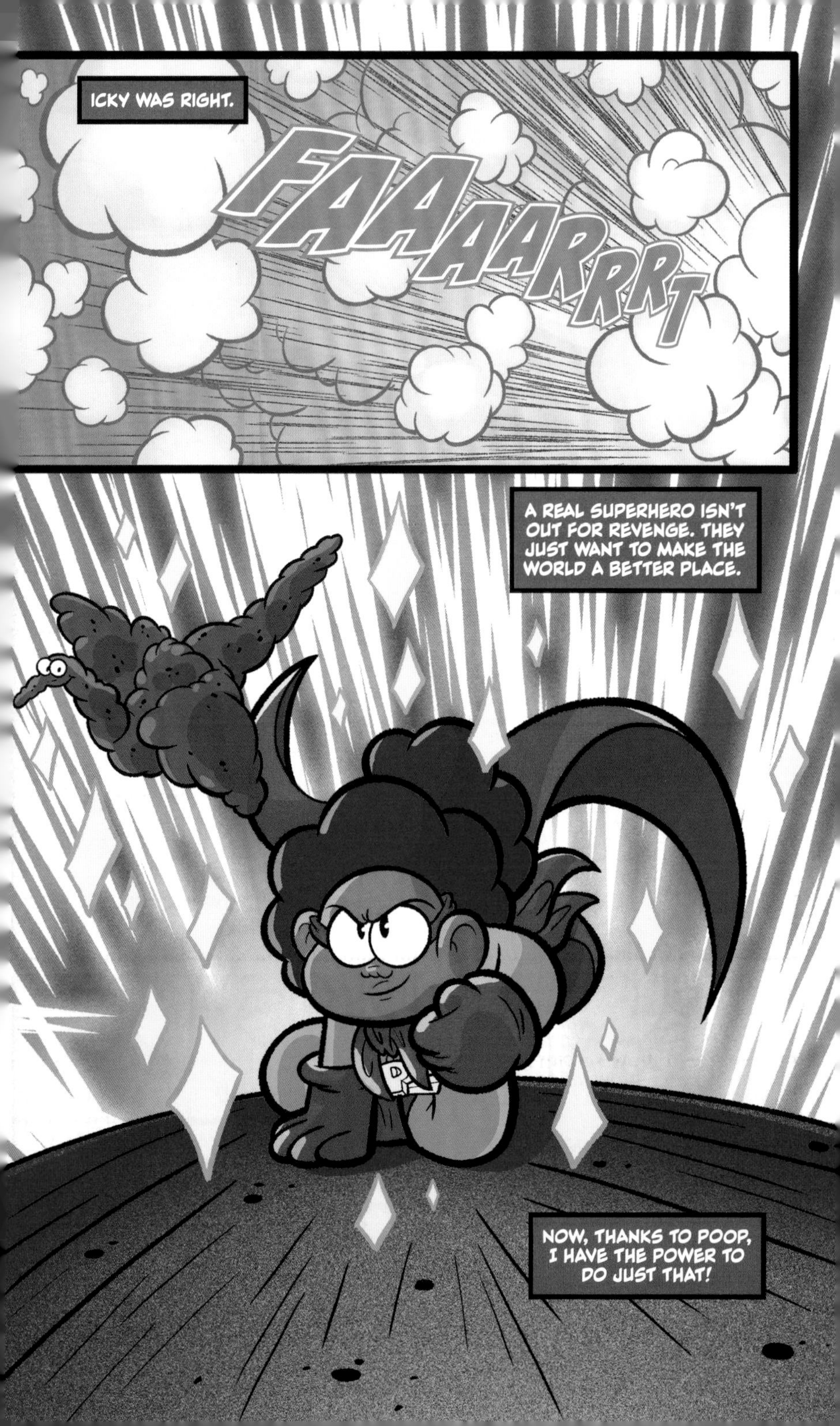
ICKY WAS RIGHT.
FAAAARRRT
A REAL SUPERHERO ISN'T OUT FOR REVENGE. THEY JUST WANT TO MAKE THE WORLD A BETTER PLACE.
NOW, THANKS TO POOP, I HAVE THE POWER TO DO JUST THAT!

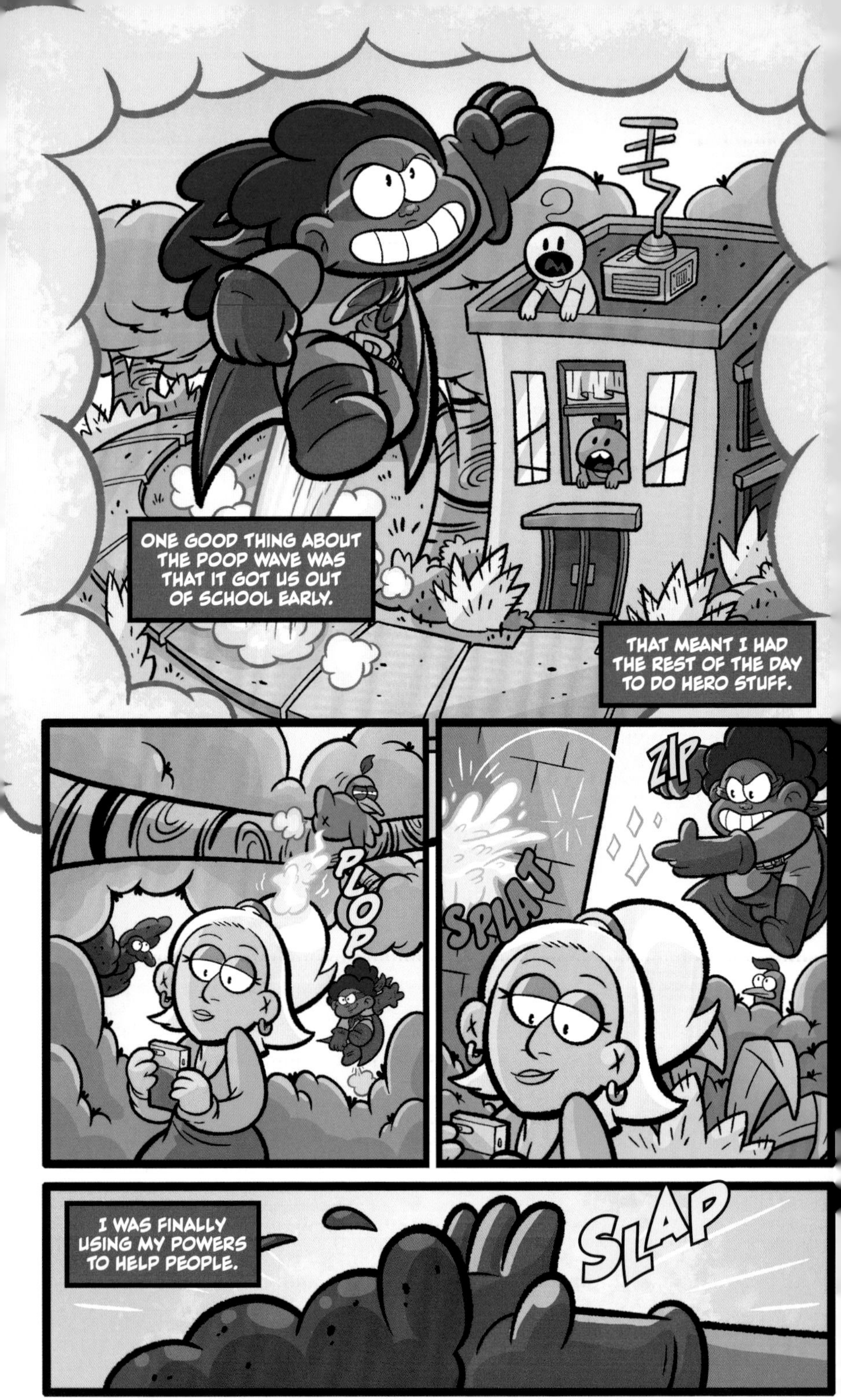
ONE GOOD THING ABOUT THE POOP WAVE WAS THAT IT GOT US OUT OF SCHOOL EARLY.
THAT MEANT I HAD THE REST OF THE DAY TO DO HERO STUFF.
PLOP
ZIP
SPLAT
I WAS FINALLY USING MY POWERS TO HELP PEOPLE.
SLAP

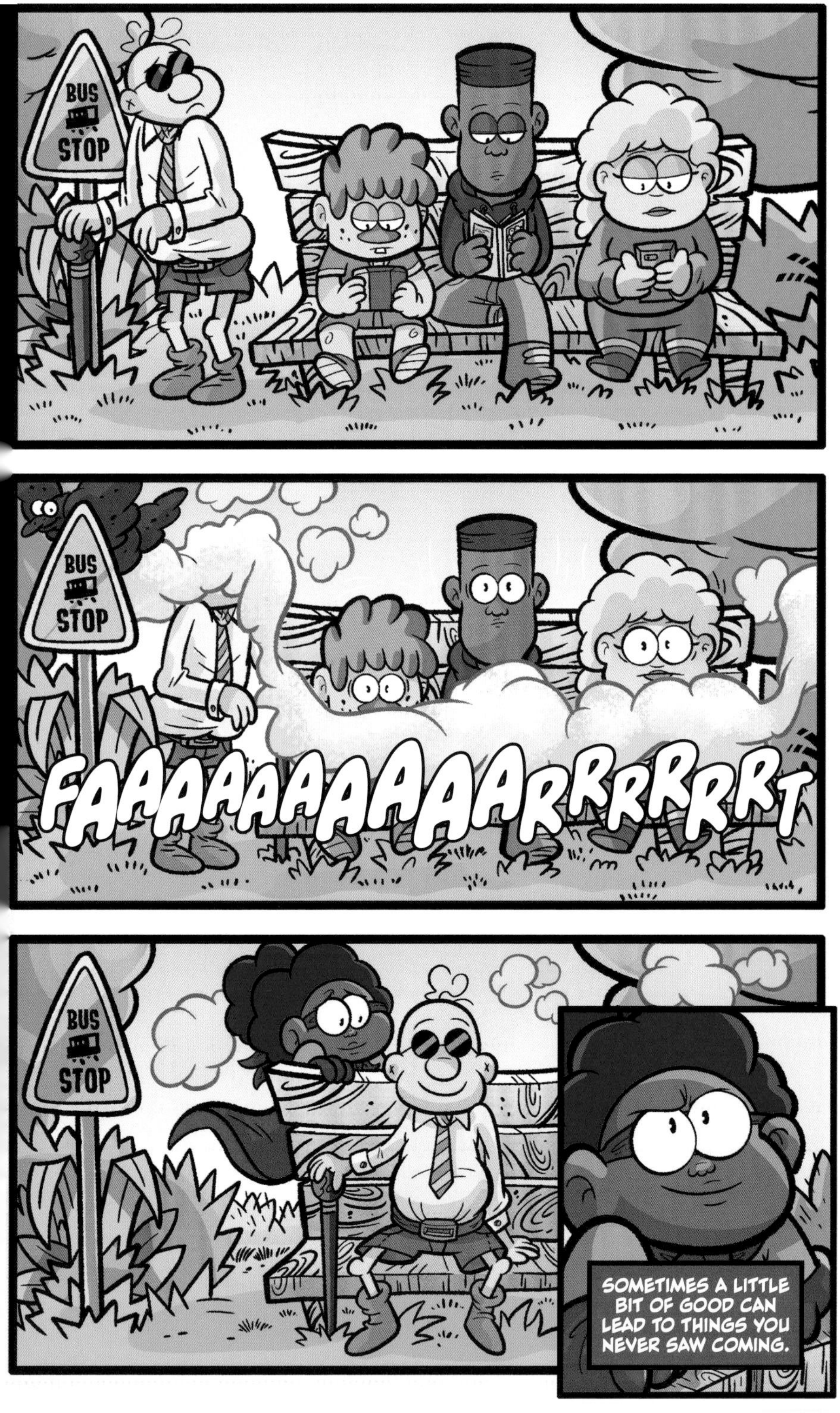
BUS STOP
BUS STOP
FAAAAAAAAAARRRRRRT
BUS STOP
SOMETIMES A LITTLE BIT OF GOOD CAN LEAD TO THINGS YOU NEVER SAW COMING.

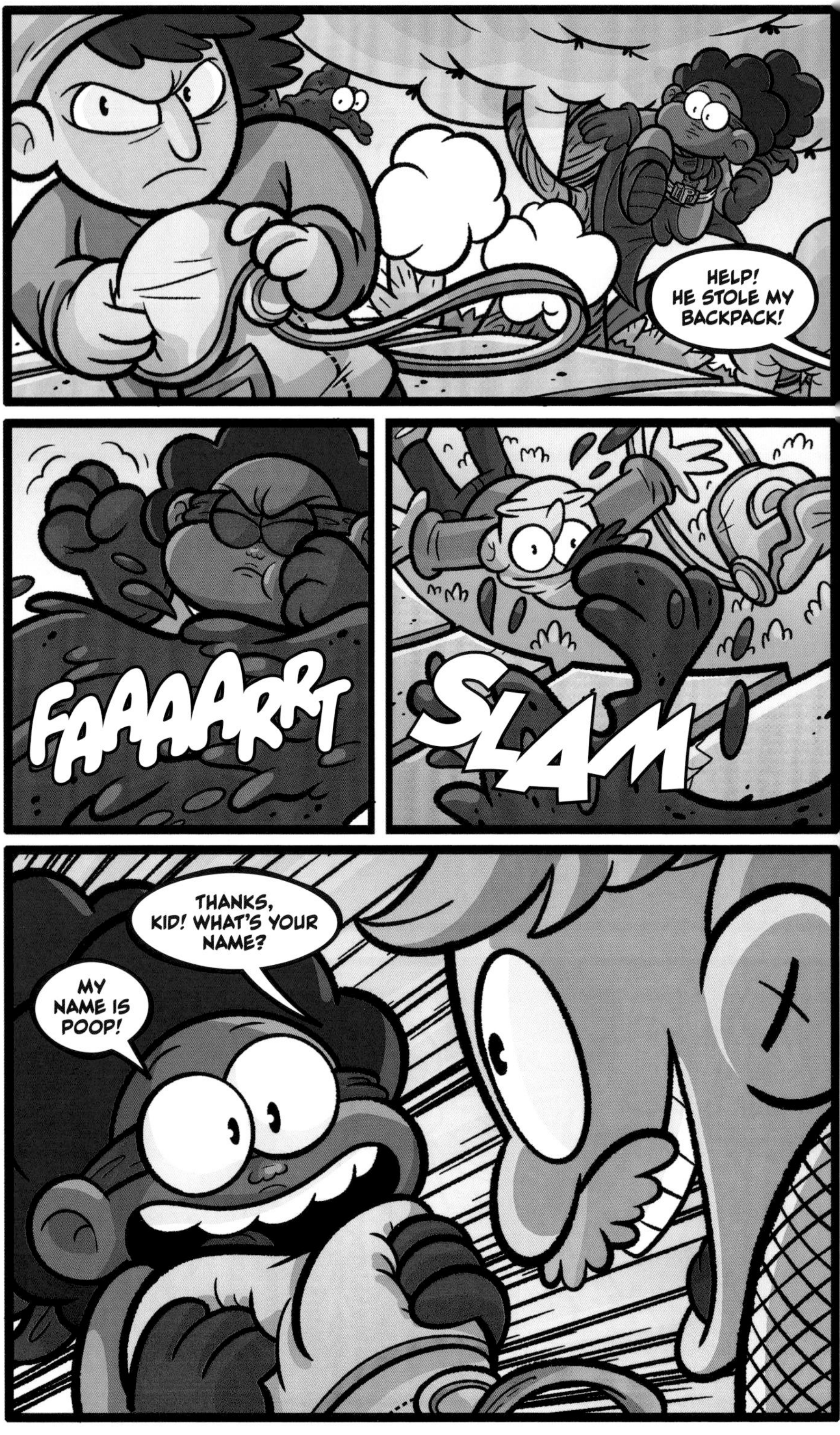
HELP! HE STOLE MY BACKPACK!
FAAAARRT
SLAM
THANKS, KID! WHAT'S YOUR NAME?
MY NAME IS POOP!

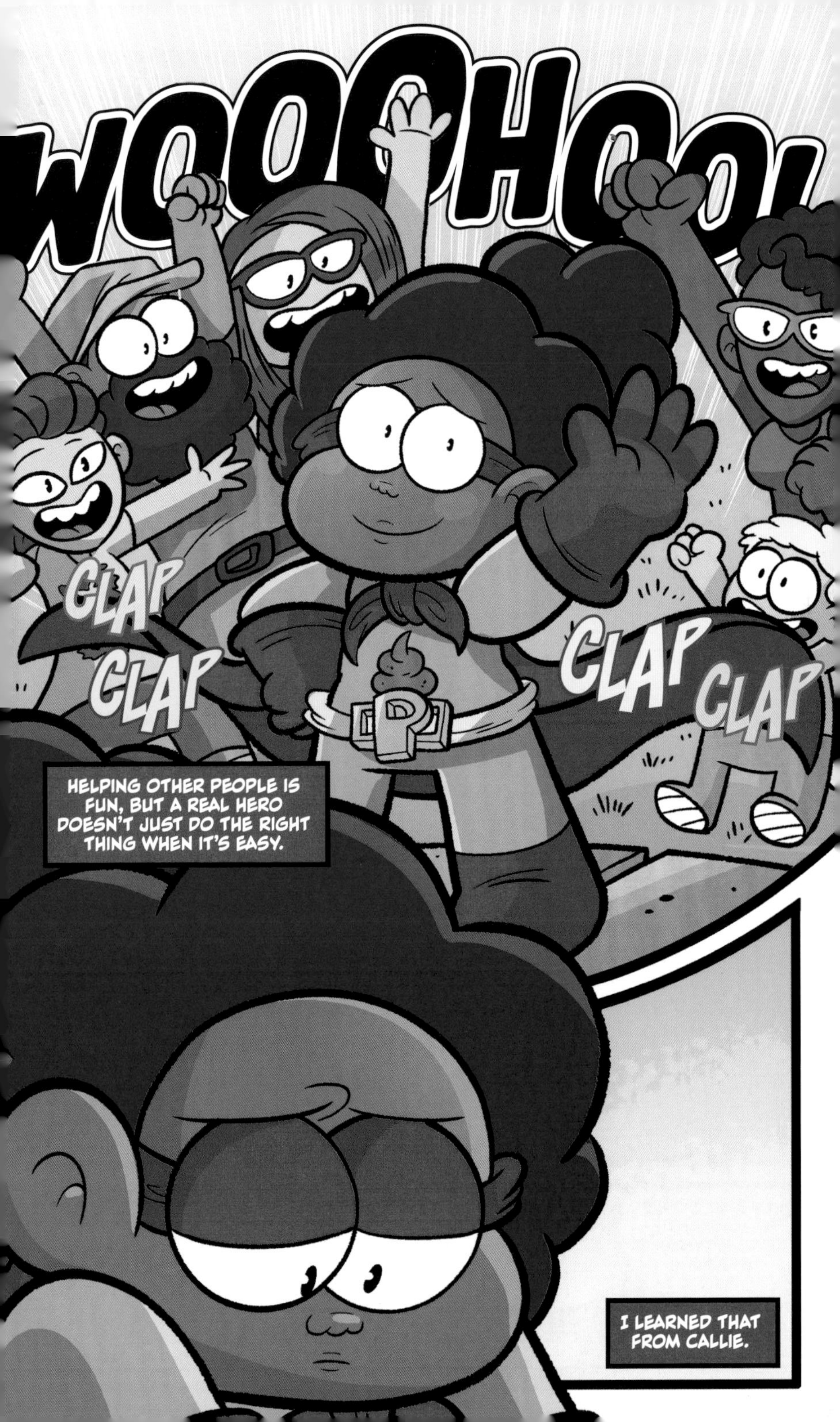
WOOOHOO!
CLAP
CLAP
CLAP
CLAP
HELPING OTHER PEOPLE IS FUN, BUT A REAL HERO DOESN'T JUST DO THE RIGHT THING WHEN IT'S EASY.
I LEARNED THAT FROM CALLIE.

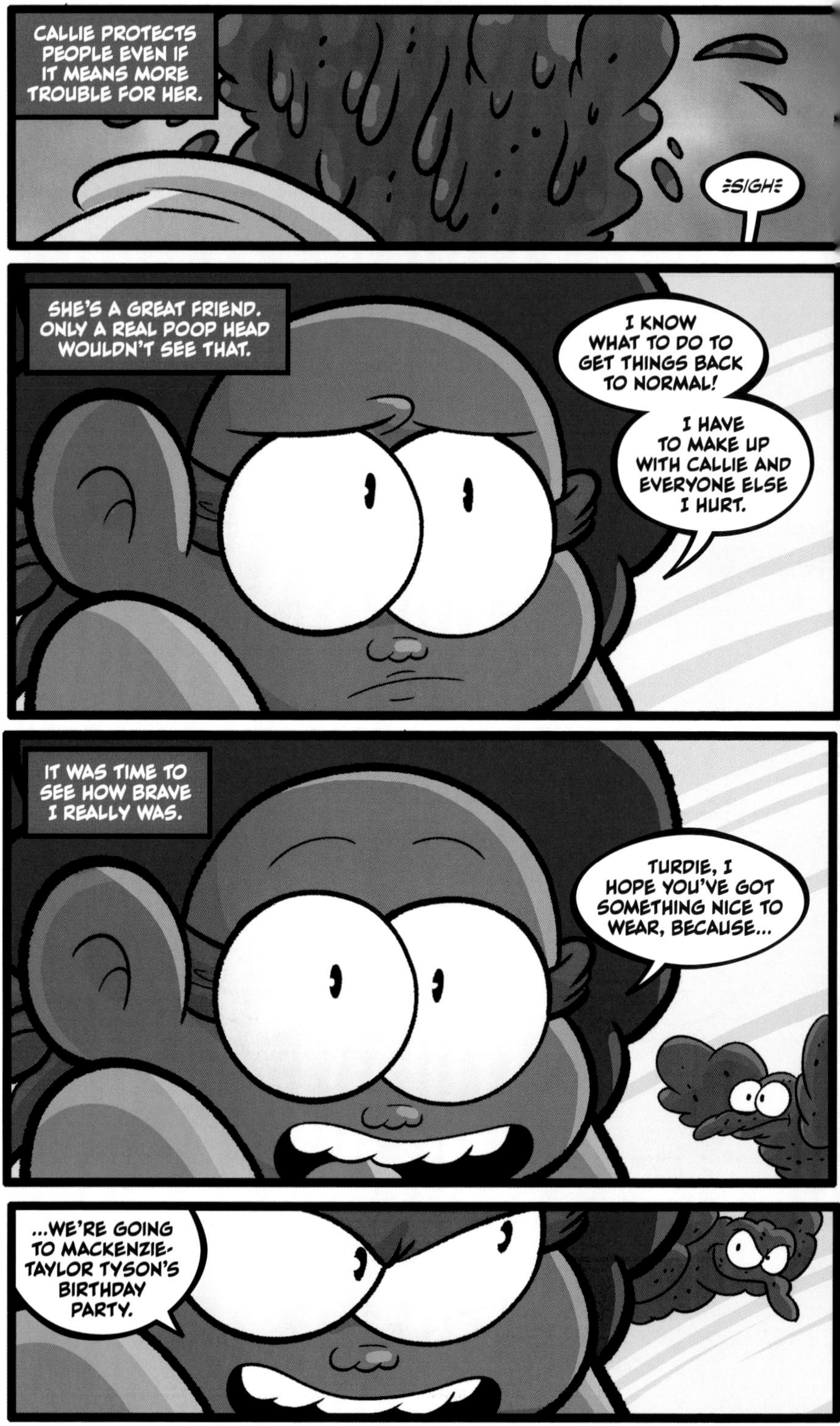
CALLIE PROTECTS PEOPLE EVEN IF IT MEANS MORE TROUBLE FOR HER.
SIGH
SHE'S A GREAT FRIEND. ONLY A REAL POOP HEAD WOULDN'T SEE THAT.
I KNOW WHAT TO DO TO GET THINGS BACK TO NORMAL!
I HAVE TO MAKE UP WITH CALLIE AND EVERYONE ELSE I HURT.
IT WAS TIME TO SEE HOW BRAVE I REALLY WAS.
TURDIE, I HOPE YOU'VE GOT SOMETHING NICE TO WEAR, BECAUSE...
...WE'RE GOING TO MACKENZIE-TAYLOR TYSON'S BIRTHDAY PARTY.

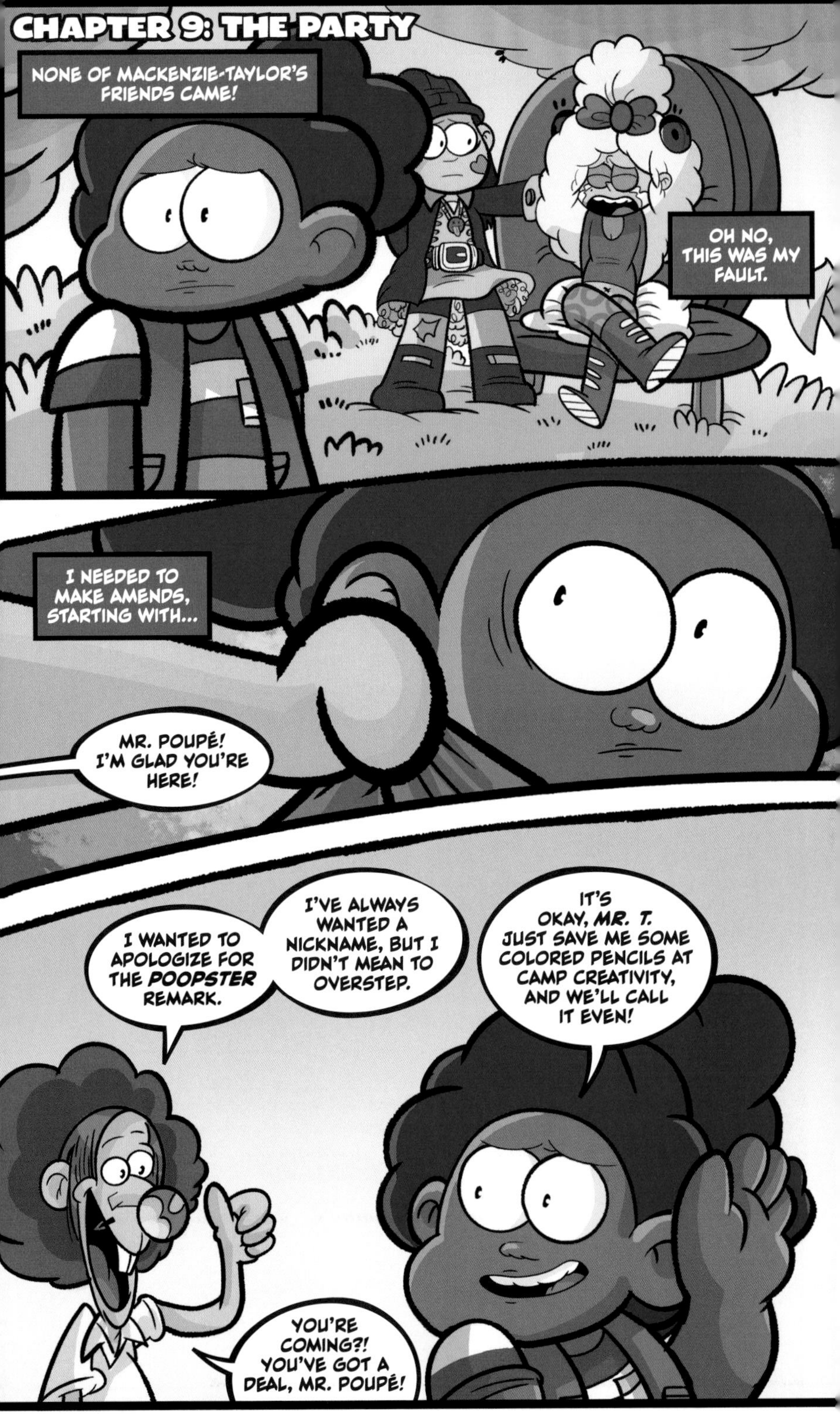
CHAPTER 9: THE PARTY
NONE OF MACKENZIE-TAYLOR'S FRIENDS CAME!
OH NO, THIS WAS MY FAULT.
I NEEDED TO MAKE AMENDS, STARTING WITH...
MR. POUPÉ! I'M GLAD YOU'RE HERE!
I WANTED TO APOLOGIZE FOR THE *POOPSTER* REMARK.
I'VE ALWAYS WANTED A NICKNAME, BUT I DIDN'T MEAN TO OVERSTEP.
IT'S OKAY, *MR. T.* JUST SAVE ME SOME COLORED PENCILS AT CAMP CREATIVITY, AND WE'LL CALL IT EVEN!
YOU'RE COMING?! YOU'VE GOT A DEAL, MR. POUPÉ!

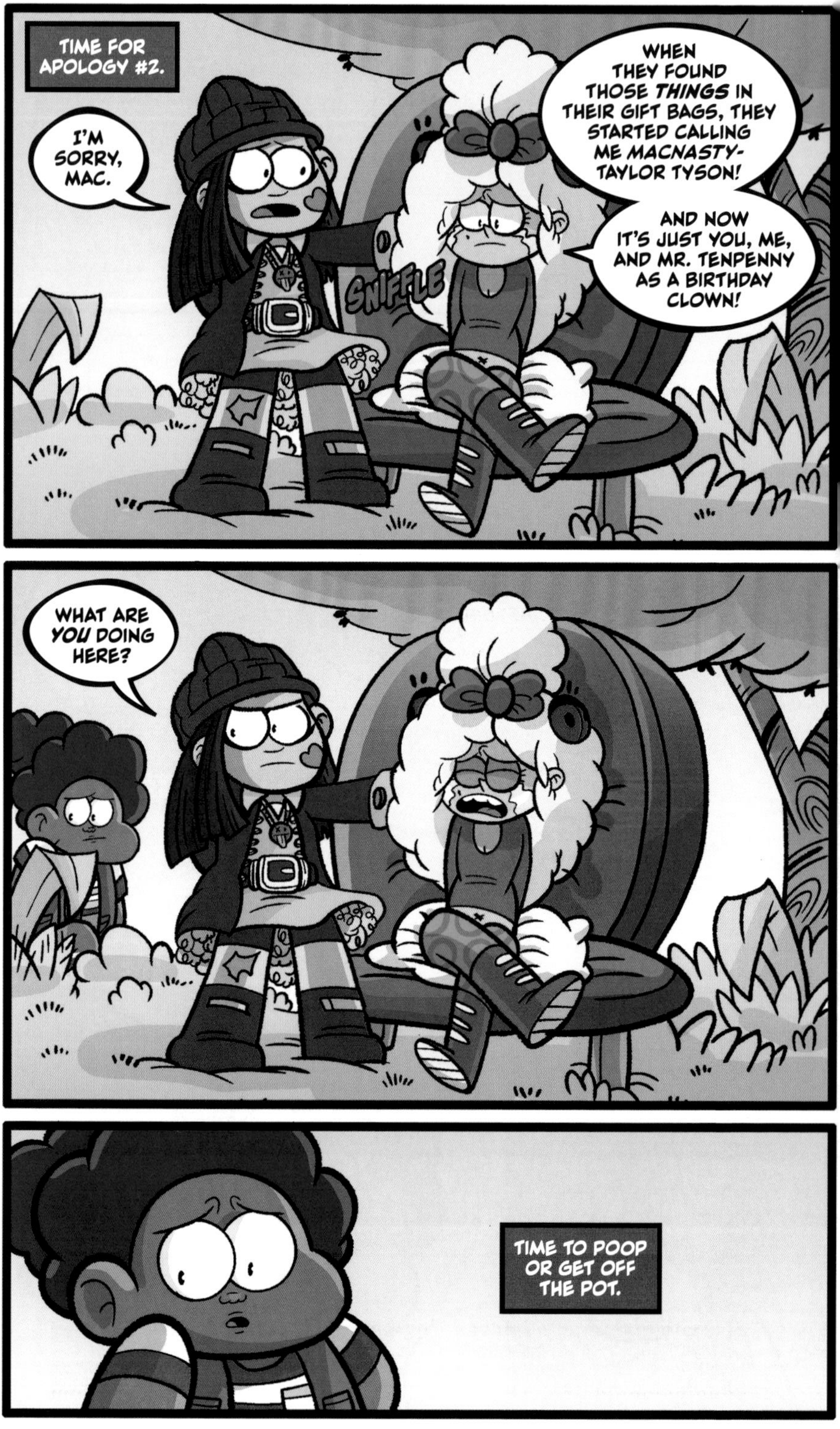
TIME FOR APOLOGY #2.
I'M SORRY, MAC.
WHEN THEY FOUND THOSE THINGS IN THEIR GIFT BAGS, THEY STARTED CALLING ME MACNASTY-TAYLOR TYSON!
AND NOW IT'S JUST YOU, ME, AND MR. TENPENNY AS A BIRTHDAY CLOWN!
SNIFFLE
WHAT ARE YOU DOING HERE?
TIME TO POOP OR GET OFF THE POT.

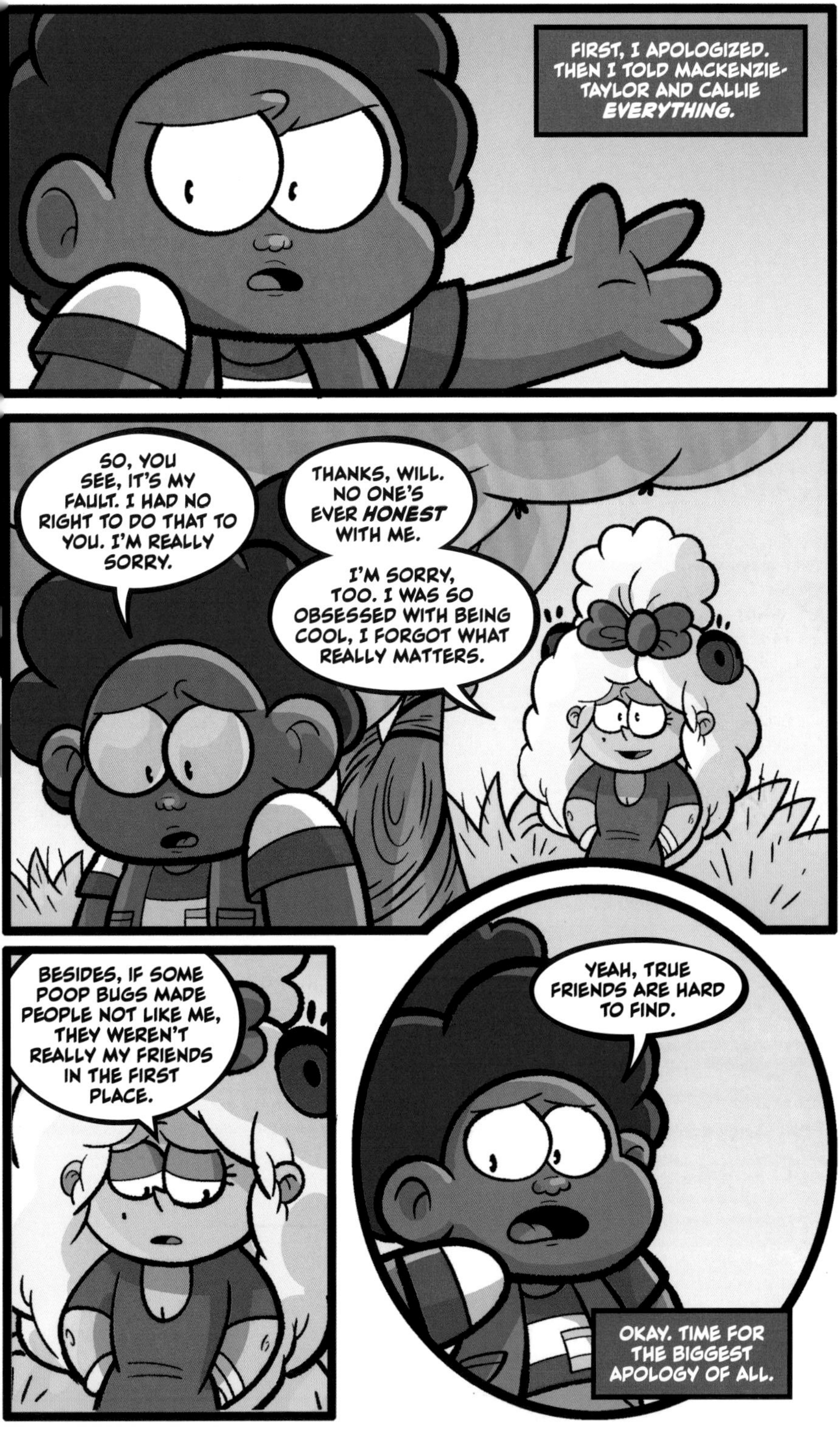
FIRST, I APOLOGIZED. THEN I TOLD MACKENZIE-TAYLOR AND CALLIE *EVERYTHING.*
SO, YOU SEE, IT'S MY FAULT. I HAD NO RIGHT TO DO THAT TO YOU. I'M REALLY SORRY.
THANKS, WILL. NO ONE'S EVER *HONEST* WITH ME.
I'M SORRY, TOO. I WAS SO OBSESSED WITH BEING COOL, I FORGOT WHAT REALLY MATTERS.
BESIDES, IF SOME POOP BUGS MADE PEOPLE NOT LIKE ME, THEY WEREN'T REALLY MY FRIENDS IN THE FIRST PLACE.
YEAH, TRUE FRIENDS ARE HARD TO FIND.
OKAY. TIME FOR THE BIGGEST APOLOGY OF ALL.

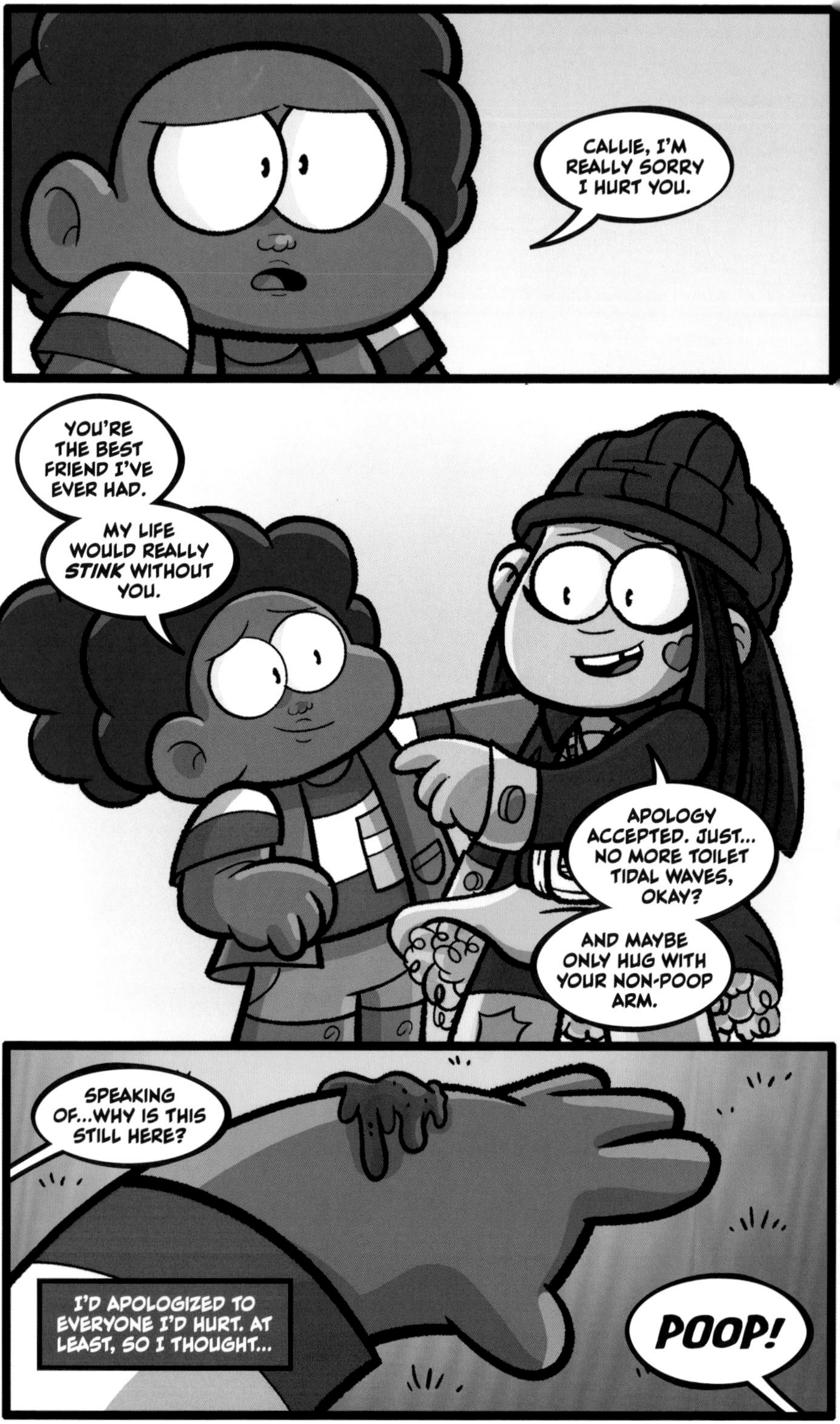
CALLIE, I'M REALLY SORRY I HURT YOU.
YOU'RE THE BEST FRIEND I'VE EVER HAD.
MY LIFE WOULD REALLY *STINK* WITHOUT YOU.
APOLOGY ACCEPTED. JUST... NO MORE TOILET TIDAL WAVES, OKAY?
AND MAYBE ONLY HUG WITH YOUR NON-POOP ARM.
SPEAKING OF...WHY IS THIS STILL HERE?
I'D APOLOGIZED TO EVERYONE I'D HURT. AT LEAST, SO I THOUGHT...
POOP!

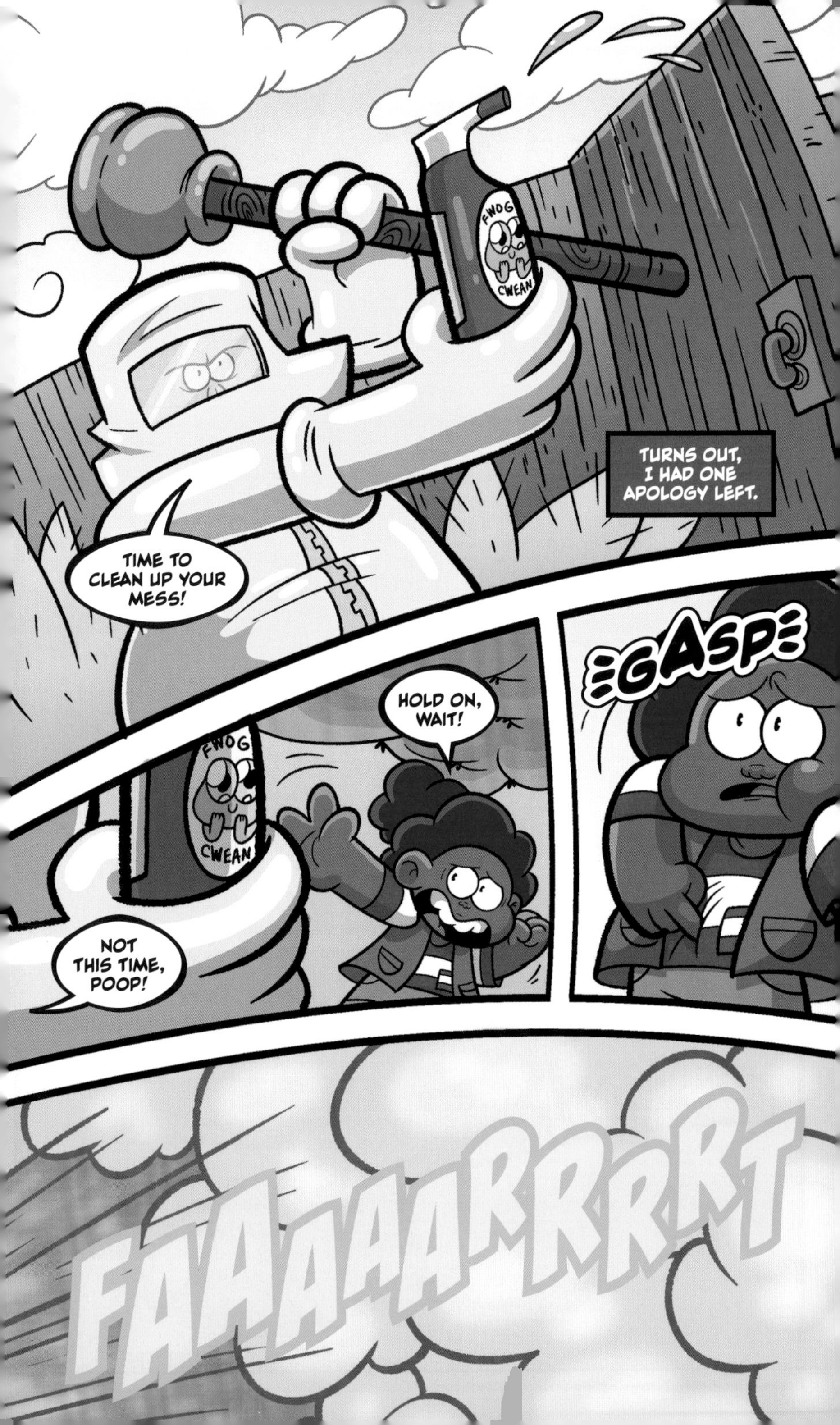
FWOG
CWEAN
TURNS OUT, I HAD ONE APOLOGY LEFT.
TIME TO CLEAN UP YOUR MESS!
HOLD ON, WAIT!
FWOG
CWEAN
NOT THIS TIME, POOP!
GASP
FAAAAARRRRT

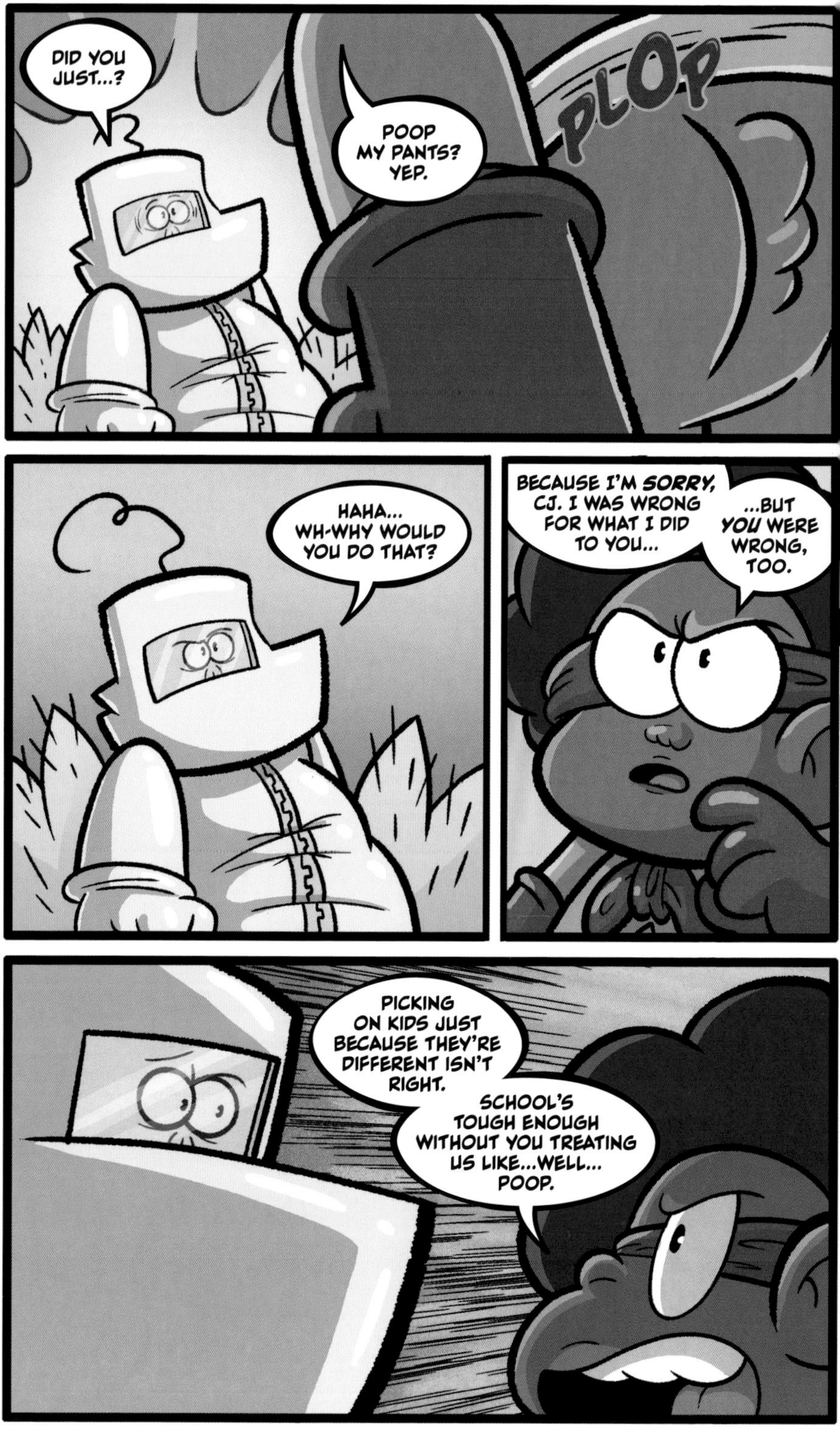
DID YOU JUST...?
POOP MY PANTS? YEP.
PLOP
HAHA... WH-WHY WOULD YOU DO THAT?
BECAUSE I'M *SORRY*, CJ. I WAS WRONG FOR WHAT I DID TO YOU...
...BUT *YOU* WERE WRONG, TOO.
PICKING ON KIDS JUST BECAUSE THEY'RE DIFFERENT ISN'T RIGHT.
SCHOOL'S TOUGH ENOUGH WITHOUT YOU TREATING US LIKE...WELL... POOP.

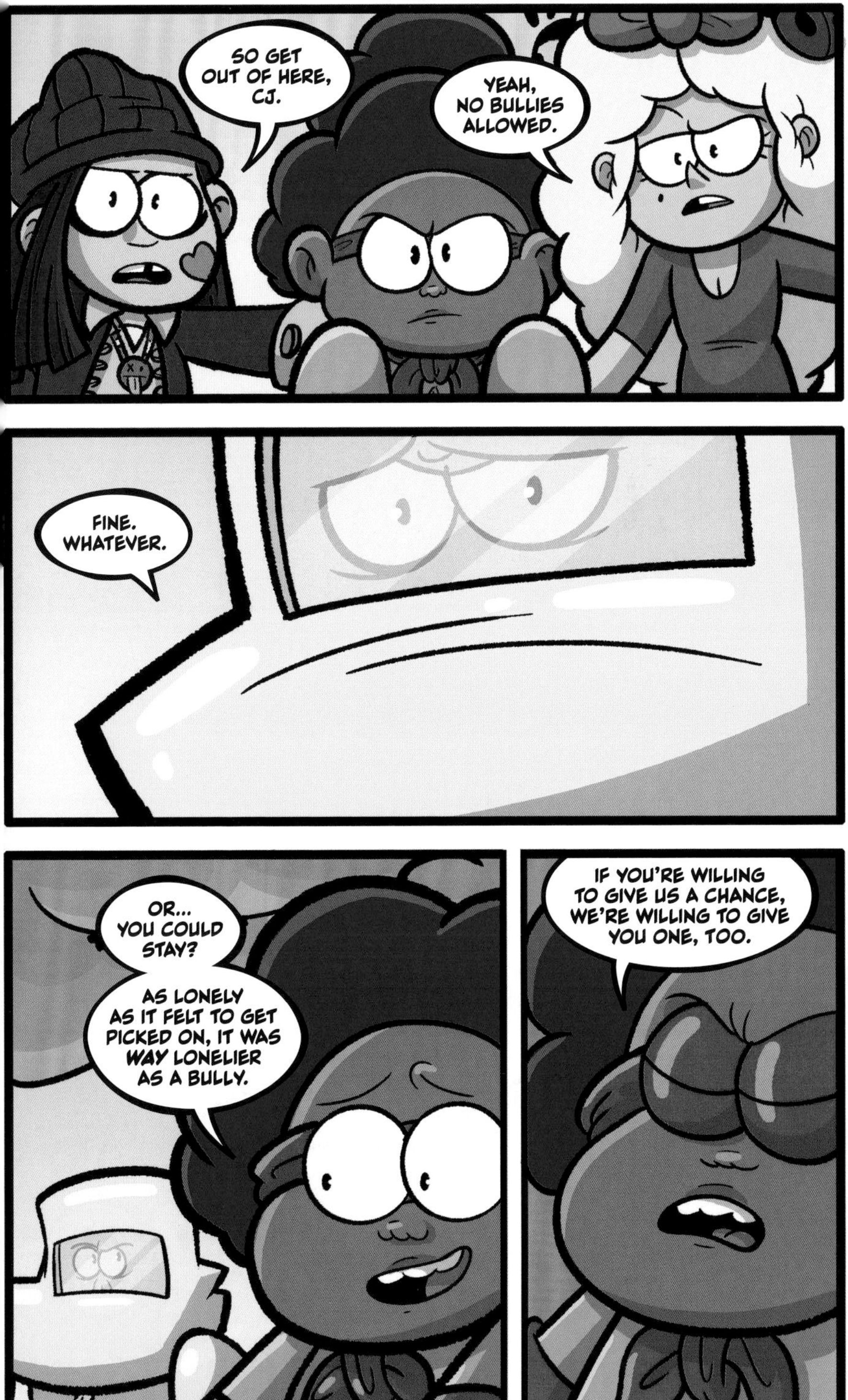
SO GET OUT OF HERE, CJ.
YEAH, NO BULLIES ALLOWED.
FINE. WHATEVER.
OR... YOU COULD STAY?
AS LONELY AS IT FELT TO GET PICKED ON, IT WAS WAY LONELIER AS A BULLY.
IF YOU'RE WILLING TO GIVE US A CHANCE, WE'RE WILLING TO GIVE YOU ONE, TOO.

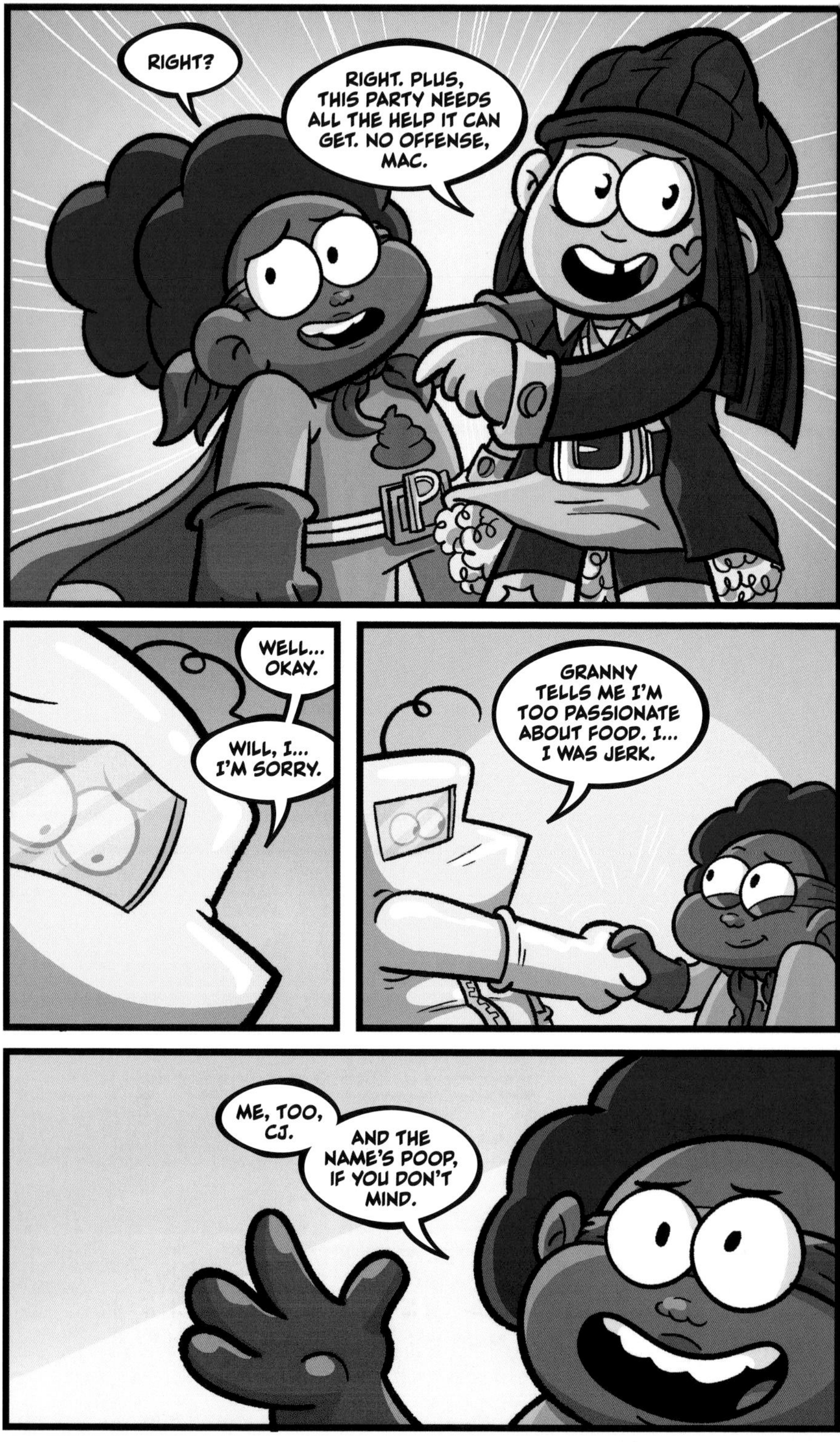
RIGHT?
RIGHT. PLUS, THIS PARTY NEEDS ALL THE HELP IT CAN GET. NO OFFENSE, MAC.
WELL... OKAY.
WILL, I... I'M SORRY.
GRANNY TELLS ME I'M TOO PASSIONATE ABOUT FOOD. I... I WAS JERK.
ME, TOO, CJ.
AND THE NAME'S POOP, IF YOU DON'T MIND.

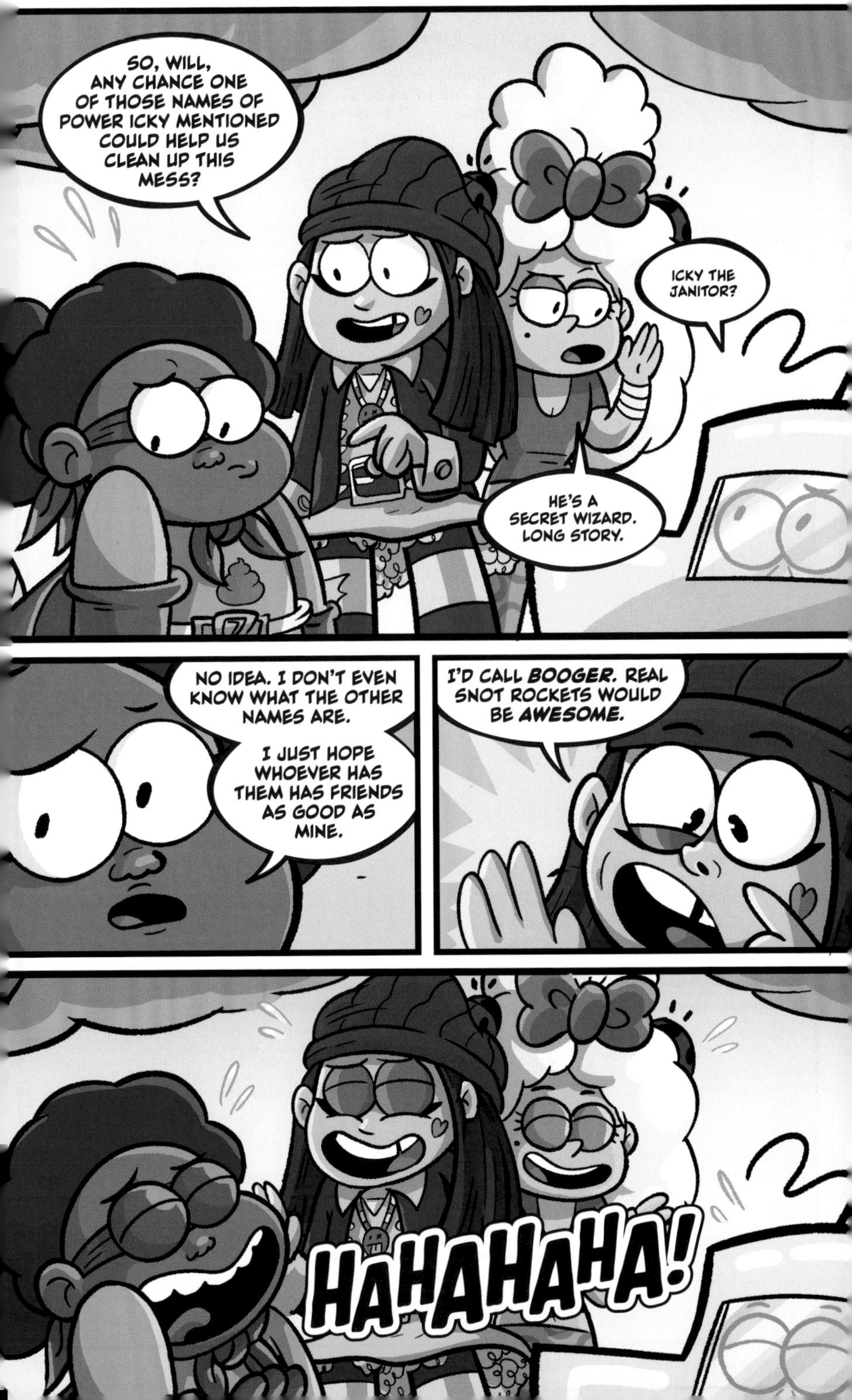
SO, WILL, ANY CHANCE ONE OF THOSE NAMES OF POWER ICKY MENTIONED COULD HELP US CLEAN UP THIS MESS?
ICKY THE JANITOR?
HE'S A SECRET WIZARD. LONG STORY.
NO IDEA. I DON'T EVEN KNOW WHAT THE OTHER NAMES ARE.
I JUST HOPE WHOEVER HAS THEM HAS FRIENDS AS GOOD AS MINE.
I'D CALL *BOOGER.* REAL SNOT ROCKETS WOULD BE *AWESOME.*
HAHAHAHAHA!

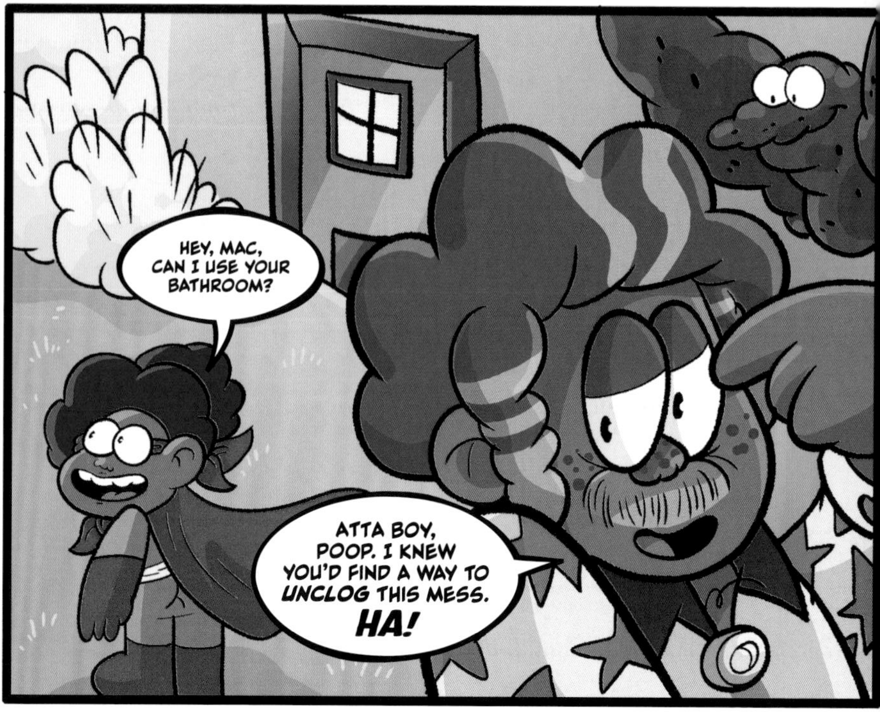
HEY, MAC, CAN I USE YOUR BATHROOM?
ATTA BOY, POOP. I KNEW YOU'D FIND A WAY TO UNCLOG THIS MESS. HA!

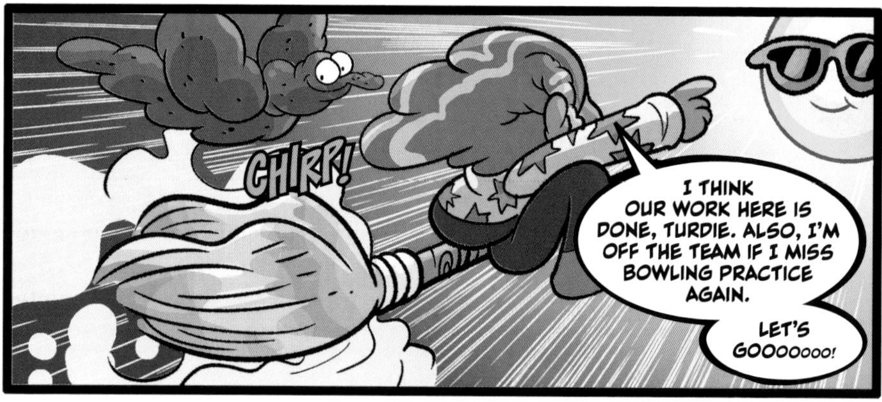
CHIRP!
I THINK OUR WORK HERE IS DONE, TURDIE. ALSO, I'M OFF THE TEAM IF I MISS BOWLING PRACTICE AGAIN.
LET'S GOOOOOOO!

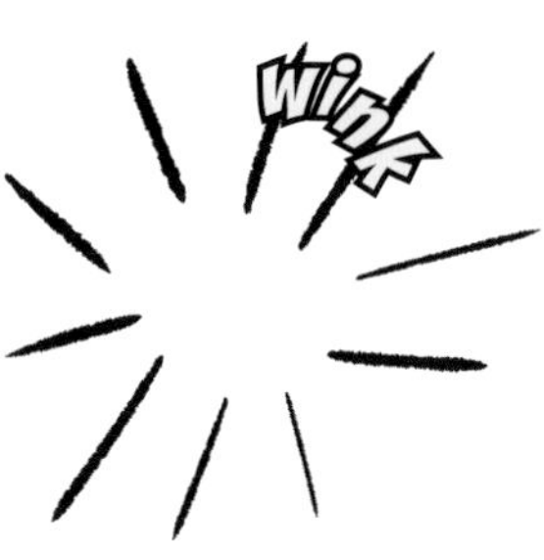
WINK

THE END.

THE CREATORS

BEN KATZNER is a Midwest-raised writer and comedian based in New York City. Ben's musings can be seen in places like Insider, Buzzfeed, and USA Today, and you can catch him doing standup on stages across the country. *Hello, My Name is Poop* serves as Ben's graphic novel debut.

IAN MCGINTY is an animator, artist, writer, and voice actor. His comics work include *Adventure Time, Steven Universe, Invader ZIM*, and much more. His own animated pilot, *Welcome to Showside*, has over a million views and is currently being developed for a series.

FRED C. STRESING is a colorist, artist, writer, and letterer for a variety of comics. You may recognize his work from *Invader ZIM*. He has been making comics from the age of six. He has gotten much better since then. He currently resides in Savannah, Georgia, with his wife and two cats. He doesn't know how the cats got there; they are not his.

ANDWORLD DESIGN is the design and production studio founded by veteran letterer **Deron Bennett**. His talents have been recognized with multiple Eisner, Harvey, and Ringo nominations for best letterer.

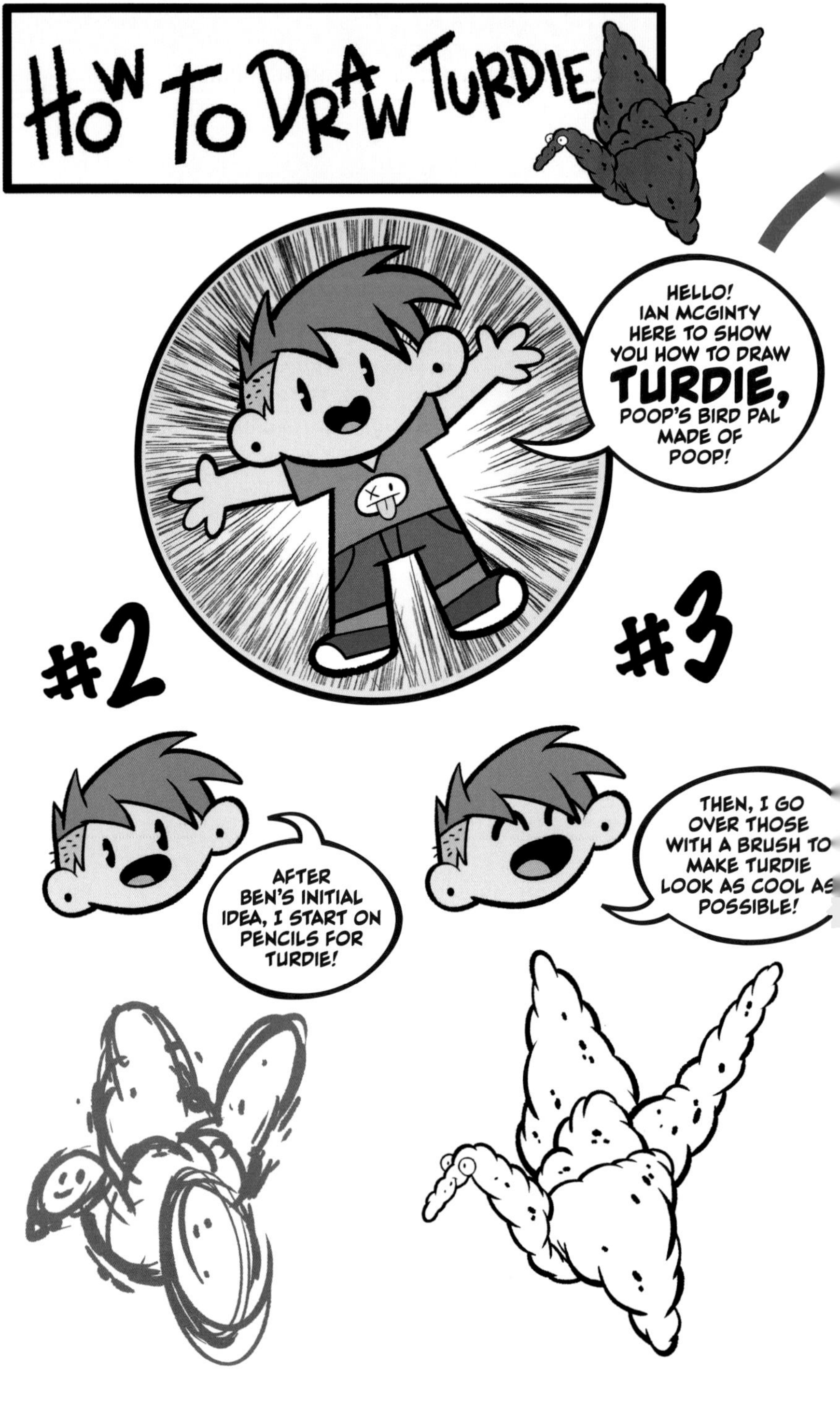
HOW TO DRAW TURDIE
HELLO! IAN MCGINTY HERE TO SHOW YOU HOW TO DRAW TURDIE, POOP'S BIRD PAL MADE OF POOP!
#2
AFTER BEN'S INITIAL IDEA, I START ON PENCILS FOR TURDIE!
#3
THEN, I GO OVER THOSE WITH A BRUSH TO MAKE TURDIE LOOK AS COOL AS POSSIBLE!

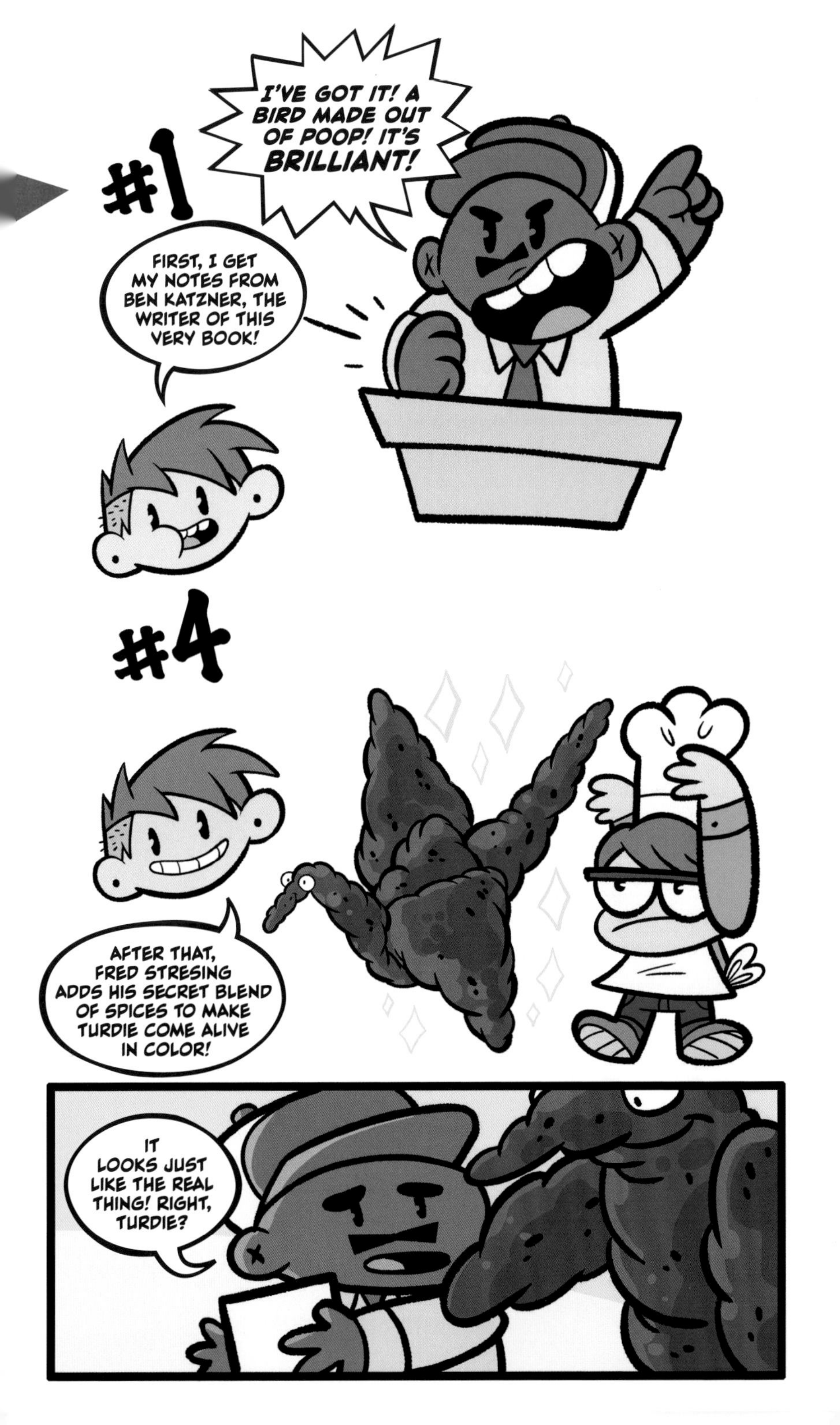

#1
I'VE GOT IT! A BIRD MADE OUT OF POOP! IT'S BRILLIANT!
FIRST, I GET MY NOTES FROM BEN KATZNER, THE WRITER OF THIS VERY BOOK!
#4
AFTER THAT, FRED STRESING ADDS HIS SECRET BLEND OF SPICES TO MAKE TURDIE COME ALIVE IN COLOR!
IT LOOKS JUST LIKE THE REAL THING! RIGHT, TURDIE?

WONDERBOUND

YEAR ONE — 2021

Wonderbound publishes science fiction, fantasy, and spooky original graphic novels for the young and young at heart.

Grab a ticket to wonder! readwonderbound.com

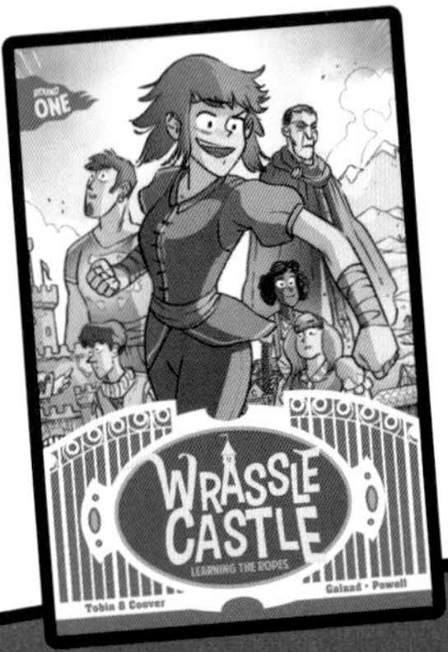

ONE
WRASSLE CASTLE
LEARNING THE ROPES
Tobin & Coover
Galaad • Powell

WRASSLE CASTLE BOOK 1: LEARNING THE ROPES

Written by Colleen Coover & Paul Tobin
Illustrated by Galaad
Lettered by Jeff Powell

IN STORES: 9/21/21
Price: $9.99

ISBN: 9781638490098

VERSE BOOK 1: THE BROKEN HALF

Written & Illustrated by Sam Beck

IN STORES: 9/28/21
Price: $12.99

ISBN: 9781638490104

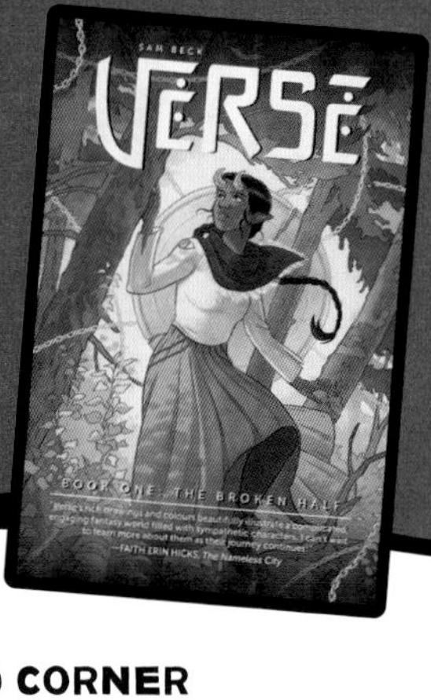

SAM BECK
VERSE
BOOK ONE THE BROKEN HALF

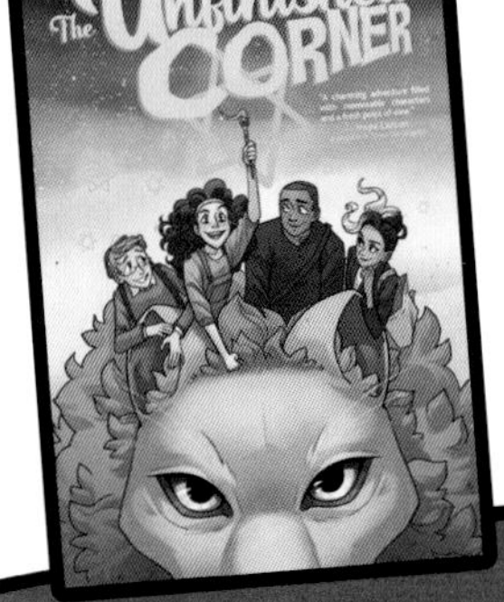

Colman • Petrovicz • Cogar • Campbell
The Unfinished CORNER

THE UNFINISHED CORNER

Written by Dani Colman
Illustrated by Rachel "Tuna" Petrovicz
Colors by Whitney Cogar
Letters by Jim Campbell

IN STORES: 10/19/21
Price: $12.99

ISBN: 9781638490111